ALSO BY NEIL GRANT

*The Ink Bridge*

*Rhino Chasers*

*Indo Dreaming*

*From Kinglake to Kabul*
(edited with David Williams)

# THE HONEYMAN & THE HUNTER

## NEIL GRANT

**ALLEN & UNWIN**

SYDNEY · MELBOURNE · AUCKLAND · LONDON

**Australian Government**

**Australia Council for the Arts**

*This project has been assisted by the Australian Government through the Australia Council, its arts funding and advisory body.*

First published by Allen & Unwin in 2019

Allen & Unwin
83 Alexander Street
Crows Nest NSW 2065
Australia
Phone: (61 2) 8425 0100
Email: info@allenandunwin.com
Web: www.allenandunwin.com

 A catalogue record for this book is available from the National Library of Australia

ISBN 978 1 76063 187 1

For teaching resources, explore
www.allenandunwin.com/resources/for-teachers

*Tiger of One Thousand Bees,* photo composite and cover design by Amanda Gibson, Rare Metal Design
Maps by Amanda Gibson, Rare Metal Design
Set in 9.3/14 pt Tarsus by Amanda Gibson, Rare Metal Design
Font design by Khyati Trehan, Indian Type Foundry
Printed in Australia by SOS Print + Media Group

10 9 8 7 6 5 4 3 2

www.neilgrant.com.au

*For Marjorie Grant (1937–2017) –*
*whose homeland vanished as surely as Didima's.*


*And for Amanda –*
*who knows the storms and the lulls.*


*And also for Emma, Matisse and Calum –*
*for whom India is much more than a story.*

*The fish in the water is silent, the animal on the earth is noisy, the bird in the air is singing,*

*But man has in him the silence of the sea, the noise of the earth and the music of the air.* —*Stray Birds*, Rabindranath Tagore

# Central Coast

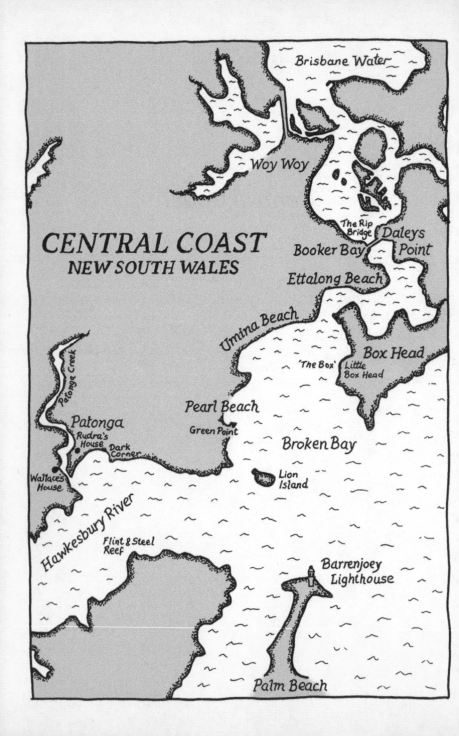

# 1

RUDRA SOLACE IS CROSSING THE CHANNEL with his best mate, Maggs Briley – Rudra with his heart clambering in his chest and Maggs powering through, born to it. The summer storm has left bruises in the sky – great welts of cloud up high and others, blotchy stains, above the headland. Last night's rain set the creeks to flooding, vomiting branches and beer cans from the neck of Brisbane Water. The outward tide is in their favour, helping them to the break that is spitting and cracking in the middle distance.

This is a sharky paddle – all the talk that ever was points to it. 'Men in grey suits' hazing boats. A local nabbed by a tiger off Lobster Beach last summer (or the one before), returning shaken and pulpy, stitched and glued back together at Gosford Hospital.

*We are just meat,* thinks Rudra. Him on his old six-four with glass as yellow as a smoker's fingers. This board has lived for too long beneath his house, that much is obvious. *She'll never win a beauty contest,* as Maggs says, *but at least she floats.* Rudra isn't a surfer, not really, but when your best mate calls and school's out for summer, you have to go.

Maggs, on the other hand, has a brand-new McCoy he's been saving for this swell. He snaps at least one board a season – pulling in when he should not, in Rudra's opinion. Maggs has neoprene skin. He fits well here on the Central Coast.

The paddle is long and brutal, and Rudra's arms are burning by the time they reach the line-up. There are a couple of guys from school here and some older surfers on longboards. Rudra doesn't know the school guys well – ex year twelves, finished exams and back at year zero. They were once the gods of the corridors and open spaces, cruel rulers. Now they are fallen.

One of them is called Judge Dredd; sometimes just Judge. Because of his dreads, Rudra imagines, or maybe because everyone just dreads being around him. Not much going on upstairs with these guys – they will never conquer the world. Maggs gives them a nod and paddles right inside. Past the longboarders who stare at him like he's a piece of flotsam. Past the year zeros shooting him foulies. Not giving two shits. Cocky as.

The first wave of the set breaks – tumbling wide, sucking Maggs up and spitting him down the face. As Rudra claws his way over the lip, he sees Maggs pull in and set a rail for a barrel that is one hundred per cent guaranteed.

Rudra sits there for a moment, stilling his heart. The next one in the set is smaller and one of the longboarders paddles hard, moving his whole upper body like a beached seal, legs beating the air behind him. But he misses, slapping the water in disgust as it carries on towards the year zeros, and to Rudra.

Dreadlocked Judge paddles. *He'll never make it,* thinks Rudra. *Too far out.* So Rudra goes for it and, as he does, he feels the wave rise and steepen. All the chunky energy – born over a hundred sea miles out – unwinds itself beneath him. He jumps into a crouch and cuts a track across the face. He knows there is nothing fancy in his style – everything about it suggests a down-the-line bolt from danger.

'Hey!' Rudra hears the shout behind him. 'My wave!'

Rudra checks quickly and glimpses the wall hammering at Judge's broad shoulders. Technically Rudra should pull out. But he doesn't. Judge is way too far inside and he, Rudra, is in perfect position.

The wave knows it too – willing him on, throwing out little fringes of white from its lip. And the sun sneaks through, and it's all going to be okay. He sets up for the barrel – one of only three in his whole surfing life so far. Judge is already shrouded in foam, sucking gulps of sand. Maggs, paddling back out, rips a howl that blesses this wave and their friend-ship and makes this a sacred run at whatever. And the wave stretches on and on and folds over like a blanket and Rudra crouches and drives for the winking eye of headland and then he is out into the summer air and the sea is hissing like Dr Pepper.

He paddles back to the line-up, all smiles, the taste of adrenaline bright and coppery on his tongue.

Maggs high-fives him. 'Where'd you pull that from?'

And Rudra tries to be cool, to stifle the elation that is brimming over. But all he can do is smile.

A segue (Media Studies, year nine) makes the transition from one scene to the next, smooth and unsurprising. From this scene, where he is smiling and the sun is shining and his best mate has just seen him on the wave of his life, there should be a *segue* into what happens next. But there is no segue. None at all. Just a jump cut – a blunt chop to the back of his head.

'That was my wave, you maggot,' Judge snarls.

Rudra fixes his gaze on the Southern Cross tattooed on Judge's overworked right delt. Anything but look him in the eye.

'No you don't,' shouts Maggs paddling over.

Judge's mate growls and blocks his path. The longboarders mutter their agreement.

'Sorry, mate,' starts Rudra. 'I didn't think you were going to make it—'

Judge Dredd holds up his hand. 'It was a drop-in, plain and simple.'

'Plain and simple,' chimes the mate.

'Bit like you, really.' Judge nods at Rudra.

'Sorry?' *Me? Plain and simple?*

'A drop-in.'

'What?'

'Why don't you go back to where you came from.'

'Patonga?'

'Don't be smart with me, curry-muncher.'

'Got nothing to do with that wave,' says Maggs.

Judge turns on him. 'Why don't you play with your own kind?'

'Forget it, Maggs,' says Rudra.

'Yeah, listen to what your girlfriend tells you,' says Judge's mate.

'I'm going in,' Rudra says to Maggs, and turns for shore. He paddles with his head down, stifling the big wrongness punching through doors inside him.

Maggs catches up. 'Why do you let them push you around like that?'

'I don't care, Maggs.' His tears are a little too close, settled, as they are, between the weave of his words.

'Well, you should. This is yours too, you know. Your coast. Your waves.'

'I dropped in. It was his wave.'

'The guy's a kook.'

They paddle in and ride the shorey to the sand, lie there for a while, letting the waves gently tug and push.

'Thanks,' says Rudra.

'For what?'

'For what you did.'

'It was nothing.'

It was something. But Rudra can't find the speech marks to put around it. Can't find a way to get it out.

Up West Street they go. The tired old strip mall reels past like a Sunday drunk – pockets out, crusty duds and a gap-toothed smile. Pedestrian crossings rise from the gluey road, bringing the summer traffic to a crawl. Phlegmy air is coughed over the town. Umina is a little grubby and too real-world for the Sydney set. Better they stick to Terrigal. Better they sail over to Patonga and forget this even exists. Here, it's mug-a-cinos and meat pies, with not a hipster beard or pair of black-rimmed glasses in sight.

Up West Street they go, carrying their boards under their arms, twisting to avoid the pedestrians heading east.

'Do you ever think about it?' asks Maggs.

'About what?'

'Being Indian?'

'Well, I'm not really, am I?'

'Half, you are.'

'I don't think it counts.'

'Some think so.'

'They don't count.' Rudra wishes it were truly so.

The sun has burnt the cloud away and the day is warming. The storm is just another memory with cockatoos, impish, swinging from the powerlines; glossy ravens cawing as they stride through carparks.

They stand in front of Mr Chicken's Charcoal Chickenery and look up at Magg's cracked bedroom window above, with its stained lace curtains billowing. They remind Rudra of the flowing guts of fish, flung to the pelicans and hanging for a moment in the water before they are scooped away by bills as big as pillowcases. It makes him shiver to think of it. And how tomorrow, he'll have to work the nets with his dad and Wallace. Have to take their boat beyond the bay and pray for prawns. Yesterday, and the day before, Cord was up to his elbows in the engine's innards. Sleeved with grease and oil, slowly boiling.

Things have not gone well lately. They need to fish to keep the boat going, they need to keep the boat going to fish. And Rudra is caught between these two competing currents with the irrational fear he is the cause of all their bad luck.

'Let's dump these boards,' says Maggs. They go round the back where the weeds and the trash have their tangled empire.

Maggs has mostly lived here with his mum since his folks split up three years back. He had a brief spell up at Macs Beach while his mum took off and did *god-knows-what*.

That's where his surfing came good. The flat above Mr Chicken's is a shithole and he knows it, but he can walk to the surf and, *Hey, it's not forever, man.*

They hide the boards in the long grass and Rudra calls his mum. She tells him his dad is in Sydney organising something for the boat. Cord's been doing that a lot lately. Something bad is going down; something big that Rudra would rather not know of. When his father is out the house breathes easy, though, and Rudra is glad of the break.

'Fancy coming to mine?' Rudra asks Maggs.

'Is Cord home?'

'Nope.'

'You got food?'

'I believe we do.'

'Then the answer is *oui*.'

Rudra stares at him.

'French.'

'I know it's French, dumb-arse.'

Maggs rescues his pushie from a tangle of kikuyu. 'Let's ride,' he says, thumbing the tyres.

'I don't have a bike.'

'Plenty of bikes to be had.'

'I'm not flogging one.'

'Property is theft,' says Maggs.

'What are you talking about?'

'I heard it somewhere.' He sits on the bike, hanging his arms over the bars. 'Anyways, it's not stealing if you bring it back.'

'No way known, Maggs.'

It's hard to keep up when you're riding a sixteen-inch Barbie bike with glitter tassels, plastic pedals, and your knees higher than your hips. Rudra tries to catch Maggs but he is far gone and riding like this is his whole goddamn life – hands-free, hair a halo, the Lord of Single Speeds.

At last they begin the fall to Patonga. The verges blur and the creek swells into view. Rudra carves slow loops between the white lines, feeling the wind quicken in him. The summer is long and the summer is good and there is much to happen.

They hit the flat and Rudra pumps the pedals again. Amy Parwill is propped on the post outside the fish-and-chip shop. 'Nice bike,' she yells and Rudra, half-heartedly, flips her the bird. He couldn't care less about her and her stupid stupidity.

Rudra's mum is out the front of their house, sitting in the shade of the old jacaranda. The house is ancient – a fisherman's cottage painted flat onto the Patonga canvas a hundred years back, struggling now to fit in among the jaunty, nautically-themed holiday houses.

'Hi Nayna,' calls Maggs, and Rudra's mother winces. She prefers *Mrs Solace*. That formality is just bred into her – old-school India stuff, all about respect. *You can't fight your history,* she says to Rudra, and battles it every day. 'Watcha reading?' asks Maggs.

'Just the newspaper.'

'Anything interesting?'

'They're bringing Mungo Man back to his country.'

'Mungo Man?'

'He lived, died and was buried on the shores of Lake Mungo. Out in far west New South Wales, over forty-two thousand years ago. He must have been an important man in his tribe, because he was covered in ochre. Some geologists found him in nineteen seventy-four. He'd *uncovered* himself, apparently.' Nayna smiles at the thought of a man dead for forty-two thousand years doing anything of the sort. 'The wind, most likely – erosion, you see. The scientists took him to Canberra for tests without asking the local people for permission.' She shrugs. 'Different times, Maggs. But he's going back now. Back to his home and his people.'

'Well, good on them, Nayna, for setting it right.' Maggs sounds like a voiceover bloke in an old film. Nayna narrows her eyes, not sure if he's taking the piss.

'When's Dad due back?' asks Rudra.

'Not for hours,' Nayna replies, leaning back in the deck-chair, sipping her sweet tea.

'We're just going to hang out,' Rudra tells her.

'And what does that involve?' His mother folds her news-paper in half and then quarters.

'The usual.'

'Such as?'

'Cooking meth, prison tatts and the dark web,' says Maggs, smiling.

Nayna nods, blessing all three activities. 'Be good,' she says. And, as they disappear inside the house, 'Hey, where did you get this bicycle, Rudra Solace?'

No need to answer. Doorways are time portals and you get to leave the past behind. In the kitchen, they rifle through the pantry and raid the fridge.

'Not from the carton, Maggs,' says Rudra. 'Mum'll kill you.'

Maggs lets loose a thick milk-burp. 'Only if she sees me.'

Rudra makes his speciality: three rounds of toast each, butter, Vegemite, avocado, chilli flakes.

'This should be a thing,' says Maggs, 'if it wasn't so spicy, curry-muncher.'

Rudra glares at him. 'Only you, Maggs.'

In his room, he cranks 'Porcelina of the Vast Oceans'. A tide of soft guitar and cymbals washes through the room. Rudra lies on the bed and closes his eyes, feels the room pulse like a jellyfish. The lead guitar smashes in – a savage set pounding a lonely beach, spewing muttonbirds and shark eggs. By the time Billy Corgan is singing about seashells hissing lullabies, Rudra is fathoms down.

Then Maggs goes and breaks it. 'It's a little bit shit, this old music,' he says, turning it down.

'It's not old, it's *classic*. Ninety-five.'

'We weren't even born.'

'Whatever.'

'Speaking of old, who's this chick?' Maggs picks up a framed photo.

'That's my *didima*.'

'Your what?'

'My grandmother – Mum's mum. From India.'

'Nice sari.'

'Dickhead.'

'Thanks.'

'I've never met her.'

'You want to?'

'I guess.'

'Over there?'

'India? Doubt it.'

'You're not curious?'

'About what?'

'About where you come from?'

'I'm from here.'

'You know what I mean.'

The old ute pulls up outside, crushing the gravel in the driveway, its tappets ticking like a time-bomb. Rudra kills the music. 'Shit, Dad's home.'

'And?'

'He's not supposed to be.'

'I feel like saying g'day.' Maggs heads for the front door.

'Maggs!' Rudra shouts. Too late, Maggs is at the door already, waving.

'G'day, Mr Solace.' At least he doesn't call him Cord.

Cord ignores him, slamming the door of the ute. Rudra shuts his eyes and feels the flakes of rust rattling down inside the window cavity. Inside himself.

'Tea,' Cord says to Nayna, not looking at her. He gathers armfuls of paperwork and moves towards the house. Closing her book silently, she pushes out of the deckchair.

'How's the fishing?' asks Maggs, like he's got a death wish or something. Rudra grabs his wrist.

'I'll have it in my office,' Cord says to Nayna. She follows him inside.

'You'd better go,' says Rudra to Maggs.

'I think I'll stick around.'

'You're an idiot.'

'Maybe.' Maggs goes to the kitchen, Rudra following like a gallows bird. 'Can I help you with the tea, Nayna?'

'I'm fine, thank you.'

'I'll help,' he says.

Cord shuts his office door and the old house growls and settles.

Nayna makes the tea and carries it through to Cord on a metal tray. Rudra and Maggs stand quietly in the kitchen. The clock on the kitchen wall gets loud. *Snik. Snik. Snik.* Chopping time into bite-sized chunks, each one hanging in the air before being executed by the next.

'You should go,' says Rudra again.

'I'm staying,' says Maggs leaning back against the counter.

There is a sound of metal attacking timber. An alarm of sorts. It could be the tray falling to the floor, Rudra thinks; hopes. Then there is a quiet that he plummets into, a furious fist closing over him. It is not a peaceful absence of sound; it is a violent exorcism of the world.

'We should check,' whispers Maggs.

'Wait.'

The door to Cord Solace's office creaks open and Nayna appears. Rudra is struck by how dignified she looks as she walks towards the kitchen. She is carrying the tray – and on that tray Cord's mug, now split in two. Wordlessly, Nayna steps on the bin pedal and disposes of the broken china.

14

# 2

IT'S DARK. DARKER THAN SQUID INK. Zero moon.
A light breeze comes up from the bay, bringing with it oyster
flesh and the scent of floodweed. Rudra can feel the worry
high inside him, rising still, like bait in a craypot.

Today, he will work the boat, beside Cord, solemn as a
priest. And those nets will rise from the sea full of treasure
and promise, and the junk – the weed and the jelly blubber,
the swimmer crabs – will fall back to the sea. He can picture
it falling through the water in slow motion, the bubbles like
strings of pearls.

He will pull the nets because that is what his father does,
and his grandfather did, and his great-grandfather. All
fishermen. *Solace & Sons* is stencilled in black on the crates
they fill with fish – a wish-fulfilling prophecy of sorts.

Rudra checks the time on his phone. It's two hours until
dawn. High tide two hours after that. He wishes he had a
real clock, like in the kitchen, so he could hear time passing.
He lies quietly on his back, feet splayed like a gorge, the
sheet slung between. Hands keeping track of his breathing
in the dark, knotted over his chest.

Now his dad is awake – his steps bold across the uneven boards of the kitchen, the old house shivering beneath him. The kettle neck finds the tap and the kettle finds the stove. Mugs and milk are found and placed. Then there's a knock at the door and a stab of light.

'Rudra, get up.'

He rolls onto his side and feigns sleep.

The door opens wider. Three steps to his bed. A rough hand on his shoulder. The tang of fish blood. 'Wake up.'

Rudra keeps perfectly still, holding the whole world together with this tension. If he breathes, it will shatter. His dad returns to the kitchen. The kettle screams and is dragged from the heat. Rudra imagines the teabags crumping softly into mugs. The sound of water being measured onto them, followed quickly by milk.

When his mum makes tea, she boils loose leaves in a pot with sugar, sometimes a cinnamon stick and a few cardamom pods; the milk in there too. It rolls up like a storm swell, thick with bubbles, the froth clotting like cloud. *Too sweet*, his dad grumbles. *Too sweet by half.* But it reminds her of her beginnings.

The tea is dumped on his bedside table. The spillage pools on the timber and sucks the colour from the varnish. 'You got ten minutes. Eat on the boat.' Not a word wasted. Cord's speech is always just a bunch of lonely phrases looking for something to bind them. People say Rudra's can be the same. But he balances this with some of his mum's long-windedness.

He is packing his bag when Nayna comes to the door. She leans against the jamb, her hand covered by her thick plait. When she smiles, the darkness around her eyes makes Rudra want to look away.

'You sure you want to?' she whispers.

Rudra nods. *Have to.*

'This summer only, okay?'

'Dad wants it.'

'I want to make sure you know it's only temporary.'

'Sure.'

He sorts through his half-empty bag so he doesn't have to meet her stare.

'I want more for you, Rudra.'

Dawn is unromantic, awkward and brutish; clambering over the top of the headland as they cross the pier, making the Norfolk Island pines look more like giants than they have ever been. Rudra's dad is in front carrying a shoulder bag, a twenty-litre jerry can of diesel swinging at the end of his long arm. The deckhand, Wallace, is wheeling crates of ice. No one says a word for fear of cursing themselves. They've lost three days, what with the storm, the swell and the dodgy engine. At least now the water has cleared. They need a couple of good digs to make it through – to pay for the breakdowns and the diesel and to put food, other than fish, on the table.

They walk the pier, the occasional splash of ice hitting the concrete. When Rudra was little, the lower landings of the pier would terrify him. Spread like stingray wings on either side of the pier's solid spine, they were made of pitch-covered sleepers. On the highest tides they were swamped and made horrifying sucking noises as waves rose and fell. Below lay teeth of the sharpest oyster shells, and dark shapes crossed back and forth in meaningful patterns. It was the gaps between the boards though, and their horrific possibility, that built Rudra's fear. Crossing them, he would shake at the thought of falling; the water was different there, oily, dismal, rank with fish blood, swim bladders and purple spirals of gut.

Now, those spaces are so small it is hard to believe they ever got to him. Now, summer is here and year ten is done with, and year eleven pants across the great divide. This is his new dark space – this gap between, this summer – another fear altogether. *Abstract nouns*, he learnt in year eight, are things you cannot see or touch, but they are real. You need to believe in them because they belong to the world as much as *boat* and *sea* and *sky*. Words like *I can't* and *I must* (*failure* and *responsibility*) which he learnt when he was just a child. How they cling to him now, feeding and growing. Some of these words are so thinned out he can barely voice them, but he can feel them alright. They are inside his bones, like electricity, charging his marrow and making his joints ache.

In the days when they shared a common life, his mum would take him down to the beach and there they would scrawl his fleeting fears below the tide-mark with a broken stick. She promised that the sea goddess would come and take them from him. And sure enough, when high tide had come and gone, his thin scratchings were erased and so was the fear.

Now he can't be fooled so easily. Water can erase words but those feelings remain. Magic has left this world and now Google has an answer for everything. The tides are caused by the pull of the moon – gravitational forces, nothing more.

The sea goddess is just another Instagram influencer or YouTube make-up artist.

'Rudra, give Wallace a hand.' His dad is on the tender. He has the top off the Evinrude and is going through the daily routine of coaxing it into life.

'We need a new outboard,' says Wallace, pulling a pouch of Champion Ruby from his pocket and expertly rolling himself a smoke.

'We'll need a new deckhand if you don't shut it.'

Wallace tightens his lips over his rollie as he lowers the crates into the bottom of the tender. He knows better than to backchat – tried it on for size once and regretted the shit out of that little error. Had to swim home from halfway across the bay, midwinter swell, sharks deep down, chill water coursing out of the Hawkesbury.

The tender tosses a broad wake and gulls follow them out to *Paper Tiger* – the boat Rudra has known his whole life. She swaggers on her anchor, stern to the wind like an obstinate child. The tinnie nudges her gently. They climb on board and get her ready to go.

Fishing is partly about invisible lines, Rudra knows, carving bays and the river into different grounds – places you can go, places you can't. Closures, they're called, and they stop boats as surely as a sandbar. Fisheries' patrols enforce the lines when maps are ignored or forgotten. There's one line drawn across the mouth of the Hawkesbury – argued and won some years back by the fishermen down at Brooklyn to stop boats running twin gear down the river. *Paper Tiger*

only runs single gear – one net and boards. There are places that she cannot go though, spots like Pittwater, Brisbane Water, Cowan and Berowra, held aside for things like recreational fishing and oyster leases. Cord often complains about the unfairness of the setup – how the government favours weekend anglers over those trying to eke a living from the water.

Rudra hopes that today they'll fish the Hawkesbury. There is something comforting about being nestled between two banks. Plus, the river is sheltered from the ocean swell and there is no need to put the 'birds' (the black, gull-winged stabilisers) into the water to stop seasickness.

But they turn left as they motor out of Brisk Bay, heading towards Lion Island.

'Why're we heading for the sea?' Rudra asks Wallace.

'The fresh, mate,' replies Wallace. 'It's pushing the prawns into the bay.'

Rudra has been around enough fishing slang to know the 'fresh' is the flood of freshwater pushing from the estuary after the storm. He curses it as they break from the bay but is soon busy with Wallace, filling the icebox beneath the sorting table and scouring seagull shit from the deck. They work rhythmically, the sea rolling under them. The first tinge of light creeps into the sky and Lion Island looms like the predator it is.

The island has always held some fear for Rudra. Something about its shape beckons and repulses depending on the angle and time of day. The place is a nesting ground for fairy penguins and muttonbirds, their burrows nestled among the banksia and bitou bush. It is protected, and park rangers swing by every now and then to check no one has landed on the tempting crescent of beach. It's well known that sharks prowl off the point, rubbing out the dark smudges of penguins as they pass overhead.

'You know why your dad wants you out here?' says Wallace.

Rudra winces. He knows Wallace's days on the boat are numbered. His dad talks about him as if he is just another expense. And Rudra is free labour no matter how you look at it. *You don't pay family*, Cord has always said.

Wallace clamps his hand on Rudra's forearm. 'Don't worry, mate. No hard feelings, eh.'

'I don't really want to be on the boat.'

'Don't let the old man hear you say that.'

'I know nothing about fishing. He never told me anything until now. Guess he hoped some miracle would deliver him a better son.'

'Let me tell you something about fishing and me. I been on and off boats since I was little. I'm infected with it and it's some bad disease, let me tell you. On the days I'm not fishing I'm still thinking of it. Dream about it too.'

Wallace clenches and unclenches his fists; just to bring warmth back into his hands, Rudra thinks.

'I only work by the grace of Cord Solace. When he's sick or there's too many prawns or squid for him to handle on his own.' He looks Rudra squarely in the eyes. 'I love this boat. Even though I know she isn't mine and never can be.'

'You should get your own, Wallace.'

'Need cash. Got none.' He straightens his back and tucks a pre-done rollie into his mouth, then sparks it up and blows a plume of smoke over Rudra's head. 'So it's down to me today, to educate you about this fishing lark.'

Rudra should know about fishing. It should be in his blood. He looks down into the water, gone crystal clear, the night's darkness still clinging to some spots.

'School prawns,' Wallace begins, 'is what we're after. Their eggs are dropped at sea and go through a cycle – turning at special times into altogether new things. You got those posters in school, Rudra, where monkeys slowly turn into humans? Prawns are like that – one lifetime – five different animals. Like them Russian dolls with all those other dolls perched inside, just busting to get out.

'When the prawns are still little, they get the signal that winter is coming and they should head to the Hawkesbury. This is a place they've never seen, Rudra, but up the Hawkesbury they go – into the shallows and deeps, over sunken logs and oyster leases.

'They sit out the winter in the river and then, when the time is right, they get another signal. When they get a dark moon, they begin to migrate from the Hawkesbury back to sea. Their little heads are buzzing with the pull of it. They need the deep waters to mature-up and get ready to spawn. But they don't know that yet, all they got is this burning need to go. So they swim, they crawl and they gush backwards out of the Hawkesbury.

'And that's where we come in. Us with our nets and our boats. That's the gold we're after. That's what pays for this boat and the food in our bellies.' Wallace takes a drag of his smoke and blows two rings into the clear air, one through the other like it's a target.

Cord's voice explodes out of the cabin: 'Shoot that net away!' And they get busy feeding the net over the back of the boat. The winch brakes are released and the otterboards drop from the gallows into the sea. That sea, like so much trapped sky, and them clattering over it. Once underwater, the boards spread the net like a greedy mouth, guiding it towards the bottom. Wallace waits until he knows there is enough wire out for the net to be on the bottom. He gives it a little distance – watching the angle made by the wire against the surface of the sea – and then locks the winch off.

'Your dad'll set the boat to two and a half knots now,' he says. 'Any faster and we'll miss the prawns. Any slower and the net will mud-up like buggery.'

'What's happening down there?' asks Rudra.

'Those prawns are hiding in the sand. That's where the tickler chain comes in. Remember it hanging under the bottom lip of the net? It's going to work now, grubbing the prawns from the sand.' Wallace points at the water, under it. 'See them? See them?' Rudra does not see them. 'You see them, alright. You picture them huffing back with quick flicks of their tails. But too slow for the net. It swallows them up like a greedy bastard.'

They trawl out in a nice clean line, away from the shark net and the closure from Green Point, at Pearl Beach, over to Little Box Head. A tight turn and back again, towards Green Point; Cord's eyes on the plotter screen, tracking the shot. Rudra and Wallace waiting. Three digs around – that first shot an hour of hoping, with their path on Cord's screen winding like a cyclone eye.

Then they winch the net. It comes up slowly, with Rudra holding his breath.

'With those storms,' says Wallace, 'there'll likely be a lot of kelp.'

The winch drags the net to the end of the gallows, and when the otterboards rise from the depths Rudra grabs the lazy-line. Its other end is attached to the cod-end: their bag of gold. The net is winched higher on the gallows and they grapple the cod-end onto the sorting table.

'You can do the honours, mate,' says Wallace, and Rudra pulls at the drawstring, the knot releasing the cod-end like a purse. There is a bit of weed with the catch, but it looks big enough to kick the morning off nicely. They go to work, tossing the weed into the water. Soon they are left with a good pile of prawns on the table, flipping and turning in the warm morning. Wallace smiles. 'Nice dig,' he says and, as he shoots the net again, Rudra begins to sort them for size, washing them and slipping them into the slurry of ice and salt water. By the time this is done the next haul is ready to be brought in.

They do three more shots that morning, before the tide changes. The sun climbs into the cloudless sky and Broken Bay fills with pleasure boats. The ferry to and from Palm Beach skips past every half-hour. People appear on the beach – joggers and their dogs, early morning swimmers.

The shots are decent, mostly free of kelp. After the last dig of the day, a massive forty kilos of golden school prawns sit on the sorting table, the light glinting off their backs.

They break back into Brisk Bay not much after midday, the icebox jammed with prawns. While the rest of Patonga were sleeping, they were making money. They moor *Paper Tiger* and trundle their iced prawns to Cord's old ute. 'I reckon this lot's worth the trip into Sydney,' says Wallace. 'If they're the only prawns on the market floor tomorrow morning, we'll make a killing. I'll run them in with Rudra if you want.'

'Rudra can help me on the boat,' says Cord. 'Reckon it'll be another big day tomorrow. More like this and we'll be back on top.'

Rudra is nervous about being on the boat alone with his father. With Wallace around, he has an ally. Without him, Rudra feels as if he has had the shell ripped from him and he is horribly exposed to Cord's quick temper.

morning, we'll make a killing. I'll run them in with Rudra
if you want.'

'Rudra can help me on the boat,' says Cord. 'Reckon it'll
be another big day tomorrow. More like this and we'll be
back on top.'

Rudra is nervous about being on the boat alone with his
father. With Wallace around he has an ally. Without him,
Rudra feels as if he has had the shell ripped from him and
he is horribly exposed to Cord's quick temper.

# 3

THE NEXT DAY, AS IT TURNS OUT, is not a big day – at
least not in a fishing sense. *Paper Tiger*'s motor vomits oil
into the bay and Cord, knuckles skinned and greasy, sets to
work fixing it once again. Prawns go uncaught, bills will not
be paid.

In the evening, Rudra is in his bedroom when he hears
the sound of his dad's voice, one notch above normal,
through the thin walls.

'She's not coming. End of.'

There is a break where his mother must be talking but
her voice is so low that he cannot hear it. He can picture
the head wobble she does when she is trying to say *yes*,
or trying to say *maybe*, trying to convey she understands,
trying to calm or reassure.

'I'm not talking about it anymore.' A classic Cord Solace
shutdown.

Rudra creeps to the door. They are in the living room.
He can see the back of his dad's head, the scars beneath
his number-one haircut like gill slits. He can see his mum,
her hands pressed as if in prayer against her lips. And they

seem further away than ever, a distance that cannot be crossed. Rudra often wonders why they even got married.

This much he knows. His mum, out here from India at nineteen, studying physics at Sydney Uni – a bright girl from a rural village who earned her way to boarding school in Kolkata. Refusing her childhood ghosts and building a wall of books to keep out the gods and goddesses that pound on it nightly.

Kolkata, she tells him when he is still small enough for her lap, is the home of the fearsome goddess Kali. Kali, the black one; she who dances on corpses, who drinks blood, his mum says, wincing but not refuting the words. Rudra, cowering in the corner while Kali's tongue, dripping red, reaches for him. His mum says not to fear her; Kali is powerful but she is also a protector, a destroyer of the demonic *asuras*. She tells him these stories, then tells him not to believe. She is ashamed – he can see this even at age five. *Folk stories,* she calls them, but Rudra sees beyond that, even then.

Rudra's dad, fearing Kali so much he banishes her statue. *She is only a keepsake,* Rudra's mum tells him. *To remind me of Kolkata. She is not a goddess. There is no such thing.* And Rudra wants to say, *But what about the sea goddess taking my words? How can you pick and choose your stories?* Rudra sometimes pulls black Kali from her hiding place. She's a statue no bigger than his hand; she is cool, even among the old jumpers at the back of the wardrobe. He touches her garland of skulls and that lolling black tongue, and feels that she is real and they are a part of each other. He also feels terrible confusion at a shame so deep, buried in jumpers, hidden from the world.

His mum met his dad at the fish market, in Pyrmont. She was there with friends, eating squid tubes and fresh crab. She loved the market – the smell reminded her of the Sundarbans, a vast tangled mangrove swamp in West Bengal. Here, the steel tang of fish; there the glitter of scales. Her, as a child, placing them on her fingernails, dancing for her parents, in the lamplight.

Cord was twenty-three and had inherited his father's boat. He had big capable hands and deep blue eyes. She liked the way he walked and told her friends so. *So confident, that one,* she said, pointing at him. *He knows the world.* She was bold, six months into her science degree – a girl who had escaped the village and saw everything open before her.

One of her friends stopped the fisherman and asked about his catch, then asked him to sit and have coffee. He was busy, he said. Had to offload the fish and get back, he said. And it should have stopped there. Could have, so easily.

*I was wild back then*, she tells Rudra. A *wild and stupid girl. I bought a whole mackerel – sides barred green, its underbelly plump and glossy. Such beauty you cannot imagine.*

Cord was leaving when she stood in front of his ute. Back then she thought she was in control. She handed him the fish through his open window and he looked at her like she was mad.

That night, he laid the fish on his bench and slipped the filleting knife from the vent to the gill slits. With a quick flick, he pulled the guts into a bowl. Cold, pink and red, smooth. Something caught his attention and he grubbed out a piece of paper. He unfolded it to read *Nayna* and a Sydney phone number.

Things twist on the smallest point. A tremor far at sea, down deep where no one can see. And these things, they wash through time, collecting people, carrying them, building speed and force, until they erupt one day like a tsunami on a white sand beach.

In the living room, his mum is sitting beside his father on the couch. Rudra's eye is pressed to the narrow gap between the hinge side of the door and the jamb. No more than a pinkie's width to see it all. The TV is on but the volume is down. There is silence and space between Nayna and Cord. A space where Rudra would sit when he was younger, not understanding then he was both buffer and glue.

'She's my mother,' says his mum.

Silence rises from his father like smoke. Rudra can see the outline of his jaw, chewing on the bitterness.

'And she has no one left. I am the only child. She will die now my *baba* has gone.'

'That old witch will go on forever.'

'You don't talk of her like that.'

'I don't want to talk about anything.'

'You never do.'

'She's not coming. You're not going. End of.'

'I have saved some money, Cord.'

'Good. I need cash for repairs.'

'I worked for it. All last winter, when you couldn't fish, I was serving food in that damn restaurant.' *She never swears.* 'I put food on our table and I saved some money. For a time such as this, Cord. For now.'

'Then send her the money and be done with it.'

'That's not how it works in an Indian family. I have responsibilities.'

'This is not an Indian family.'

Rudra turns from the lounge room and slips out the front door. The cicadas are drilling the night as he walks down the street. At the end he takes a right, turning away from the sea and walking up the creek edge.

The water is brassy with moonlight as he picks his way between the sawtooth edges of oyster shells. On the other side of the creek, Wallace's light beckons to him as he doubles back towards the creek mouth.

There is a good stock of dinghies on the foreshore. When the pub closes, the men will clamber in and row back home, splashing water on their faces in the hope of sobering up. Some holiday boats are turned over against the weather, waiting to be rowed over four times a year, filled with wine, cheese and Hawkesbury oysters. Rudra flips a boat and drags it down the sand, leaving behind a slim furrow. *It's borrowing*, Maggs's voice whispers, *it's not stealing if you bring it back*. It's not as if it's a local's boat or anything – that is Rudra's invisible line. Slipping the oars in the rowlocks, he pushes out.

Water tocks on the hull as Rudra moves towards the far bank. The tide is running out so he angles above Wallace's landing, pulling on the oars, feeling the tightening in his shoulders. When the bow hits the sand, he jumps out, dragging the boat to Wallace's jetty and tying it off. He climbs the rough concrete steps to the house and knocks on Wallace's door. The cicadas are now in a wild fury and the trees on the escarpment are restless.

Wallace appears, framed by the doorway, bleary-eyed. Rudra can see red wine tusks at the corners of his mouth.

'Come in,' he says, backing into his home.

Wallace built this place himself, over time, from scrounged materials. Not a pretty house, but it serves its purpose: to keep Wallace dry, mainly, and warm, mostly.

Wallace's dog, Tangent, is asleep on the couch. He is grey around the muzzle now but still perky in the way of all little dogs. He gets called a chihuahua a lot. *I'm a miniature pinscher – a minpin,* he snarls. *So get it straight or I'll have a piece of you.* The dog wakes and rolls his belly at Rudra. His tail moves lazily. Rudra sits beside him and, pulling him onto his lap, rubs him behind the ears.

'Wanna watch TV?' Wallace asks, flicking on his old black-and-white. Rudra has never seen one of these relics anywhere but at Wallace's. *Because it makes everything look arty. Like a* National Geographic *photo.* For this Wallace turns the sound down, so it provides a backdrop to his life – moving wallpaper – to be ignored or watched as he sees fit. The cicadas outside get shriller and shriller until it seems like the air will combust. Rudra doesn't know how to start this conversation.

He looks around the room as if seeing it for the first time; exactly how it is rather than just the container that has always held Wallace. The kitchen crammed in one corner with walls streaked with sausage fat. The raggedy furniture worn shiny, stuffing stumbling from cuts. Sun-bleached photos of the mullet run stuck to the wall with Blu Tack – the killing of so many fish. The whole place shabby and old and on the brink of being forgotten by the world.

And there in the middle of all those photos, one makes him feel as if he is falling through himself. It is of Rudra with his mum and dad, when he is maybe seven or eight. He can even remember the bright-blueness of that very day. They are about to hop on the ferry to Palm Beach. They got fish and chips that day, and he tamed those seagulls, oh yes he did. His mum called him *Master of Seagulls*. There she is, shading her eyes against the sun, bright as polished brass. She is smiling, her dark hair lifted by the lightest of breezes. But his dad, he is coming right down the lens – reaching through time and space and, finding his son, pushing his fists high inside his chest and crushing Rudra's heart.

'What was Dad like back then?' Rudra asks.

Wallace answers, almost apologetically, 'He's always been a hard man, Rudra. Hard to like and hard to know.'

'And Mum?'

'She was special, your mum.'

'Still is,' says Rudra. Cord Solace's fist is around her heart too. Rudra squeezes his eyes shut for a second, watching tiny flashes of light arc on the inside of his lids. 'I should get back,' he says, barely a whisper.

'You only just got here.'

'I know.'

'Well, you know where I am if you need something.'

'Thanks, Wallace. Have a good night.' Rudra closes the door and walks to the jetty. Patonga's lights hit the water so softly it looks as if there can be no malice in the town. As if, behind every window, in every lounge room, there is calm.

# 4

PEACE COMES TO THE SOLACE HOUSE and stays for
a while. Fixing the boat takes up most of Cord's time and
the arguments burn themselves to silence. But this isn't a
comfortable peace – the kind that Sunday afternoons are
cut from. Instead, it is more like a truce – an uneasy and
purposeful forgetting.

And then, all at once, war returns. Rudra shelters from
the bombardment in his bedroom. The shells sing their
destructive song, and sometimes it seems like shouting,
and sometimes it seems like tears. And sometimes it is just
heartbreaking silence. He doesn't know why that feels the
hardest of all.

His dad goes fishing without him. He takes Wallace. And
Wallace won't meet Rudra's eye. He leaves Tangent at the
Solace home for company and Rudra sits in the deep shade
of the verandah with the little dog on his knee, feeling his
heartbeat quicken with the wind.

Restless energy forces Rudra to act. He calls Maggs and
they arrange a meet-up. Together they cross the Rip Bridge
in search of flathead.

The water, smashing its way through the narrow nip in the bay, is rarely at peace. The bridge connects the far side of the coast with the peninsula and cuts the long trip from Booker Bay to Daleys Point down to mere seconds. They watched a video about the bridge at school. An *engineering marvel,* the voiceover called it, spanning the troublesome rip in *one graceful leap.* Rudra has never trusted the bridge though. Even now, when he crosses it in a car, he holds his breath from one side to the other, counting the expansion joints as they clunk beneath the tyres.

The concrete pavers that form the footpath rattle as they walk. The railing is barely a metre high. Rudra looks down to the coursing water and oyster-scabbed rocks below. They spot Judge and two of the year-zero heroes loitering at the railing halfway across.

'Let's turn back, Maggs,' says Rudra.

'Why?'

'We'll get more fish off the pier at Ettalong.'

'Toadfish?' Maggs shakes his head. 'That's not fish. The spot we're going is the bomb. Flathead'll be on the menu tonight.'

Rudra pulls his cap down over his eyes. With his red bucket and his rod, he feels like a kid heading to the beach.

As they approach the year zeroes, Judge pipes up. 'Well, lookee who it is, lads. It's Daggs and his faithful sidekick Curry Boy.'

Tangent growls way down in his throat. Maggs pushes his cap back with the tip of his rod. The footpath is narrow. There is nowhere to go.

'Nice tatt,' says Maggs, nodding to Judge's Southern Cross, the stringy script below it: *Remembering Cronulla 2005.*

'You must've been like seven years old when the riot went down.'

'My uncle was there, you little dog. Protecting the beach from *invaders*.' He sneers at Rudra.

'Whatever,' says Maggs. He rests his rod against the rail and looks eighteen metres down to the churning water. 'Jumping, are you?'

'What's it to you?' says Judge.

'Just concerned, that's all. Might break a hip or something. Should leave it to the younger fellas.'

Judge spits. 'S'pose you're going to tell me you've jumped before.'

'Might've.'

'Bullshit.'

'Maggs,' hisses Rudra. 'Don't get sucked in.'

'Yeah, Maggs. Listen to the curry-muncher. He knows what's best for you.'

'Piss off,' says Maggs.

'What?'

'You heard me, shitbird.'

'Cheeky.' Judge lunges at Maggs. 'Little.' He catches his arm. 'Arsewipe.' Turns Maggs's arm up behind his back. 'Give us a hand here, lads,' he yells to his mates. 'Let's learn him some manners.'

'Leave him!' But Rudra knows it will do no good.

The three year zeroes wrestle Maggs to the bridge railing. Tangent runs in circles snapping at their ankles.

'Let's dangle him,' shouts Judge, excited now, kicking out at Tangent. Maggs is a fish on a hook, his fight trembling into their arms. They get him up and over the rail. They lower him – one at each leg and one holding the back of his shirt. Maggs goes limp; he knows better than to fight this one.

'Let go,' says Judge to the guy holding Maggs's shirt. The guy backs away, hands up in mock surrender.

'You'll kill him!' yells Rudra.

'Say you're sorry, Daggs.'

'Piss off, Judge,' Maggs replies.

'Be nice, mate. I got your life in my hands.' He turns to his other sidekick. 'Let go of his leg. I got him.'

The other year zero is unsure. 'I got him!' yells Judge, grabbing the other leg. His mate eventually lets go and Judge shakes Maggs above the water. A fishing boat slows to look. There are two-foot standing-waves beneath the bridge and legends of broken spines and bleeding lungs.

'Say. You're. Sorry,' says Judge, jerking Maggs at each word. Maggs's left shoe comes loose and Judge fumbles. Judge's hand slips from the ankle and loses hold of the toes.

Maggs falls.

Rudra runs to the railing in time to see Maggs managing to flip his legs back under him, hitting the water feet first, as straight as he's able. It is not a pretty entry – a low scorer by Olympic standards. The water flowers white for a moment, fizzing. Then all trace of Maggs is swallowed by the churning rip.

'Shit, Judge,' says one of the year zeroes. 'You might've killed him.'

'We should look for him,' say the other one. 'He could be in trouble.'

'Be in more if we stick around,' says Judge. 'I reckon we get gone.' Could be fear in his eyes.

Rudra shouts, 'Bastards!' as they run from the bridge.

He chases after them before veering off and taking the J-shaped footpath that leads down to the water.

Rudra reaches the water's edge and looks out over the lumpy water. He scans left and right but sees nothing. *No! No-no-no-no-no!* The words, machine-gunned from deep inside do not sound like his own. He runs twenty metres up the bank towards Woy Woy before the sheoaks and mangroves stop him. 'Maggs,' he calls. 'Maggs!' Tangent empties a volley of yaps into the air. 'Maggs!' The name scours the back of Rudra's throat. 'Maggs!' He runs back to the spot where he saw Maggs fall. 'Maggs.' His voice fails. 'No, Maggs. No.'

Then, from around the mangroves at the water's edge, Maggs drags his sorry arse. He is limping, carrying his surviving shoe in one hand, carefully picking his way through the oysters. His nose is bleeding.

'I can't believe they dropped me,' he says.

# 5

FINALLY, SHE ARRIVES, LIKE SHE WAS always going to. She stands on their doorstep mid-afternoon, small, with a battered cardboard suitcase. They have never met, but she is so familiar – that smile, the tips of her ears poking from her hair. Rudra thinks he should probably hug her, but he shakes her hand like the stupid kid he is and leads her to the kitchen.

Nayna is bent over the stove, stirring soup. She looks up and blinks once, twice. They stand apart from each other, the wooden spoon hovering, dripping soup to the floor. And then they are together, his mother and grandmother, and their eyes are closed and they don't speak.

The shoulder of his grandmother's sari is wet with tears by the time she hugs Rudra. She smells of fenugreek, and it is the most exotic and the most normal smell he has ever come across. She holds him out at arm's length.

'What a strong boy you have become, Rudra. Like your *dadu* – your grandfather.' She looks at her daughter. 'Does he know this word, Nayna? Have you taught him Bangla? So much like him, don't you think, Nayna?'

Nayna waggles her head.

'Of course he does. Your *dadu* would be so proud. So proud. Where is your husband, Nayna? Are you keeping him a secret all these years? No photos or nothing like that.'

'He's fishing, Ama.'

'Fishing, is it? Well, it is not the best but it is not the worst. It is good to be busy, Nayna. A lazy man is trouble. I have always said that. But look at me. I talk too much. Can you make me a cup of *cha*, Nayna. Nice and sweet. I have presents for you. Here in my bag, they are. Let me sit down and I'll show you. You will like them.' She winks at Rudra conspiratorially. 'I brought *ladoos*.'

'Ama, you shouldn't.'

'Phhft!' She purses her lips on the sound. 'It's nothing.'

'It's illegal, Ama. You have to declare all food at customs.'

'It's *LADOOS*, Nayna, not drugs.' She shakes her head at Rudra as if his mum is simple. 'We'll have some with *cha*. You like *ladoos*, Rudra?'

'I—'

'Of course you do. What Indian boy does not like *ladoos*?'

'I don't know that he'll like *ladoos*, Ama.'

'Just put the *cha* on and don't be a bore. You were always such a serious little girl, Nayna. She was, Rudra. Always one for rules.' She purses her lips again. 'Well, some rules.'

'Ama.' His mother's eyes are flames.

'I'm not saying a thing.'

'Good.'

'But—'

'Ama!'

'Let's have some *ladoos*.'

They are eating *ladoos* and drinking *cha* when Cord Solace returns from the sea. He smells of seaweed and prawns and there is salt in his hair. Nayna places her hands around his biceps as if restraining him. She looks right into his eyes, speaking slowly as if to a dangerous dog. 'This is my mother, Cord.'

Cord blinks as though to make her disappear, but still she remains – five foot of her, from grey wisps of hair to slippered feet.

'Ama, this is Cord – my husband.'

'Pleased to meet you.' Rudra's grandmother's mouth tightens around the words.

Cord ignores her. 'Nayna, we need to talk.'

'Cord, please.'

'In the other room.'

The kitchen vomits Cord into the hallway.

Nayna watches the weave of her own fingers. 'I am sorry, Ama.' Then she leaves Rudra alone with his grandmother and goes in search of her husband.

'So, Rudra,' says his grandmother. 'Have you heard of Rabindranath Tagore – the most famous of all Bengali poets?'

Rudra shakes his head.

'Such a pity,' she says. 'Still, there is time.'

The walls muffle his parents' voices but it is clear what they are saying. Rudra can picture his father, legs apart. His mother, clutching at straws.

There is a knock at the front door and Rudra takes the opportunity to leave the kitchen. It is Wallace and Tangent. The little dog turns circles when he sees Rudra.

'Ah...hi, mate.' Wallace rubs his stubbly head with his palm. 'It's just your dad said to come by. Said he had some pay.' He looks beyond Rudra. 'If I'm interrupting, I can come back later.'

'Come in,' says Rudra and Wallace follows him down the hall into the kitchen. 'Wallace, this is my grandmother – my *didima*.' He looks to his grandmother to see if he has the pronunciation right.

'Didima, is it? Please to meet you, Didima.' He takes Rudra's grandmother's hand and shakes it vigorously. 'Wallace. Wallace Gully.'

Tangent jumps up, barking.

'And this is Tangent. He's a dog.'

'We have dogs in India, you know,' says Didima sharply. She grimaces. 'But usually not in the kitchen.'

'He's a bit special, this one, Didima. Aren'cha, Tangent?' Tangent agrees wholeheartedly.

Rudra's parents return to the kitchen – Nayna first, Cord following like a cloud.

'Wallace.' His father nods a greeting.

'Boss.'

They stand for a moment, awkwardness unfolding like a banana lounge between them. 'Nayna,' says Rudra's father, turning to his wife.

She snaps out of her stupor. 'Ama, you have to leave.' The words come out like a rush of water from a burst pipe.

'But I just got here. It's been so far.'

'I know, Ama.' Rudra's mother seems like she is on autopilot. 'I will pay for a hotel while we find you somewhere to stay.'

'Nayna, is this you speaking?'

'Ama, please.'

Cord speaks up. 'You can't stay here. There's no room.'

'She can stay with me,' says Wallace.

They have all forgotten Wallace standing there and, like a flock of curious birds, they swivel in unison to look at him.

'You can stay with me, Didima. I got heaps of room. Too much, really.'

Didima looks grey and crumpled. 'That's very kind—'

'Then it's settled.' Wallace nods. 'Rudra, grab her bags and walk her to the boat.'

'Boat?' Didima seems unsure.

'The creek's a bit deep to wade on this tide.'

Cord fills a glass at the sink. He says over his shoulder. 'Rudra, get your grandmother's bags. Quickly now.' This is clearly the end of the conversation.

They walk down the long, tree-lined street – Rudra tugging Didima's unruly suitcase, its wheels slowly disintegrating on the rough surface. Didima's shoulders are rounded by the blows she has just taken. 'My daughter,' she says to no one in particular. 'All this way.' Then, her hand against her chest as if someone has torn at her heart, 'So sad.'

The tide is on the turn by the time they get to the creek. Rudra helps Wallace pull the dinghy to the water, then places his grandmother's battered suitcase in the bow.

'You can sit here, Didima,' he says.

'I know where I can sit, Rudra,' she says, straightening her back. 'I am from the Sundarbans. We are very familiar with boats.' Rudra sees that nothing will keep this woman down for long; that this is from where his own mother draws her strength.

Wallace nods approvingly and slips the oars in the rowlocks. 'Come on then, Didima, let's get you to your new home.' He helps her into the boat and lifts Tangent on board. The little dog runs to the box and perches on Didima's suitcase.

'Is the dog coming too?' Didima asks.

'Can't leave him here, can we?'

Didima seems to consider it, but Wallace breaks in. 'You coming, Rudra?'

'I might swim over.' He watches to see if Didima has registered this. If she knows water, she'll see how tricky this tide is. She'll notice Wallace having to hold the tinnie against its force.

'You sure, mate?' says Wallace. 'The current's moving a bit.'

'I'll be right,' says Rudra and, throwing his shirt in the boat, dives into the creek. He knows almost immediately that he has misjudged. He's done this swim plenty but usually he would never attempt it at this point in the turn. It's only thirty or forty metres over, even with the tide this full. He starts strong, stroking hard into the water, eyeing the opposite bank like it's his. But pretty soon Wallace and Didima are alongside him.

'You okay?' Wallace shouts.

'Fine,' Rudra manages, putting his head down and powering ahead. After ten or so strokes, he lifts his gaze to see where he is. Wallace and Didima are almost at Wallace's jetty. He can just make out Didima's hand shading her eyes; looking his way. He is nearly at the mouth of the creek now. There are mangrove sticks in the water and his shoulders are on fire.

He gives up and, floating on his back, allows himself to be carried into the bay. The water is calmer out here and the clouds are mere papercuts on the blue of the sky. He can hear his heart thumping and bubbles popping, and he is happy for this release – to allow the current to carry him.

'Why is Cord such an arsehole?' The words tremble off his tongue. And then to himself, so even the fish can't hear, *Why would he turn Didima away? His wife's mother. My grandmother. Does family mean nothing?*

He never met his dad's dad, nor Cord's mother. They were both dead before he was born. And there is the mystery of his uncle – an absence never discussed but there all the same, like the warmth on a seat after someone has left the room. A blurry photo in their hallway – him just a smudge in their collective history left for Rudra to wonder over. So many mysteries in this family. So many boxes unopened.

He hears Wallace before he sees him – the tonking of water against the hull of the tinnie, then Wallace's face eclipsing the sun.

'What are you doing, mate? Scared the bejesus out of Didima. Old girl's having kittens. She made me row out here to save you.'

Rudra pulls himself over the gunnel and drops into the dinghy. Tangent is all over him, ragging his tongue on his face. They row to Wallace's in silence. Wallace is good like that. He usually knows the right time for words and the right time for holding back. Rudra keeps Tangent on his knee, feeling the little dog shiver. As they near Wallace's jetty, he sees Didima sitting on her cardboard case, her sari pulled over her head.

'Oh, Rudra,' she says as they dock. 'I was worried. Sometimes the sea is hungry for young men like you.'

'I was fine, Didima.'

'Of course you were. But I am an old lady. You cannot worry me so.'

'Sorry, Didima.'

Wallace ties the dinghy off. 'Let's get you settled and put the kettle on. Rudra, grab Didima's bag for her.'

They climb the steps to Wallace's shack. It looks very worn. The paint, dull and flaking; the mismatched tin. Didima struggles with the climb. Even though it is no more than twenty steps, she stops three times for breath as if she is ascending from a dive. Her sari has fallen from her head, revealing a mist of grey hair. Rudra wonders exactly how old she is.

Wallace opens the door, throwing his arms wide dramatically. *Ta-da.* Didima puts her hand over her mouth and Rudra closes his eyes.

'Oh, Wallace,' she says finally.

*She hates it,* Rudra thinks. *Now where will she go?*

When he opens his eyes again, Didima is smiling. 'It is a palace, Wallace,' she says. 'I feel like a *rajkumari* – a princess.'

'You are that, Didima. Plonk yourself here.' Wallace brushes the dog hair from his favourite chair. Rudra feels relief wash over him. His grandmother will be fine here. She likes the house. She likes Wallace.

'I'll put the billy on,' says Wallace. 'And when you've got your breath, we'll set you up in the spare room.'

'You are too kind, Wallace. Isn't he kind, Rudra?'

'He's kind, Didima.'

'Come and sit beside me, Rudra, so I can see you.'

Rudra does as he is told, even though he is sixteen and beyond all that. Didima takes his hand, and the feel of her skin is like newspaper from an attic or behind the plaster of an old wall: thin and cold and dusty, with dark blotches here and there as if her ink has bled through. He wants to pull away, disgusted by the oldness of her. And then he is disgusted by his disgust. He repeats to himself, *She is my grandmother, she is my grandmother* ...

She sees it, his disgust. It is in her eyes – a sadness gathering, harlequin bugs souring the summer.

'Here, we go, Didima,' says Wallace. 'A nice cup of tea. Put your feet up here. Tangent, git down from there!'

The little dog looks up at him with his round moist eyes and doesn't move.

'Doesn't listen to me. Does what he likes. Still, he's a mate. Can't argue with that.' He scoops Tangent into his lap. 'So, where you from, Didima?'

'The Sundarbans.'

'India?'

'Near Kolkata. Between there and Bangladesh. It's where all the rivers decide to come together before they give themselves up to the Bay of Bengal.'

'Hmmm,' says Wallace, considering this for a moment. 'Is it pretty?'

'The most beautiful place on earth.'

'Big call.'

'It's quite like here.' She smiles. 'But a bit nicer. I can see why your mother chose it, Rudra.'

'Well,' says Rudra. 'She didn't really choose *it*, Didima. She chose my dad.'

Didima's lips tighten for a moment on that thought. 'Well, it is beautiful. Nearly as beautiful as the Sundarbans. You'll come one day, Rudra, to see your home.'

'This is my home.'

'This is where you live, but India is your *home*.'

Wallace shifts on his seat, looks out the window. 'Looks like the wind is coming up,' he says, trying too hard to change the subject.

'It's my home, Didima. I come from here.'

'But do you feel like you belong?' asks Didima.

*I am from here,* he thinks. *I am of here.* He has lived in Patonga his whole life. That is surely enough. But Judge's words still sting. *Curry-muncher. Drop-in.*

Didima places her cup on the table. 'I wrote to Nayna so many times, you know,' she says. 'But she replied so little. And not at all in these last years.'

Rudra doesn't know what to say. 'She is busy, Didima. She thought of you a lot. Told me stories about you.' It wasn't a lie. When Cord was out of the picture, Didima was all his mum wanted to talk about. But Rudra also knew how proud his mother was and that telling Didima of her misery could be seen as defeat.

'Still, she could have written more. I am old and she is all I have.'

Wallace slurps the last of his tea and grabs Rudra's mug. 'You should be getting back,' he says. 'Your mum and dad will be expecting you for dinner. I'll run you over in the boat.'

'I can swim.'

'I know you can, mate. For Didima's sake though.'

'Will you be okay, Didima?'

'She'll be fine,' Wallace says. 'Tangent will look after her. Won't you boy?' The little dog yaps a quick yes.

Rudra's *didima* throws her arms around him, and she is so dry, so papery, it is like hugging a cicada shell.

'Thanks, Wallace,' he says as they close the door.

'What for, mate?' Wallace replies. 'She's family.'

# 6

THE NEXT MORNING, AFTER BREAKFAST, Didima turns up on the doorstep.

'Is your father home?' she asks Rudra.

'He's on the boat.'

'Good,' says Didima, nodding as if to herself. 'He's not a kind man, is he, Rudra?'

'Not often, no.'

Didima's eyes narrow. 'Was he *unkind* to you when you came home last night?'

'No more than normal.'

'To my Nayna?'

Rudra wants to hold back and make it seem like things are normal in the Solace household. He doesn't want Didima to become tainted by Cord's poison; to let it out in the world. 'She's not supposed to see you,' he blurts.

'Not supposed to?'

'Not really.'

Didima swallows as if she has a chicken bone lodged in her throat. 'Is she here?' she asks.

'She's in the garden. Reading. She has to do the lunch shift.'

'Work?' asks Didima.

'At Second to Naan.'

'Sorry?'

'It's an Indian restaurant. In Umina. A friend drives her.' Rudra doesn't know why he offers up all this information. It's not like Didima is Federal Police.

'She's a cook?'

'She waits tables.' There it is – more family shame. And he sees it hit Didima fair in the stomach.

'She is a *waitress*?'

Rudra knows the word is *waitress* but Didima makes it sound so wrong – so unclean. 'She's been saving money. Trying to help with things around here,' he tries.

'She was studying science, Rudra. My daughter is a scientist, not a *waitress*.'

'Well she's not a waitress until one. Until then, she is reading a book.' He pauses, nodding to the back door. 'In the garden.'

'So like her, always with a book. I used to tell your grandfather she'd drown in those words. Do you like books, Rudra? Are you a reader?'

'Not so much.'

'We all need just the right amount of education, you know. But don't drown in those words, Rudra, not like your mother. And all the good it did her. A *waitress* – well I never. Now, how about you make your *didima* a nice cup of *cha*.'

She herds Rudra down the hallway and seats herself at the kitchen table.

'I'll get Mum,' says Rudra.

'Leave her be. We'll have a nice lollygag, you and I.'

Rudra fills a saucepan at the sink and puts it on the stove.

'Didima, can I ask you a question?'

'Of course you can, my grandson.'

'Didima, why words like *lollygag*?'

'Those damn Britishers,' she says. 'When they finally let us be, they left behind all their rubbish. I don't think even they would even use such words these times. Twenty-two languages of our own and still we cling to these stupid words. It is hard to let things go.'

'True,' says Rudra, grabbing a handful of tea from the caddy and adding it to the water.

'Some people say I speak English even better than Bangla. That is because I was able to get an education. Just the perfect amount. Some good fortune came from some bad fortune.' She waggles her head. 'And this story I will tell you one day.'

'You speak very good English, Didima.'

She smiles, obviously happy with the praise from her grandson. 'No spicy things in the tea, Rudra, okay. This *masala cha* is no good for my stomach.'

'Okay, Didima.'

'Plenty of sugar, though. And boil the milk nice and hard.'

'Yes, Didima.'

Rudra pours in the milk and adds three heaped teaspoons of sugar.

'Don't skimp, Rudra. It's not like you are poor. Make it nice and sweet for your *didima*.'

Rudra adds another scoop. The pot begins to boil and foam. He turns the heat back, allowing it a rolling boil for another minute, then pours it into two small glasses.

'Any of those *ladoos* left, Rudra?'

'I ate them.'

'Good boy. Come and sit beside your *didima*. Tell me what you are going to do after school.'

Rudra sits like an obedient Indian grandson. He looks out the window to where his mother is sitting under the jacaranda, her book on her lap, head thrown back in sleep.

'I don't know what I am going to do, Didima.'

'You are young yet.'

'I'll be in year eleven soon.'

'And you are clever. We always had brains in our family. Always.'

'Dad wants me to be a fisherman.'

'In the village, they'd always come to your *dadu* for solutions. He was a solution-*wala*. From a very good family.'

'Fishing's been our family business forever.'

Didima steals Rudra's hand. Hers is warm from the *cha* cup. 'Listen to me, Rudra. The sea doesn't care about you. Why should you care about it?'

'I don't know if I want to keep on with school.'

'But you are clever, Rudra. Just the right amount of education, *na*?'

'Didima, you don't know that.'

'I know our family, and we are all clever. Your *dadu* was a solution-*wala*. He worked on solutions. For the whole village, Rudra. And it was a big village we came from.

'He was wise and kind, your *dadu*, and your mother, she was clever. But she and her foolish choices, they were the undoing of her. There is a difference between wisdom and cleverness. She wasn't so wise sometimes.'

'Didima, you can't say that.'

'I can say it, and I will. I won't stay silent and let you become an Australian.'

The words shock Rudra. 'But I *am* Australian, Didima.'

'That's preposterous. You are my grandson. We are a clever family.'

Rudra lets it pass. Tries another tack. 'Your father was a honey-gatherer.'

Didima drops Rudra's hand. 'Who told you that?'

'Mum.'

'But my *husband* was a solution-*wala*. A big man in the village. The village is one of the biggest in the Sundarbans.'

'What's wrong with being a honey-collector?'

'Anyone can be a honey-collector. Or a *fisherman*.' She spits the word and looks hard into Rudra's eyes. Then she takes his hand again, so gently. 'Your mother went to school and university in Kolkata. She was such a clever girl.'

'She still is, Didima.'

He pulls his hand from Didima's. 'I'll get Mum,' he says.

'Rudra,' she calls as he escapes the kitchen.

There have been big hauls up the Hawkesbury – past Peats Ferry Bridge and towards the lower stretches out to Flint and Steel. The town has been alive with the news, fishermen wheeling crates of prawns down the pier, beers shouted in the pub. Everyone in on the game. Out on *Paper Tiger* Cord Solace works in fuming silence, piecing her tired motor back together for the fourth time this season.

Eventually, she is ready to go. Just after midnight, Cord, Wallace and Rudra motor away from Patonga and cruise up the Hawkesbury, burning fuel on the promise of a decent go at the prawns. Past Dangar Island, Cord pushing the boat between the gappy teeth of the old stone pylons. On beneath the steel rail bridge, pooled with light, the last train out of Central pushing towards Wondabyne. Rudra sees the people as though framed orange portraits – dead on each other's shoulders, winding into the greasy blackness of Mullet Creek and down to Woy Woy, while Cord Solace and his crew pass Long and Spectacle Islands.

Wallace and Rudra stand at the stern looking at the swirl of white leading a trail all the way home. Wallace lights up and a bitter cloud of smoke mingles with the diesel fumes.

'Didima's a good old stick,' says Wallace.

'Yeah, I guess.'

'I like her.' Wallace turns his back on the river and looks sideways at Rudra. 'And you should too. She's your blood.'

'I do like her.'

'But?'

'I dunno. It's like she expects me to be the Instant Indian.'

'She's teaching me how to cook,' Wallace says. 'Real Indian food – like back home.'

'So it looks like you get to be the Instant Indian.'

'Not me, mate. I know exactly who I am.'

After the freeway bridge at Mooney Mooney, they shoot their net, trying three short digs near The Vines before heading over to Davo's. Nothing but weed and trash – an old bicycle frame comes up knobby with rust and a crusting of oysters. At four in the morning they head back to the mouth for one last dig near Flint and Steel. Cord has this feeling that they will get lucky there.

'I don't like this place much,' says Wallace.

'Why not?' asks Rudra.

'Too much stuff hidden under. Chunks of reef, sunken logs, dead boats.'

'Boats?'

'Your dad never told you?'

Rudra snorts. 'He never tells me anything.'

'It's the Bermuda bloody Triangle. Boats come here to die.'

'I think you're mixing that up with the Elephant's Graveyard.'

'Whatever you reckon. But there's plenty of dead boats beneath, and it makes it a fearful place.' He looks into the night, his smoke down to a stub in the corner of his mouth. 'One of them boats you may know better than you think.'

'What do you mean?'

Wallace shakes his head. 'Forget it,' he says, as he feeds the net into the dark water. Cord slows the boat and begins a shot parallel to the shore. Across the water, Rudra can see the lights of Patonga winking at him – so close he can almost snuff them with his fingers. The light is beautiful in reflection; so much treasure against the velvet. Suddenly there is a grab at the net and the boat shudders.

'What's she stuck on?' shouts Cord, throttling back.

Wallace tugs on the foot-rope. 'Dunno. Something big. If we tear her free there'll be a stack of mending to do.'

Cord swears, punches the roof of the cabin. 'I'm going to have to pull her free. No other option.'

'You know what's under there, don't you?'

'I know well enough,' Cord says between his teeth.

'You know if we get into a pulling competition it'll win. We'll go under.'

'The nets will tear first.'

'Better hope,' whispers Wallace.

*Paper Tiger* strains against the net. The ropes tighten until Rudra thinks they are going to break. Now they are tight as guitar strings. Now they are shedding drops of water. Now they are singing into the night – songs of tension and danger. Rudra looks for cover, imagining where they might lash out when they go.

Suddenly, the net pulls free and the boat lurches forward. Rudra watches as the net comes up from the secret deep, the otterboards breaking the surface and rising to the gallows.

'Grab the lazy line,' Wallace calls. And Rudra does, swinging the cod-end, when it appears, up and onto the sorting table. It should be full of prawns. Should be, but isn't. A long gash in the net has seen to most of that.

It's light. Way too light. And Rudra knows all the secret repercussions of this; knows all the muttered curses and silent treatments. Curiously, though, when the net hits the table, it clunks as if there is something solid in its core.

'How's it look?' shouts Cord. But he knows already; knows it to be worthless.

They go to work, hooking out the weed and smaller prawns, the crabs and jelly blubber. Putting everything, apart from the prawns, back where it belongs. It goes like this for a minute, maybe less, before Wallace uncovers something.

'What *is* it?' asks Rudra, reaching forward.

'I wouldn't go touching it,' Wallace warns, his hand on Rudra's bicep.

Rudra holds his breath. There is a clicking in his ears that could be the snicking of crab claws.

'What are you two bozos staring at?' Cord yells from the

cabin. 'I'm not paying you to stand around. Get the prawns on the slurry and we'll head for home.'

Rudra can see that Wallace is not going to touch the thing. He himself is weighing up the lesser of two fears: Cord Solace or the object on the sorting table. He knows how this traps him. Knows his dad to be a bully.

'Get on with it!' screams Cord. 'Dump the shit. Keep the prawns.'

It is slippery with seaweed. Rudra's finger sinks into a dark hole oozing with black sand. The smell is repugnant, thick and oily and full of decay, but he manages to pull the thing free without retching. He knows he should toss it back into the water. But the smoothness of it lures him; the hairline cracks that snag his nails are intriguing.

How to describe a thing without naming it; without truly knowing what it is? Rudra wants to say *box* but it is too smooth, less angular. How can he talk about its geometry without calling it something else? Perhaps it is entirely new in this world. Maybe they have dredged a new species from these familiar waters.

The thing is in two pieces, hinged with a glint of copper wire at the back. The top piece has the flattened sleekness of a racing bike helmet. The 'helmet' has two large holes at the rear (into which his fingers disappear alarmingly) and one at the front, with a fragile whirlpool growth that reminds Rudra of cave formation – a shawl of bitter bone. At the bottom of the bike helmet is a grill of sharpened pegs, two larger than the other and raked back as if designed for tearing. The bottom piece has a mirrored set of sharpened pegs, smaller but just as deadly looking. Could these be teeth? And if they *are* teeth, would this then be a skull?

'Throw it over,' hisses Wallace, backing against the gunwale.

Grabbing the hose, Rudra drenches the object in water. Silt gushes from it, and weed and lugworms and tiny crabs. *Like water spiders*, he thinks. Yes, like water spiders. He almost recognises the collection of shapes that make up the object; assembles them in his mind like a three-dimensional jigsaw. Not believing what he has made.

Rudra has seen many skulls in his life. The small, space-ship skulls of wallabies that sit well in the palm of your hand; the masses of muttonbird skulls – seemingly folded from paper during September storms. But this is so new. Even the human skull (Yorick) who lurks behind tough-ened glass in the science room, does not come close to this menace. Maybe it can't be a skull. Maybe it shouldn't be.

His dad guns the engine and a cloud of diesel smoke coughs itself into the night. 'Get moving,' he yells.

Carefully Rudra washes the object. He pulls the sea-things from it so it belongs up here. Scrapes its surfaces with his nail until it is yellow-brown, even white in patches.

'I told you, *dump the crap*. We're only after prawns.' Cord stops at the door of the cabin. 'What is that?'

He approaches the sorting table slowly. He picks the object up, looks at it close. His nostrils flare, his eyes widen and his top lip, Rudra notices, has the slightest tremor – hardly noticeable, but there for sure.

Without taking his eyes from the thing, Cord whispers at Wallace, 'Put the prawns on ice. Get rid of the weed.' With that, he takes the object into the cabin.

# 7

NO SLEEP. TOO FEW PRAWNS. The sun is a little too bright this day, the leaves too green, the air too soft, the insects too shrill, the birds too raucous. The world is too cruel. When they come up from the bay, Cord, Wallace and Rudra are painted with a grey brush while all about them is colour. In the playground the kids' laughter seems directed at them – at their failure. Cord carries the object in a gunny-sack. They don't talk about it or what it could be, but the question is burning inside Rudra. He knows Cord will take it to his office, where he will hide it. Where he hides everything, including himself.

All morning Rudra battles sleep. Around midday, Maggs calls.

'S'up?'

'Nothing.'

'Wanna do something?'

'Nup.'

'How was fishing?'

'Shit.'

'I guess we'll catch up soon.'

'Yup.'

The line goes dead. He is weightless. The connection severed, he floats off into the gasping void. *It's just lack of sleep*, he says quietly to no one. *Nothing more.*

The day begins to burn. The cicadas go wild for it but everything else is still. The house settles and moans. His dad locks his office door behind him and leaves the house.

Rudra puts on The Smashing Pumpkins. He lies on the bed and listens to Billy Corgan assure him that the world is a vampire. And he believes it, despite all his rage. Why not? Today is a waking dream.

Rudra wonders about the thing that came up in the net. He saw the way his dad looked when he seized it from the sorting table – like he recognised it from somewhere. It is in Cord's office now – Rudra has seen its dark shadow drying on the windowsill. He wants to see it up close. Wants to turn it over in his hand, examine it. But Cord has the key in his pocket. And Cord has his fury.

Rudra sits at his desk. He pulls out an old exercise book and opens it to a blank page. He begins to draw, although art isn't his thing and he can never could make what is in his head appear magically on the paper. Always coming out wrong until the paper, tired of his eraser, grows worn and grubby. Still he tries – drawing the half-helmet, attempting the smoothness of it and some hairline cracks that he remembers now. He sketches two large holes on each side and one at the front into which, he wishes still, he could ease his fingers. Below this hole, he details the grill of pointed pegs, two larger than the others, curved, stalactites guarding the mouth of a cave. His hand moving quickly now, shading in, brushing crumbs of rubber from the paper. The hinged flap assembles itself, with more pegs, curving upwards – stalagmites or teeth – he doesn't know. He recalls the glint of copper wire holding this flap in place and his pencil scratches this in too.

When he finishes, he holds it at arm's length. He rips it from the book and, Blu Tacking it to the wall, views it from the doorway. Then he approaches it from an angle, sneaking up and peering at it so closely that the breath from his nostrils laps back at him. Eventually and inevitably, it crunches itself into a ball and drops itself into his bin.

Rudra curls on his bed and slips in his earphones. He closes his eyes and imagines the ocean, a street away, sucking at the rocks and pier, swirling into the river mouth. Billy Corgan sings to him of 1979. Of a time Rudra will never know. He knows what Maggs would say – *who cares what Billy thinks or sings*; that Billy doesn't know where his own bones will rest, much less theirs. The music is soft but it has a menace grinding inside. Music is the bait, he realises. Beneath it, the barb. The deep swallow. The guthook.

He feels himself slipping under. He tries to make it back to the surface. He realises he has missed one song, or maybe two. He fights sleep for the enemy it is. He is irrational at the end of this long day – at the edge of dreaming. His bed is so comfortable. He has known it his whole life. This house that grows around him is like a forest of kelp, so familiar. He drifts towards the sound of the ocean. Gives himself up.

The beach up near the dunes is fringed with pumice, blue with night and frosted where the new scar of a moon edges it. And on that sand, prints, waiting for the sea goddess to accept them. Prints too big and too foreign for this shore. Prints with a central pad, four toes, the slight impression of claws.

*He tracks them up the beach towards the creek, notes the lazy scuff of the leading paw, the careless way the animal has moved. He loses the prints in the scrub near the caravan park but by the cyclone wire, in the dusting of sand, the prints resume. Round by the kids' jungle gym, wires strung like a trap.*

*Then round the camps – the big square tents pitched, beers cans in piles. Them all snoring inside, forgetting what they left – jobs in warehouses and caryards, a square of burnt kikuyu beneath that Hill's hoist, periods four and five in classrooms with peeling posters. They are alive for these hot, sunlit weeks and it will keep them going for another year.*

*Up by the gutting tables, there is blood. On the ground. So dark it eats the light from the moon. There a finger – or could be a chunk of bait. And there an ear – or could be an abalone heart. The prints here are mangled, worked together into a frenzy.*

*He moves around to the river mouth, seeing the sway of a night animal, the quiver of its flanks. Its eyes are so round and yellow, the pupils as black as the deep pulling in the grey-blue wash, the frenzy of trees up on the headland, the boats straining against their ropes. And he slows and he slows. And every time the animal looks up, he is frozen into a rock, a tree stump.*

He wakes to a furious heartbeat, feeling the realness of the dream slowly dissolve. *Only a dream*, he whispers. *Only a dream. Only.*

# 8

HE FINDS WALLACE DOWN AT THE PIER mending the net. Tangent is curled in a tight little ball in the netting.

Rudra sits down beside Wallace on the wooden bench. 'What's happening?'

'Don't ask,' says Wallace. 'And especially don't ask *him*.' He points the net needle to where the dark figure of Cord is sitting in the stern of *Paper Tiger*. From this distance Rudra can see he's on his mobile. Out there in the bay he gets good reception, so he often uses it as his office – calling suppliers, arguing over prices. Now, it's obvious from his body language that he's shouting, even though the offshore breeze bundles his voice towards West Head.

Rudra grabs a spare needle, a flat piece of beige plastic with a hole in one end.

'Wanna hand?'

'You hold it, Rudra, I'll run the needle along.'

Rudra pulls the tear together while Wallace runs in and out with the needle loaded with nylon string. Wallace is quick. It's one of the many reasons his father uses him. No one can mend a net as neat and fast.

'Been thinking about that thing,' says Rudra.

'What thing?' asks Wallace.

'The thing we pulled up in the net.'

'What about it?'

'It's like Cord had seen it before,' says Rudra.

Wallace doesn't look up from what he is doing; his needle keeps shuttling along. Rudra follows its hypnotic movement, staring first at the diamond patterns of cord and then through the holes between. *Is it the holes or the cord that make the net?* he wonders. *The things you see or those you can't?* The intruding thought only stays a moment before he pulls his mind back to the job at hand. The muscles between his thumbs and forefingers are growing weak but Wallace's needle doesn't stop, his quick fingers running it along the tear, drawing the edges together.

'I got another question for you,' Rudra says. 'What was that about the sunken boat out at Flint and Steel?'

Wallace pinches the bridge of his nose. 'It's just a boat, Rudra,' he says, 'We snagged it with the net. End of.'

*Not that easy, Wallace. No way.* 'You said I might know one of those boats better than I think. What did you mean?'

'Ask your old man.'

'Yeah, right.'

'It's just an old boat, Rudra. Stories, that's all. This place is full of stories.'

'Why do I feel like you're keeping something from me?'

'Hold the net, mate. And stop driving me crazy with your questions.'

Rudra looks out to *Paper Tiger* and the silhouette of his father. All that blackness, with the sun eating into him like quicksilver.

When they finish, Rudra walks with Wallace and Tangent towards the creek. The morning has collapsed over town like a broken beast. It's only ten, but it's already boiling and the cicadas are crazy-making in the trees. As they approach the creek, he notices a dark hump near the gutting table.

When they get close, he sees it is an animal, or what remains of one. Tangent noses the carcass – a mess of peeled-back skin, the sinew on the hind leg exposed like a strip of bark, the black meat already blown with flies, a gaping hole in its belly – guts all stripped out. *Eviscerated*: Rudra remembers that word, because it sounds like what it is, all full of knife and sharpness.

'Gotta be a dog,' Wallace says. 'A big dog. To do all that damage.'

Rudra tries to shake the dream from the night before but it hangs on to him. The animal is a wallaby, or the remains of one. He helps Wallace drag it towards the creek, him on a leg and Wallace on the tail. Seems wrong to feel its body jarring over every rock and tussock.

'Help me in the boat with it.'

But Rudra doesn't want to touch it anymore. It disgusts him, with its craned-back head, kelp trunk tail and glassy eyes.

'What's the matter?' asks Wallace. 'You know we can't just leave it here. What'll the tourists think? Some great dog out there hunting at night? They'll never get their kids to sleep.' He pokes the wallaby with his toe. 'Come on, Rudra, give us a hand. It's food now, nothing more. Stop thinking and start doing.'

Together, they dump the animal in the boat. 'You'll need to come over with me. I can't lift the bloody thing up the hill on my own.'

They row over in silence. Tangent licks at the carcass. 'Stop it,' growls Rudra. 'You'll get it soon enough.'

Between them, they carry it up the steps and Wallace drags it to the shed. When he exits, Rudra can see past him to the carcass hanging from a rope in the gloom. 'It won't go to waste. Keep Tangent in food for a month,' says Wallace. 'But best we keep this from Didima, eh?'

# 9

ALL TIME IS MARKED FROM SOME significant point.
The Buddhists, the Christians and the Muslims all believe
they are living in different times. In the long and drifting
summer, Rudra begins to mark time from the appearance of
his grandmother, as if his life has pivoted on this point and
will never be the same.

On day five after Arrival Didima, Maggs turns up unan-
nounced on the Solace doorstep.

'Sorry about the other day,' Rudra says.

'What other day?'

'After I'd been fishing. The phone call – I was kind of
weird.'

'You're always weird, mate.'

'You coming in, or what?'

'Your dad home?'

'Nup.'

'Lead on.'

As they walk down the hall, Maggs stops at the lounge
room door.

'Never been in here.'

'It's just a lounge.'

Maggs swings open the door. The room smells of moth-balls and damp. There's an old floral couch with its back to the door, and two overstuffed chairs by the fireplace.

'I will never understand why this family doesn't own a TV. Or have internet. You fellas are locked in another time.'

'TV rots the brain.'

'Says Cord Solace. It's like he's Amish or something. Which is fine if you like that sort of thing. But all that time staring at the walls – kinda creepy, mate.'

'We do other stuff. Listen to music or the radio. Read books.'

'Weirdos.' Maggs grabs a book from beside a chair. 'I never picked your old man as a reader.'

'What do you mean?'

'Well, he doesn't talk much. People who read – they talk. They use big words. They quote shit all the time. That's not Cord. Not by a long shot.'

'I think he uses books as an excuse *not* to talk. I don't even know if he reads them.'

Maggs shows Rudra the cover of the book he is holding – *Man-eaters of Kumaon* by Jim Corbett. 'This book?'

Rudra shrugs and Maggs drops the book back on the table. He moseys over to the old record player in the corner. 'This is true vintage.'

'Don't touch that.'

'Must be a hundred years old.'

'You can't touch it. It's not allowed.'

'So many rules in your house, dude.'

'It's my great-grandmother's – my dad's gran. I've never heard it played.'

'You guys really are Amish.'

'Always the low-hanging fruit for you, Maggs.' If you didn't have Facebook, you were Amish. If you didn't have the latest iPhone – Amish. To Rudra it made no geographic sense – the Amish were American. 'It's just Cord being Cord. You know how he is.'

'I do indeed. He's definitely, *definitely* Amish. Part Amish, part Taliban. Such a fun guy.'

'You hungry?'

'I am hungry, Rudra. Starving. Famished. In need of sustenance.'

They go to the kitchen and sit around the table eating toast and drinking milk.

Rudra says, 'Remember Mr DeNicola called milk *purified blood*?'

'Worst science teacher ever.'

'Hippy.'

'That too.'

'Spoiled milk for everyone. Forever.'

'It's only a name.'

'He also called eggs *liquid flesh*.'

'He's a weird dude.'

Rudra sips his milk gingerly. 'We pulled something up in the nets the other night,' he says.

'Prawns, I hope.'

'Something stranger.'

'What was it?'

'It was like some sort of skull.'

'A skull? Like a dolphin skull or something?' Maggs looks up from his milk. 'Do dolphins even have skulls?'

'Pretty sure they do, Maggs. But this didn't look like it came from a dolphin.'

'Maybe a seal? Seals have skulls, right?' Maggs struggled with biology. At the end of last year, he'd asked Mr DeNicola whether fish had nipples.

'It wasn't a seal.'

'You still got it?' says Maggs, leaning forward. 'Show me.'

'Cord took it when we were on the boat. He's hidden it.' Rudra takes a sip of milk. 'I had this strange dream too. About some kind of animal, here in Patonga, that didn't belong here. It was out to kill something.'

Maggs places his hand on Rudra's shoulder and puts on a look of mock sincerity. 'Rudra, is it *the drugs*?'

'I'm being serious.'

'You're being weird.'

'There was something in that dream, Maggs. Something a bit too real.'

Maggs sculls his milk, brings up a thick burp. 'Ah, purified blood.'

'I dream about an animal killing something and the next day,' continues Rudra, 'Wallace and I find a dead wallaby by the creek.'

'Oh-kay then.' Maggs does crazy eyes. 'You dream an animal kills something and then that thing dies. You are seriously a god, Rudra.' He rocks back in his chair and laces his hands behind his head. 'And I am your best mate. God's best mate – that's me. Bet I'll get free pizza and Kendra Mayhew will want to pash me ... finally.'

'Can you be serious for once in your life?'

'You're smoking your socks, mate. You can't dream something and then have it happen. It's just bloody coincidence.'

'Maybe.'

'Definitely,' says Maggs. 'But I reckon we need to find that skully thing you pulled up in the nets. That is interesting.'

'I saw a look on Cord's face when he saw it. It was like he recognised it.'

'Bullshit. It came from under the sea. Unless your old man is a fish, it is unlikely that he recognised it.'

'Maybe.'

'Imagine how much stuff is under the water of that bay. Your old man just happens to jag something he's seen before. What are the odds of that?'

'Slim.'

'Slim Dusty, Fat Boy Slim, Slim Shady. Between slim and exact zero. There's no way.'

'It just looked like it, that's all. Maybe I was wrong.'

'You are wrong,' says Maggs. 'But I still think we should find the thing. Where would he hide it?'

'If it's anywhere in the house, it'll be in his office.'

'What're we waiting for?'

'It's locked.'

'It just so happens, Rudra, my man, that I have been preparing for this very situation.'

'How so?'

'Two words – *lock picking* and *YouTube.*'

'That's three words. And what if Cord comes home?'

'That's what's wrong with you, Rudra – too much of the *what-ifs.*' Maggs stands up and brushes the crumbs from his shorts. 'Has Nayna got hairclips?'

'Well, yeah.'

'Let's get busy then.'

Rudra retrieves two bobby pins from his mum's dressing table. Maggs peels the plastic coating from one with his teeth and bends one of the arms to ninety degrees. He puts a little kink in the peeled arm. He bends the head of the other pin up, inserting it deep into the lock and holding it with a little pressure. Slowly, he slides the peeled pin on top, jiggling the bottom one as he goes. Rudra holds his breath. At any minute, Cord could arrive home.

'Can you make it any quicker?' he says.

Maggs doesn't even look at him. 'It's not that simple,' he says. 'Not like in the movies. You gotta picture what's happening inside. Each little pin being pushed up so the barrel can eventually turn. And . . .' There is a satisfying click. 'The lock is open.' He turns the handle and the door creaks ajar.

The study is dark, with a shaft of sunlight spearing the dusty air. Cord never opens the curtains in here. The outside world is not permitted. Rudra only remembers being in here a handful of times – mostly when he was younger. Once without Cord's permission. Only once.

He flicks on the light, feeling the fear gnaw in his belly. The room is roughly square with Cord's cheap old desk at one end. On the far wall, bookshelves rise from floor to ceiling, crammed with non-fiction – shipping charts, *Knots and Splices*, *Birds of the East Coast*, diesel engine manuals, logbooks. The top shelf is a graveyard of peeling spines and strange titles, hunting books similar to the one that Maggs picked up in the lounge room.

On the left wall there is a single photo. An old black-and-white image, speckled with time. A fringe of jungle, a dirt path worn shiny, a brick temple in the background. Two men with waxed moustaches and starched shirts. Gun barrel straight. Eyes in the middle distance.
man in a turban with a dense thicket of a beard. And,

at their feet, something mauled with age, bleeding silver bromide, torn up from the photo's edge to beneath their boots.

'Come on,' says Maggs. 'We haven't got all day.'

They cross the floor to a symphony of creaking floorboards. The old house is built on sand, and white ants work day and night at the stumps. It amazes Rudra that termites will eat and eat until they sense the light pulsing through the veneer they have created. Then they will stop. And what amazes him more is how a windowsill or doorjamb can look like solid wood, yet he can push his finger right into it.

Sometimes too, the bearers come adrift. Then the whole place floats for a season, the floor spongy, the house springing like a boat at anchor, until the re-blockers arrive to set things right.

Rudra opens the top drawer of the desk and finds the key to a filing cabinet. The door opens, releasing an angry swarm of manila folders. Rudra slides in his arm and feels around. Nothing. Meanwhile, Maggs rifles through the desk drawers like a professional. He pulls out an old pistol, points it at the bookshelf and pulls the trigger. *Click*. A blue flame appears at the tip of the barrel.

'A cigarette lighter,' he says. 'Your old man got a licence for this?'

Maggs slides it back into the drawer, picks up a battered old Akubra from a chair and slips it on his head. 'We need to think like Cord. Where would he hide things?' He walks to the window and, twitching the curtain open, peers outside. 'Hey, imagine he came home right now and found us going through his stuff. That'd be an amazing *what-if* for you, Rudra.' Maggs lets the curtain fall back into ce and moves back towards the desk. He stops abruptly, cking his head on one side. 'Hear that?'

'What?'

'Listen.' Maggs steps back towards the window.

'What?'

Maggs springs off his left foot and a floorboard rattles back into place. 'That.' He grins like a fool. 'Hear it?' He demonstrates again and the floorboard rattles. 'Get that letter opener.' He begins rolling the rug back from the window.

Rudra passes him the letter opener and, working it under one of the boards, Maggs prises the board up. The next one comes up too, releasing cool, slightly fetid air. With the torch on his mobile, he drenches the cavity in light. The beam comes to rest on a large rectangular steel box with a handle on each short side. He hands Rudra the phone and manoeuvres the box from its hiding place.

Once it is sitting on the floor, he says to Rudra, 'You should do the honours.'

Taking a deep breath, Rudra flips the catch and opens the box. At one end there are a pile of envelopes – twenty, maybe more. He pulls them out and hands one to Maggs. 'They're all addressed to Mum,' says Rudra. 'From India.'

'And they're unopened,' says Maggs, flipping an envelope over to show him. Rudra catches the neatly printed name *Prinika Thakur*. His *didima*.

'Let's put them back.'

'You don't think this is weird?'

'Course it's weird,' says Rudra. 'But it's not what we came for.'

He places the letters back in the box and removes a cloth-wrapped bundle. Placing it carefully on the floor, he peels it like an orange.

'What is it?' asks Maggs.

Rudra runs his hands over it, feeling its cold, damp surface. He picks it up and holds it to the light. They are both silent. He slips his fingers into the two round holes and then into the vee-shaped hole below.

The front door rattles open, creaks on its hinge and then slams shut. An echo of fear reverberates inside Rudra. Quickly, he rewraps the object. 'Hold the door,' he hisses at Maggs, 'Don't let him in.' But what good could it do?

Maggs is too slow off the mark, anyway. Suddenly, Cord Solace is looming over them.

'I didn't,' says Rudra.

Cord grits his teeth, his jaw muscles bulging. He begins to shake; earthquake anger – magnitude nine on the Fark! Scale. Maybe the pictures on the walls are rattling, or maybe it is Rudra's heart. Maybe the grey men in the photo are bleeding from their eyes. Maybe the day is darkening and the sky is falling.

His dad lunges towards him and, as he does, Rudra dodges. Cord Solace is a big man and he drops heavy. When he smacks the floor, Rudra is up and over him and through the door and along the hall and out the front with Maggs beside him, running as they never have, splitting at the roundabout, Maggs heading towards the creek and Rudra towards the bay, with the bundle of whatever under one arm. His dad comes after him like a hurricane, his footfalls thundering over tar and dirt. Rudra makes for the pier, the sea turfing white arrows from the tops of waves. The wind and the cries of gulls and the pelicans with their backs to it all. The kite screaming from the pines.

Leaping into their tender, he lobs the object into the bow. He grabs the outboard's ripcord and yanks. The motor splutters. His dad is on the pier now, roaring at him. Rudra pulls again. The motor refuses. He sees his mum now, come from nowhere, running, her hair flying behind her like a veil. His dad is four metres away. Rudra pulls again. The motor fires and catches, blurts out a cloud of blue smoke. He casts off and slams the outboard into reverse, pulls the boat round in a sweeping arc, straightens up and puts her in forward.

His wake throws a broad silver path from the pier. There are his mum and dad – her grabbing his elbow and him throwing her off. And, strangely, it reminds him of the photo on Wallace's wall, when he was eight. When he could tame those seagulls. When he was too young to see the cracks and chasms that must have been there even then.

The crossing is rough, but he knows the place he will be safe from his father's rage. Knows that Cord will drive along the coast expecting him to make landfall. He will never expect this courage from his son.

Lion Island – its back turned to him, ignoring his flight. He knows penguins nest out there and off the southern tip – a feeding ground for sharks. The boat skips over the water and he can smell a storm coming, the waves crowding together. The boat starts to leap and the motor leaves the sea screaming; then the hull makes contact with a sickening thud and lurches on like a drunk. There is nothing graceful about this crossing.

In the bow of the boat, nestled between the clamour of cold chain, is the object. Irrationally, he allows himself some *what-ifs*. What if this thing pulls him to the bottom? What if that is its purpose? What if it has been waiting for him, under all that water, all along? *Crazy-talk*, Maggs would honk. *You and your what-ifs, you little weirdo.*

The island seems close. The waves are battering the north point, ripping into the little beach that is the only place for him to land. He knows there is a channel in the rocks, he's seen it from the water, and he also knows he needs to hit straight on to avoid tearing the boat apart like a tin can.

He takes a run past the beach to get his bearings. On the way back, he swings in at ninety degrees and makes a run for the beach. On either side are the dark hulks of rock, angry and quite prepared to kill. He realises then how soft his skin is, how unprepared he is for battle. The wind is in his ears, whispering, *you will never do it*. The sharks are hunting penguins. *You are only meat*, screams the wind.

And then he is through, his bow slamming into the beach, the outboard pushed out of the water. He kills the motor, leaps from the bow and pulls the boat up the beach. Safe for now.

# 10

LION ISLAND IS A MANED HEAD snarling at the ocean and a fattened rump shunning the land. Its mouth, a cave, is fringed with gnarled banksia and ribbon grass; dripping, as if with saliva. Rudra heads for the cave to escape the wind and the rain. He saw the cave as they passed by on their last fishing trip, but knows that the whole island is a reserve and that landing is not allowed.

He skirts the narrow beach and clambers over the rocks. He begins to climb, through the rain that's coming down in sheets, making the rocks black and slick. He tucks the thing under his shirt and battles the thick scrub along the ridge, as lightning forks into the sea. When he reaches the sea cliff, he shuffles over the edge, dropping onto a rough shelf. Here the wind is at its worst – howling over the sea at him and threatening to tear him away. He shuffles sideways to the dark mouth of the cave, a large sheet of rock blocking most of its entrance. He slips through the narrow gap, feeling the pressure of rock across his torso as if he is clamped between the jaws of a beast. Inside, abandoned by summer, he sits shivering in his shorts and T-shirt. At least he is out of the wind.

Outside, a slice of sky mocks. He places the thing on the dirt and stretches out beside it. Suddenly, he is more tired than he has ever been or ever wants to be. He feels fatigue pressing on his ribs and the sides of his head. He closes his eyes and wonders why this place is called Lion Island. Lions do not belong. Aboriginal people surely had a better name – one that would have suited not only the shape but its place in the world. But the name Lion Island persists. Everything needs a name. Naming something brings it into the world. Makes it real.

Rudra reaches out his hand and touches the nameless thing. Can he call it a skull? Not quite yet. He looks beyond it to the chaos outside. He pulls it to his stomach, curls around it like a seed husk, warms it. Imagines it erupting like the flame trees along the bay road. And he drifts.

*The animal can see everything – the twitching of muttonbirds beneath the sandy soil, cicadas pitching through the sky, the dark lust of sombre mopokes chanting in the trees. It can smell blood and bone; and the sinew behind its knees tightens at the chance of them. It is a brutal remembering of past kills, an excitement that bruises through its body like a drug.*

*It takes to the water, snarling at the salt. The animal needs sweet meat to relieve it of its anger. It knows where to find it. Swimming is no problem – broad pads are paddles, the skin between them so like webs you might think it belonged there and nowhere else. The tail is a rudder, three foot of bone and sinew allowing it to swim for hours and still hunt and kill. It is built for this and nothing else. When it arrives, it is to the sound of snapping and tearing, to the tang of unleashed blood. Its tongue brushes the tips of his teeth so lightly. And deep in the tidelands they wait and wish it would not come.*

Rudra wakes to the thrum of a motor across the sea. And he remembers he left the dinghy on the beach. If he had thought a little harder, he would have camouflaged it with branches and seaweed. It could be the park ranger or it could be his dad. Either way it will be bad.

The storm has retreated, leaving stillness about the island. He smells Champion Ruby on the still air as he leaves the cave. Down on the beach, Wallace pulls a rollie from the corner of his mouth, staring up at Rudra as he descends the hill. Tangent is running around him like a mad thing, and when he spots Rudra he comes bounding forward.

'Yer dad's looking for you,' Wallace says. He jerks his thumb back at the tinnie. 'You need a tow back?'

'I'm right.'

'You gotta come home, you know. Sooner or later you'll have to face Cord's music.'

'What'd he say?'

'Said nothing. Your mum, though, she's worried about you.' Wallace takes a drag at his smoke. 'How come you got that?' he asks, pointing at the object.

Rudra holds it up. 'We took it, Maggs and me, from Cord's office. It's the thing we pulled up from Flint and Steel.'

'You should chuck it back in the bay and be done with it,' says Wallace – a deep mistrust puckering the corners of his eyes.

They sit down. Tangent hassles the gulls along the water's edge, snapping wilfully at the air between them. The water rolls shells up the beach. Years to turn shell to sand. Hundreds more to grind stone to powder.

'I'm going to take it back,' says Rudra.

'Back where?'

'To wherever it belongs.' The words are falling untested from his tongue. He doesn't know what he is saying. It's tiredness. Maggs would say, *You're a bit emotional, mate.* Rudra looks about him. 'It doesn't belong here. I know that.' Rudra thinks back to the article about Mungo Man. Of forty-two-thousand-year-old bones willing themselves back home.

Wallace butts out his rollie in the sand and pops it into his pocket. There is an art in his silence. It means something. But it is a language that Rudra does not fully understand.

'Think I should?' Rudra pushes his toes into the sand. 'Take it back?'

'It's trouble, I reckon. But your dad will want to have his way. You need to play this one clever.' It's not an answer.

Rudra follows Wallace's wake from the beach and towards Patonga. As they enter the bay, the seagulls harangue them, turning above the boats in swooping runs, their quick little eyes rimmed with silver. Rudra sees his dad waiting on the pier, arms folded, and his mum, two steps behind, hair tricked into a bun. He feels a dart of fear or excitement inside him, he can't tell which, and draws the object to his belly as if protecting it.

Wallace ties up first but Cord doesn't even acknowledge him. His eyes are on Rudra, jaw muscles working on something invisible. Nayna puts her hand on Cord's arm and he flinches her off. The tender noses the pier and Cord reaches down and grabs the painter, forming a lazy bowline.

'We were so worried,' says Nayna.

The chainsaw cicadas suddenly stop and Rudra hears the whistling kite give one sharp shriek before she comes angling down from the pines to land on the end of the pier. His dad has never hit him. And surely he won't now, in front of witnesses.

Rudra looks past his parents along the beach towards the creek mouth, where his *didima* is picking gingerly down to the water's edge. He wants to run to her – his new-found family. To the safety of her arms. He can see now, even from here, she is staring out to sea. *What is she waiting for?*

The kite shrieks from the end of the pier and Rudra is drawn back into the moment. He unwraps the thing and shows it to the new storm-washed day. Holds it up so his mum and Cord can see it, plain, in the light. Cord holds out his hand – a hand so big, like an uprooted tree. *Play this one clever,* Wallace said. With his dad standing there in front of him, it is inevitable Rudra will give it over.

Slipping his fingers into the holes, he plucks it cleanly from the cloth and, as his mum exhales her fears, drops it gently into Cord's huge palm. Rudra will get it back again, he is sure. And then he will return it.

His dad squats down on the pier, places the thing on the concrete. 'When I was your age,' he begins and rests the tips of his fingers on the pier to balance himself, as if this is going to take a while.

'One autumn. Muttonbirds. So many we had to get a tractor onto the beach. Buried them by the thousands. They fly up to Kamchatka, you know.'

Rudra doesn't know. Doesn't know what a Kamchatka even is. But more incredible still is so many words from Cord.

'Five thousand clicks up. And five back.' He pauses and looks at the thing. Runs his hand over it, plunges his fingers into the holes.

'They get tired. Real tired. Crosswinds. Off the coast of America. They fly till they drop into the sea. And the sea doesn't care. Just keeps on doing its thing. Doesn't have any respect for what they been through. What they seen. The sea doesn't care for details.

'Me and your Uncle Tam. I don't think you'll remember him.'

Rudra shakes his head.

'You were just a baby when he...' He swallows visibly. 'Well, you were just a baby. Anyway, we found this mutton-bird still alive. Brought it home and had it in a cardboard box. Your grandad said it wouldn't live. That we should take it back to the beach. Let nature do its thing. But we were kids.' That could be a smile, but never on Cord's steel face. Could be *wistfulness* or *nostalgia* or a hundred other abandoned emotions? 'Just little kids,' Cord says. He gets up, holding the thing like a bowling ball. His fingers in the holes. The *eye sockets*, Rudra thinks accepting it for what it is.

'Your grandad got that muttonbird in the night. Took it back to the beach.' He shrugs. 'Best thing for it. Let nature do what it must.' Cord takes the bundle under his arm and starts to walk down the pier. Before he is out of earshot, Rudra hears him say, 'You'll understand why things are the way they are when you're older. Why sometimes you just got to shut up and take it.'

# 11

'IN THE END, IT WILL BE BEST,' says his mum.

'But this is my home,' Rudra replies.

'He will calm. And you will come back. For now, though, it is safest if you live with Wallace.'

'Safest, Mum?'

'Your dad is not a bad man. He wouldn't hurt you. But you took something from him and he needs to think things through.'

'Did he tell you that?'

Nayna peers into her teacup; into the leaves that predict a storm. 'He said there must be a reckoning.'

'What does that even mean.'

Nayna shrugs. 'I think he is embarrassed if this ever gets out. That his son would steal from him and there would be no consequence.'

'You say he would never hurt me. How can you be so sure?'

'I can't, Rudra. But I need to believe that there is enough good in him.'

'Why do you defend him?'

'If not me, then who?'

84

'What about you staying here?' asks Rudra.

'I will be fine.'

'How do you know?'

'I have to trust.'

'In what?'

Nayna does not answer. Instead, she draws Rudra to her and hugs him like he is eight years old and the world does not matter.

Rudra packs his bags and walks to the creek. He waits there, skimming stones across the mirrored water. Wallace arrives in his dinghy trailing a cloud of Champion Ruby. They cross the narrow channel without exchanging a word.

Didima is in bed when he gets inside Wallace's place. Her skin has a grey tinge to it that Rudra doesn't like the look of. Her breath smells like ripe fruit.

'The dog shouldn't be on my bed,' she says.

Tangent growls when Rudra tries to move him.

'Leave him. He knows I am close to death.'

'We should call a doctor.'

'We can't bring a doctor all the way out here.'

Wallace appears in the doorway. 'Do we need a doctor?'

She gives him a smile – weak but sweet. 'No doctors, Wallace. A cup of *cha* will fix me.'

'I can do that,' he says and disappears into the kitchen.

'Perhaps I will die quite soon,' says Didima, slumping back on her pillows.

'You're not going to die, Didima.'

'How can you be sure?'

'Because you're tough. Because you are the daughter of a honey-collector and the wife of a solution-*wala*.'

'I am the *widow* of a solution-*wala*,' she says carefully. 'And I am old and tired.'

'But you can't leave now, Didima. Not just when I am getting to know you.' There is a whiny edge to Rudra's voice that he doesn't recognise. 'I need to know who I am.' It comes out all wrong. He doesn't even know what it means, all clunky and full of holes, sopping with neediness. 'I need to know who Mum was before she married Dad. What your village in the Sundarbans looks like. Who my great-grandmother was.' Now he is gushing like a broken pipe.

Didima forces herself up onto her elbows. 'Come closer.' She kisses him on the cheek, her lips as crackly as cured grass. 'I'll give you those stories on one condition.'

'What's the condition?'

'When I am finished you let me go. And when I go, you burn my body and take my ashes back to the Sundarbans, to my village. And you scatter those ashes in the waters around my island. And you tell everyone you are the grandson of Prinika Thakur, and that Sarin Thakur, the solution-*wala*, was your grandfather. And your great-grandparents Sutej and Vhristi were from Baghchara.' She falls back on the pillow. 'Then you will know who you are.'

Rudra returns home to fetch some clothes. His dad is not there and the only thing he feels is relief. Nayna is in the kitchen cooking. 'Take this to your *didima*,' she says, and hands him a paper bag. 'I made her *ladoos*.'

'I think she's sick, Mum.'

'Sick?'

'She keeps talking about dying.'

'Old people do that, Rudra. It's probably nothing.'

But Rudra sees that it could be something. That, as quickly as she arrived, his Didima could slip from their lives without warning.

'Take her the *ladoos*, Rudra.'

'She'll like that.'

'And Rudra?'

'Yes?'

'I'm sorry about your dad.'

'It's not your fault, Mum.'

Nayna purses her lips. 'I wish it were different for us, Rudra.'

'You're stuck, aren't you, Mum?'

She waggles her head and her eyes well with tears.

'I'm sure it can be different,' says Rudra. 'But it will have to come from you. I know it's big, but we could try without Dad. Even just for a while.'

Nayna plants a kiss on Rudra's forehead and he leaves the house with his suitcase of clothes and a paper bag of sugary goodness.

'*Ladoos*, Rudra?' says Didima, sitting up in bed.

'Mum made them.'

She pops one of the balls into her mouth. 'Coconut *ladoos*, Rudra.' She shuts her eyes. 'My daughter made coconut *ladoos* for me.'

'I'll put on some *cha*.'

'Good boy.'

When he returns with the *cha*, most of the *ladoos* are gone.

'Oh, I ate too many *ladoos*, Rudra. Does your mother not know I have no willpower?'

'Here's your *cha*, Didima.'

'That will fix me. Plenty of sugar?'

'Yes, Didima. Always.'

'Good. Now sit here and listen to the story about the disappearing island.'

Rudra sits on the edge of the bed. Tangent groans and rolls over so Rudra can reach his belly for a scratch.

'I was born on an island called Baghchara. We were not a rich family but we were well-respected. My father's father had been a big man with the Britishers but we had fallen on hard times and soon, like most in the Sundarbans, we turned to the forest for help. This is how my father became a honey-gatherer – a *mawali*. He was the youngest of four boys in a family of ten. There were a lot of mouths to feed. He started going into the jungle with my grandfather when he was six. He never got to go to school but he was a clever man, and kind-hearted.

'My mother was an only child, which was very rare back then. Her mother, my *didima*, had died in childbirth and her father had never remarried. She was brought up by her aunt who thought of her as a slave. She was married to my father when she was ten but they did not live together until much later.

'I was born during the monsoon. They called me Prinika, which means *the girl who brings heaven to earth*.' Didima smiled as if embarrassed. 'A bit of a grand title, I always thought. But in a way the heavens do come to earth during the monsoon so maybe that is what they really meant.

'It is a worrying time in the Sundarbans – the monsoon. When the grand rivers rise – the mighty Ganga and the Brahmaputra – the people of the Sundarbans look for higher ground. It is not when the rain first falls that the floods happen. It takes a while for the water to find the sea. But when it does, it all finds the Sundarbans.

'Our island, Baghchara, was a down island – meaning, people didn't think much of it. The people who lived there were mostly fishers, woodcutters, honeymen and the like. There wasn't much for people to do on Baghchara, but I loved it. It was my home. And when you are quite young it is not as if you need much other than water to swim in and trees to climb.

'After the tragedy we moved away.' Didima looks out of the window. She can see the creek from here and the sickle-curve of the bay.

'What tragedy?'

'That,' she blinks twice as if willing away tears, 'is a story for another time.'

'You said you were going to tell me about the disappearing island.'

'And I will, Rudra. Be patient.' She smooths down her covers. 'I wonder if I might have just one more *ladoo*. Really, they are so delicious. I cannot help myself.'

Rudra hands her the bag and she pops one into her mouth.

'Coconut *ladoos* remind me of the Festival of Lights – Diwali. On Baghchara, such a pretty sight you have never seen. The water dotted with candles in small boats. The trees garlanded in lights and flowers. So very lovely.' She sighs at the memory.

'I remember leaving Baghchara. My friends on the dock. The ferryman carried me to the boat because it was low tide. The mud was sucking at his legs as if it did not want him to take me from it. I remember thinking, even though I was so young, it was a bad way to leave. But my mother could not wait for the tide. She was finished with the place.

'Many years later when I was a grown woman living with your grandfather, I heard once again about my island. Baghchara had vanished. They said the rising sea had taken it. But I think the island tilted and fell into the water because it was weighed down by all its sorrow.' She pulls a comical sad face as if to make light of her comment.

'It is a funny thing, Rudra, to have the place you were born vanish from this earth. How can I ever go back?' Didima pauses, pulling her bedsheets up under her chin. 'Have you heard of the poet Rumi?'

'Is he Indian?'

'He was from a place in long-ago Afghanistan. His family fled from Genghis Khan and he ended up in what is now known as Turkey. He longed every day for his homeland. It was like a burning seed inside him. He wrote this poem called "The Reed Flute's Song". Let me see if I can remember it for you.'

She clears her throat, and blinks as if trying to rid her eyes of smoke.

*'Listen to the story told by the reed, of being separated.*

*Since I was cut from the reedbed,*
*I have made this crying sound.*

*Anyone apart from someone he loves*
*understands what I say.*

*Anyone pulled from a source*
*longs to go back.'*

Poetry makes Rudra uncomfortable. There is too much flower and sugar involved, too much earnestness. He escapes the void left by the poem by saying, 'You told me I should take your ashes to your island after you die. That's going to be tricky if it's not there.'

Didima tilts her head as if considering it for a moment. Then she pulls her pillow from behind her, looking at it as if it is a stranger. Her eyes seem damp. 'We are made from the soil of our birthplace, Rudra. It is there we must return when everything else is done.'

'Why did you come here, Didima? Why did you leave India behind?'

'Because I needed to see with my own eyes my strong grandson. I needed to see my daughter. And I needed to tell you things.'

'What things?'

'About where you are from – the soil that makes you too.'

'But I am from here, Didima. I am Australian.' There is something a little too shrill about those last words.

'You are also from India, from the Sundarbans.'

'I don't feel anything when you talk about it.'

'That makes me sad, Rudra.'

Rudra looks at his hands – his mother's fine pink nails there at the end of his father's fingers. 'How long does it take to belong? I was born in this place, Didima. Cord is Australian.'

'When I left Baghchara, I lived for many years in a place that never became my own.'

'But I was born in Australia and I don't *feel* Indian.'

'But it is most definitely part of who you are, Rudra. You have Sundarbans mud inside you – the soil and the sea.' She smiles and pats his hand. 'Maybe you can be both Australian and Indian.' She says it as if to placate him. 'Just maybe it is possible.'

92

# 12

RUDRA FINDS HIS MOTHER AT THE kitchen table. She tries to hide the bills and the tears.

'What's the matter, Mum?'

'Nothing, Rudra, it's okay.'

'I'm not a child anymore and I'm not stupid.'

She looks at him and nods. 'You're right. When did that happen?'

'Me not being stupid?'

She slaps his forearm. 'You becoming a man.'

Rudra shrugs and, getting a milk carton from the fridge, takes a long drink.

'Rudra! How many times have I told you – fetch a glass! And so much milk is not good for you. You are not a calf.'

'Tell me what's going on, Mum.'

'Oh, Rudra, where to start?' She picks up the bills and drops them back to the table. 'The bank will take the boat soon. Then it will come after the house. I am working all the shifts they will give me at the restaurant but still it is not enough.'

'So what are you going to do?'

'We have to go to Sydney this afternoon. As soon as your dad gets back from fishing. There's a finance company who will take on our debt.'

'That sounds alright.'

'Then they will own the boat. And we will be their servants.'

'Dad'll never go for that.'

'He has to, Rudra. He has no choice.'

Rudra puts the empty carton back in the fridge. 'I'll leave school and get a job.'

'It's not going to help. This is too much money.'

'So we just let someone take our boat and house and we become their slaves?'

'*Servants*, Rudra. There is a difference.'

'Whatever. We've been fishermen forever. Grandfather, great-grandfather, back as far as it goes.'

'Your dad is still going to fish. He'll just be working for someone else.'

'He'll hate that.'

'Yes, he will, but life is full of change.' She looks out the window. 'And compromise.'

The sky is flooded with purple clouds and the pier lights wink on as Rudra steps onto it. Rudra looks across to Palm Beach, then at the black forest rising above Dark Corner. He loves it here. This place is in his marrow – its soil and sea.

On the bench at the end, Maggs is sitting, his face lit by the glow of his phone. He looks up as Rudra approaches.

'S'up?' he asks.

'Not much,' answers Rudra. 'You ready?'

'Yup.'

'Let's do it.'

'Where's your folks?'

'Sydney. Something about the boat.'

'Are they staying there?'

'They'll be on the way back. We'd better do this quickly.'

They walk slowly towards the Solace house. Small bats flit down from the trees, plucking moths from under street-lights. The village tightens around them.

'This is mad,' says Maggs. 'I mean, I'm up for it and all, but if Cord catches you again he'll definitely kill you.'

'We have to get it.'

'If it's just a skull, why do you want it so bad? Can we just get another less dangerous skull? I reckon Yorick would be piss-easy to nick. You distract DeNicola with something sciency, I put Yorick in my schoolbag. Cord doesn't kill us.'

'I have to take it back.'

'Back where?'

'I don't know.'

'You are making less sense than you usually do. Is this something to do with grandmother arriving?'

'No. Maybe. I don't know.'

'It's not healthy, mate – the three of you cooped up in Wallace's place. You sleeping on the floor. Her getting up to piss a thousand times a night.'

'She does go to the toilet a lot.'

'That's old people for you.'

'She might be sick. Maybe dying.'

'We're all dying, mate. Might be sooner rather than later for us, if Cord catches us at it.'

They are at the front of the house. They are at the door. They are inside. Their footsteps are a drumbeat in the hall – a call to arms. Maggs pulls out his makeshift lock picking kit and has Cord's office door open in minutes. He switches on the overhead light.

'Let's use the desk lamp,' says Rudra. 'If Dad comes home he's less likely to notice we're in here.'

He pauses in front of the old black-and-white photo on the wall. The hunters in front of the brick temple. A jungle backdrop. Something dead at their boots. He presses his finger to the glass – all that separates him from years of history, a thin membrane that just maybe he can push through.

'Snap out of it, Rudra,' says Maggs. 'We gonna do this or what?'

They draw back the carpet and prise up the loose floorboard. The air rushes to them, cool and damp and smelling of a bunch of yesterdays. Rudra plunges his arm down, quickly finding the steel box, pulling it up, flipping open the catches.

'Where is it?' asks Maggs.

The box is empty. Even the envelopes are gone.

'I don't bloody know.'

'What's the big deal about this thing anyway? Why is Cord so hell-bent on hiding it? And why are you so mad for it?'

'I know it sounds weird,' says Rudra. 'But I reckon it's something to do with that dream I had.'

'You mean the dream where an animal kills something and when you wake up it's happened for real? That hardly sounds strange at all.' Maggs circles his finger around his temple. 'Gotta drop that crazy talk, you little weirdo, before they put you in a coat that ties at the back.'

'Forget it.'

'I already have.'

'But if it's no big deal, then why is Cord hiding it?'

'People collect stuff, I guess,' says Maggs. 'My mad aunt has forty years' worth of *Woman's Day* stacked in her front room. There's nothing special about any one of them.'

'There is something about this thing, Maggs.'

'Man, you are losing your shit. Your Dida-whatsit arrives from India. Next minute you are a full-blown weirdo.'

It is then that lights sweep through the room. Headlights. Their old ute, suddenly in the driveway. The guttural chuckle of its old motor, spitting oil and pinging tappets. Rudra dumps the box back and pulls the carpet back over the replaced board while Maggs kills the desk lamp. They squat in the darkness.

'They'll have seen the light, for sure,' whispers Maggs. 'Let's make a run for it.'

'Sit tight, I reckon.'

The key in the front door. The light in the hallway – a bar beneath the door. The silence between his parents. Footsteps. Pause.

Rudra holds his breath.

More footsteps. The light switch snicks on in the kitchen and the kettle rattles against the tap.

'Now,' says Rudra and they open the office door, slip out and lock it behind them. Out the front door and into the pure, clear night, stars, now, prickling between the trees, them breathing the dark deep into their lungs.

'We're like bloody ninjas,' says Maggs.

'Next time we have to be more careful.'

'Next time? Rudra, there was nothing there. Cord ditched it, for sure.'

'It's somewhere close,' says Rudra. 'I know it.'

'Mate, you are a certified freak.'

'Maybe.'

'For sure,' says Maggs. 'Hey, what you got there?'

'This?' Rudra looks at the framed photo in his hand as if it has just appeared without his bidding. 'I think it might be another piece of the puzzle.'

98

# 13

'LISTEN,' SAYS DIDIMA AND HOLDS RUDRA'S HAND so he can't get away, 'while I tell you the story of the tiger and the child. It is a true story and it happened long ago.' She repositions herself on Wallace's chapped little pier so her legs are crossed beneath her. It is the morning after the ninja raid and there have been no reprisals as yet so Cord must not have noticed Maggs and Rudra had broken into his office or that the picture was missing. It is a good morning for a story, bright and safe with a breeze crossing the creek.

'It was the time when the Britishers had not long left India. I think it would have been around nineteen fifty if I have my mathematics just so. I was very young. The village men would go to the forest for honey while the bees were happiest. The *bauliya* – the tiger charmer – would make chants to protect them. The *bauliya* was needed by the forest workers but it did not come without a price. Because he was so close to the tiger spirit, Dokkhin Rai, he was often in danger of being eaten first. He could not eat pork or tortoise and if he ate crab, his ears would pop. Everyone prayed to Bonbibi – the protector – she so loved by Muslim or Hindu alike. The *bauliya* would pray the hardest.

'Dokkhin Rai was a tricky one. Himself half made of dark and half of fire. On a full moon or a new moon, the spells would not work on him. Then the honeymen – the *mawalis* – would go into the forest unguarded. My father was a *mawali*.

'In the early morning, my father would rise. He would join with the other *mawalis* of his group – five of them in all – and they would take their boat to the honey grounds. But first they would stop by the shrine to Bonbibi, beneath the banyan tree that guarded our village. There they would lay sweet herbs and flowers and chant *Maa Bonbibi Durga, Durga*. I would watch them go – their boat cutting through the early morning mist like the arrow of Krishna. And I would whisper *Maa Bonbibi Durga, Durga*, to keep my *baba* safe.'

Didima looks down into the water, where a school of tiny silver fish are sewing the shadows together. She smiles as if remembering something, but pain tightens the corners of her mouth.

'On *that* day…'

Rudra can feel what is coming, can read the inflected *that*, the infected *that* – the weight of the word on Didima's tongue.

'On *that* day,' she shakes her head slowly, 'they said Abhin, the son of the *paan-wala*, washed his cooking pot in the water. Or that he had thrown his *beedi* carelessly over the side. That is all Dokkhin Rai needs to seek his revenge. People disrespect the forest at their own risk. Or sometimes at someone else's.

'They couldn't get his body. My wonderful *baba*. He so strong, like the trunk of a *sundari* tree. His hair dark and thick, full of rich oils. His name was Sutej, which means "lustre" in Bangla.

'A tiger, once it has eaten a man, cannot turn back. It sends him mad. Or so they say. Things were different then. We were not separate from the world like now. We were part of nature. Sometimes we became food. But when we did, we fought back. Because we were equals. Now we have guns and poison. Then we had knives and spears.

'But Dokkhin Rai was cunning. He knew how to hide and when to spring out. And he would use the nights when the moon was full or hidden. Then the *bauliya's* spells do not work. And my mother, she was weak with grief.

'The tiger killed four more men that season. His reputation grew. Soon the whole of the tide country knew of him. He was Dokkhin Rai himself. People had turned their back on Bonbibi to their peril. Dokkhin Rai would have the forest and humans would be banished forever.

'Then a *gora* – a fair-faced one – came down the river from Basanti. He scared the children in the village. My mother said he could be a *haji* – a pilgrim who had been to Mecca – because he had red hair and a red beard. But us kids did not think he was a pilgrim, he did not look holy enough. Instead we knew he was definitely a demon.

'He brought a gun with him. He had heard of the man-eater and wanted to take him as a trophy. I remember him talking to the tiger-widows – including my own dear mother. I can see her white sari fringed with mud. She looked so small near him. Even as a child, I thought the *gora* seemed too eager. His eyes were bright for blood.

It wasn't just revenge, like with us villagers, it ran deeper and was dirtier. It was killing for the sake of killing. You understand, Rudra?'

Rudra nods. Yes, he understands.

'They were two nights in the jungle, the *gora* and his men. He came back with Dokkhin Rai – or the sack that held Dokkhin Rai. The fur was dirty and dull. He was already beginning to smell. The *gora* wanted to keep him. No one in the village had heard of keeping an animal forever like that. Even with an interpreter they didn't understand. He sent a message to Kolkata, to bring a man who could preserve the beast.

'The *gora* skinned that tiger. He threw that tiger's guts into the water. The dolphins fought the sharks and the crocodiles fought them all. It was no longer safe to be out at night. The crocodiles stayed around, lying on the mud flats where we used to beach our boats.

'Finally, the tanner from Kolkata arrived. It was two weeks since Dokkhin Rai had been killed. The skin was eaten through by flies. The hair was coming off in clumps. The *gora* was mad. He told the tanner he wouldn't pay him. The tanner said he'd call the Forestry Department and have him jailed for poaching. *Poaching?* said the *gora*. *I was saving lives.*'

Didima's eyes are round with the magic of the story. It is as if she is back there, still a child, wondering at the adult rage around her.

'The tanner left. He took his knives and his case with plaster of Paris. But not before he poured his jar of formaldehyde into the ground where it later killed our banyan tree. That was the place where Bonbibi lived – our protector.

'The *gora* left too, but not before he broke the skull out of the tiger skin. The headman warned him, *Don't take Dokkhin Rai from the tidelands. He will have his revenge.* But the *gora* spoke no Bangla and his interpreter, knowing what was good for him, had set out for home the day before. The *gora* wrapped the skull in a cloth and, stepping past the sleeping crocodiles, he left for Kolkata.

'But there must have been one ounce of goodness in the *gora* – as surely there is in everyone, Rudra. Or perhaps he did it from guilt. After all, he had stolen from the tidelands without giving anything in return. He took the money he was to pay the tanner and he gave it to my mother – the newest tiger-widow in the village.'

Rudra looks across the water. He knows Didima is expecting a response. 'What happened to you and your mother?'

'Your great-grandmother used the money the *gora* gave her and we went to Kolkata. We could never have afforded to go there otherwise. She left me at the Loreto Orphanage in Entally. I never saw her again.'

'How old were you?' asks Rudra.

'I was eight.'

Those three words sit there for a while.

'But this is not a sad story, Rudra. Not in the end. Your grandfather, his family saved me. They were quite wealthy, you know. Every so often, when times were good for them, they would sponsor one girl or boy from the orphanage. When I was twelve, I was chosen. They sent me money every year and I went to school – a good school. I learnt Bangla and I learnt English. Mathematics and poetry and some scientific things. And your grandfather, he was at

St Lawrence High School in Ballygunge. One day, he took me to Flurys. It is a tea room in Kolkata. Very famous and very expensive. Such cakes I have never see since. Next time, he took me to a film at the Metro Cinema in Dharmatala.

'Such a scandal. It was very bad back then. It is not good even now, Rudra. But then – a high-caste boy and a low-caste girl – absolutely not. We snuck around like this in Kolkata – the biggest city where no one would ever see us.

'His family were one of the richest in the Sundarbans. And I was the orphan child of a honeyman. But your *dadu* had a very strong mind. When I turned eighteen, against his family's wishes, we were married.'

'Did you go back to the Sundarbans straight after you were married?'

'Not at first, Rudra,' Didima answers. 'I was scared of the ghosts. And a little afraid of your *dadu*'s family. But when your *dadu*'s father died, we were compelled. And I found that rather than holding bad memories of tigers and such, that it was still very much my home.

'And that is the story of the tiger and the child, my grandson. It is your story too. Today, I am giving this to you.'

Rudra smiles at her. He picks up a flat stone and skims it across the mirrored surface of the creek. Two, three, four, five, six rings and it is gone.

# 14

THAT AFTERNOON RUDRA IS WITH MAGGS up on the boulders in Dark Corner. They would come here as kids, slipping behind the rocks when dry weather sponged the water from the pools and allowed access. There are caves here – hidden; narrow-mouthed and shallow, just big enough for a child with a torch and a taste for adventure. But they stay outside now, too grown for those games.

'My great-grandfather was killed by a tiger,' says Rudra.

Maggs is splayed over a boulder, his head resting on tree root. 'That's pretty awesome.'

'Not for him.'

'True.'

'Or my Didima.' Rudra pulls a gumleaf from an over-hanging branch and chews on it. It is bitter and pungent. 'Imagine it, Maggs – getting torn apart by a tiger.'

'Yeah…nah.'

'He was a honeyman, my great-grandfather. He'd go with the other honeymen into the forest and collect wild honey. They had all these rituals they'd do to keep the Tiger God happy.'

'Tiger God?'

'He's called Dokkhin-something and he's mad for human flesh.' Rudra spits the mangled leaf onto the rock. 'There are things that make him angry – disrespecting the forest, taking what you shouldn't, stuff like that.'

'What did your great-grandfather do to piss him off?'

'I don't think it was him. Not directly. One of the guys in his boat washed a pot in the water or threw his ciggie in. And the tiger charmer hadn't been able to do his thing.'

'There was a *tiger charmer*?'

'Yeah. These guys that knew the right words to say; the rituals to make the forest workers safe. But at certain times they just couldn't – like if the moon was wrong. That's where my great-grandfather came unstuck.'

'When he was killed?'

'First him, then four others. When word of the man-eater spread, a white bloke arrived and hunted him down. Left his skin to rot and took the skull from the Sundarbans.'

Maggs props himself up and looks at Rudra. 'You mean a skull like the one Cord has such a thing for?'

Rudra can feel the blood pounding at his temples, an empty grinding inside him. He looks beyond the shadowed fringe cast by the forest to the magnesium flare of the beach and bay. The whistling kite swoops at the water and pulls up, triumphantly with a fish in its talons. Rudra takes a deep breath and continues. 'My great-grandmother was given some money by the hunter. Enough to get her and Didima to Kolkata where she was left in an orphanage. She never saw her mother again.'

'She did okay for herself though,' says Maggs. 'Had a daughter who came here and made you – part human, part weirdo.'

Rudra ignores the comment. 'In a strange way it was the hunter who made it all possible by giving my grandmother the money that allowed them to go to Kolkata. Which then made it possible for Didima to meet my grandfather and go to school.'

Out on the bay, a fishing boat returns, trawling a cloud of noisy gulls.

'How is Didima anyways?'

'She's sick.'

'Seems like a tough old chook.'

'Still says she's dying and, that when she does, she wants to go home.'

'That's a bit mad – come all the way here just to die and go home. Kind of a waste of a trip, don't you think.'

'I don't know how we'd do it.'

'Do what?'

'Get her home. We got basically no money. Really we got minus money, even with what Mum brings in.'

'I think you worry too much, Rudra. Leave some stuff for your parents to do.'

He rises from sleep like air in a bottle of oil. His skin feels slick with another tiger dream but his mouth is dry. He tries to reorientate himself. There are the walls of Wallace's spare room, a tiny window showing winking reflections over the creek, a dark doorway. There is Didima sitting on the bed, her legs like mangrove roots. There is her hair set like smoke above her. There are her worried eyes.

'It's alright, Rudra. You were dreaming,' she says. 'I will make you some warm milk with turmeric and honey.'

'It's okay, Didima, I'm fine.'

'Nonsense. It is no trouble.' She struggles out of bed, slipping on her flattened sandals. A clank of a pot on the stove, the snick and flare of a match. After a moment, she appears at the doorway with two enamel mugs in her hand.

'Come, we'll sit outside, Rudra. It will calm you.'

They sit in the plastic chairs in front of the house. The stars are sprayed like milk froth over the headland.

'What did you dream of?' she asks.

'It was nothing,' says Rudra. 'I've already forgotten.'

Didima wobbles her head to show that it is okay if he doesn't want to talk, that she will talk instead.

'Listen,' she says, 'while I tell you the story about the singing fish. This is a nice story with no bad dreams attached.' She smooths her sari over her knees and looks up to the sky as if willing the words to arrive. Finally, she starts, 'When I was young girl, before my father was killed by that terrible tiger, my mother's cousin returned from Ceylon where he had made his fortune in mining tin. It was very unusual for people from poor villages to travel in those times but he was quite unlike anyone I have ever met. He was a bit of a show-off; I remember this, although I was young. But he brought a great many gifts into our poor house and he would sit me on his knee and tell me stories.'

She pauses to sip her milk. Rudra notices his has grown a skin and he pulls at it with his finger and drags it up the corner of the mug and into his mouth.

'My mother's cousin was from a town on the east coast of Ceylon. Do you know the story of Ceylon, Rudra?'

'I don't think so.'

'About King Ravana, capturing the lovely Sita and taking her away to his kingdom of Lanka? About the loyal monkey general Hanuman helping Rama to rescue her with a monkey army and building a bridge from Lanka to India? And when they walked back through India, people placing lamps on their doorsteps to welcome light, in the form of the lovely Sita, back into the world? This is where we now have the *Diwali* festival of lights.'

'I don't think so.'

'I don't know it matters for the purposes of this story, Rudra, other than I thought when I was a child that Ceylon...' She places her hand on Rudra forearm and whispers, 'It's now even called Sri *Lanka*,' nods at this conclusive proof, then continues, '...was a strange and magical place.'

'Why are you telling me this story?'

'To pull you away from your dream. It will help. Warm milk for the body, story for the mind. Now listen to my mother's cousin's story. One night – a good full moon in the sky – he hired a boat and an oarsman to visit the Kallady Lagoon. The lagoon was splashed with moonlight. It was very, very beautiful. The air smelled of coconut oil and sandalwood.

'When he got to the Lady Manning Bridge, the oarsman stopped the boat. It was quiet, just the sound of water around the feet of the bridge. Then the oarsman pushed one of his oars deep into the water, blade first. He motioned for my mother's cousin to put his ear to the handle of the oar.' Didima stops and blows into her cup, even though the milk is now tepid.

'And then what?'

'Well, I will tell you, Rudra. There was a sound. Soft at first, like a pinkie humming around the wet rim of a glass. Then other sounds joined – the slow sawing of a violin bow, the pluck of a single guitar string. Soon it was a whole chorus. The oarsman said, *Oorie coolooroo cradoo*. Words in Tamil, so many vowels, like bird language. A pigeon singing in a forest. My mother's cousin said those words in Tamil and then he whispered them, into my tiny ear, in Bangla. And now I will tell you in English – thrice removed. That oarsman believed the sound was made by crying shells.'

'Crying shells?'

'That's what the oarsman said. But my mother's cousin said it was fish that made the music. Singing fish. They are famous in Batticaloa.'

'Singing fish.'

'You can even look them up in the any such encyclopaedia. There are many doubting Thomases but I heard this story with my own ears.'

'But fish can't sing, Didima.'

'How do you know that, Rudra?'

'I just know it. Fish can't sing. I mean, I've heard of fish like sooty grunters making noises, but singing, Didima, that is something completely different.'

'What do you mean?'

'Only things that feel sing.'

'Like birds?'

'Yes, I reckon birds feel things – happiness, sadness, anger.'

'But not fish.'

'No. Fish don't *feel* anything.'

'You are talking about *emotions*, Rudra?'

'Yes, they don't feel emotions. They're cold-blooded. They just act on…on…'

'*Instinct* – is this the word you are looking for?'

'Yes, instinct.'

'How do you know they do not feel anything?'

'Because they're fish and I just know they don't.'

'I think until you've been a fish, Rudra, you cannot say what they are feeling.'

'That's just stupid.'

'I heard this story when I was a child, Rudra, and from that moment on I have always treated everything as if it has the *potential* to sing.'

'This is getting weird, Didima.'

They sit there for a moment, listening to the bay slowly pashing the sand from Dark Corner to the inlet. Then, Didima speaks.

'Us water people think the sea is silent, that it will give up everything without complaining, forever. It makes it easy for us to take – like stealing sweeties from child. If you don't protest then we think you are agreeing, even when you are giving up your very life. But there is always the fish song, Rudra – a protest so quiet, we believe it is not there.'

Didima wipes at her eyes with the corner of a hankie. 'Your mother was such a sweet child, you know. Always so sweet. Like coconut *ladoos* I would tell her, sweeter even, like *chomchom* or *rosogolla*.' She smiles. 'I wish she hadn't gone so far away.'

'Why did she leave India, Didima?'

'You have not asked her?'

'It never came up.'

'I'm not really sure it is my place to tell you, Rudra. But I will anyway. Because I am your *didima* and I promised you your stories.' She takes a quick sip of her hot milk and, clearing her throat, begins. 'We gave Nayna everything we could. She grew up with love and when the time came, we sent her to boarding school to be educated in all the things that would bring her into the world. We didn't want her to always have river mud between her toes. It was a lot of money, Rudra, and by this time the family fortunes were not so high. It is true that your *dadu*'s family were once rich, but fortunes rise and fall with the tides.'

'But,' says Rudra, smiling, 'Dadu was a solution-*wala*.'

Didima doesn't smile, not this time. 'He was, Rudra. But sometimes when the problem is so hard the solution is a nut hidden inside a bitter fruit.'

It is not dawn yet and won't be for a few hours. Rudra wishes for sunrise and for a good ending to the story. But Didima, backlit by the porch light, looks into her empty cup. He prods her. 'What happened next, Didima?'

'Oh, Rudra, I am sad even thinking of it.' She pauses. 'Nayna was at Calcutta University – Bachelor of Science with Physics Honours – such a clever one. The university educated some very important women. Nayna's hero was Kadambini Ganguly, who became a doctor in the time of the Britishers – one of the first women to graduate from university in such times.

'Nayna had such big dreams. And why not? Times were changing, life for women was getting better and better. For some women, Rudra, not all. Things were not perfect.' She presses her fist to her mouth. 'But the expense. Fees were one thing, and then accommodation for Nayna, and food expense.' Didima shakes her head in the remembering, the weight of the debt pressing down on her even after all this time. 'Your *dadu*'s family had some dowry things set aside. You know what dowry is, Rudra. It is the price a family must pay to a groom for the upkeep of a bride.'

'That's good, Didima. Money was what you needed.'

'It wasn't enough money that Nayna could be brought through university and we would not also starve. And then what after that? What of her future? So,' says Didima, looking at Rudra gravely, 'that is when your *dadu* came up with the solution.'

'Which was?'

'The money was not so great. Enough only for a dowry and a small wedding. There were other items – saris, silk and whatnot, handed down also. But we couldn't have the pick of the bachelors in the Sundarbans. And Kolkata was not even possible. Oh, Rudra, your *dadu* and I married for love, but it was a hard road. To push against tradition is a difficult thing; maybe even impossible in the long run.'

'What did Mum do when she found out?'

'The timing could not have been more terrible. She was home on a break and excited about an opportunity to study in Australia. A part-scholarship was possible, but still it was so much money. Then we sat her down and told her of her *baba*'s solution. We brought the steel box from its hiding place and showed her the money and the nice clothing. We told her we were doing this for her.' A sob rises in her – unbidden, a bubble of pure despair. 'Your *dadu* and I had married for love and now this.' She uses her sari to blot the tears from her cheeks. 'At first my Nayna was happy, thinking she could use the money to get to Australia. But your *dadu* explained to her it was not possible – that if she went to Australia to study we could not afford the *ongoing* costs – the food money, a place to stay and whatnot. It was the long-term solution your *dadu* was thinking of. He kept repeating that: *long-term solution* in English, as if that somehow made it all better.

'It was not the crying or the shouting, Rudra, it was my Nayna's eyes I remember. We had betrayed her so deeply.

'The next morning I made her breakfast – curds with honey, a nice hot cup of *cha*. But she was gone. And the box was gone with her.'

'She stole from you, Didima.'

'It was us that stole from her, really. Who could blame her for doing what she did. To raise a child believing one thing, then to do entirely another. We knew it wasn't right, your *dadu* and I, but I am not sure how we could have done a different thing.'

'You could have given her the money to go to Australia,'

'And then we would have lost her forever.'

'You did anyway.'

Didima purses her lips. 'We did.'

'It's okay, Didima. You got her back.'

'But her *baba* never saw her sweet face again, and for that I am always sad. She wrote to us once she was at university in Sydney, then again when she was married to your father. I kept writing to her but the letters from her end dried up. Your *dadu* said I should leave her alone, that she must take her own course now. But I am an Indian mother and I love fiercely and I love forever and I never forget my child.

'When I got her letter with news of her marriage it had one email address at the top. Of course, I could never send such a thing but your Aunty Bansari's clever son, he was able.'

'I have an Aunty Bansari?'

'She is not your real aunty, she's your *dadu's* cousin, but never mind – her son is very clever and he sent an email to your mother telling her of her *baba's* death. And when I sold our house, I came here.'

'But why did Mum never go home?'

'I think you need to ask her that. But maybe she was ashamed to give up what she had fought for. I cannot actually know her mind.'

They sit there for a while in the semi-silence. The mopokes call down from the forest above. The water licks at the pier and the rocks. Wind rattles in the leaves of darkened trees.

'I think I'll go back to bed now,' says Rudra.

'No more bad dreams.'

'Hot milk and stories are the cure.' But, in truth, those stories are now hanging inside him like the wallaby carcass in the shed. Rudra has no language to absorb them into himself. What can he make of a fish with the potential to sing or a girl (his mother, he realises with a shock) denied? He looks at his *didima*, into the eye of this storm that is engulfing him; her at the centre of it all, calmly sipping her hot milk.

As Rudra slips under the single sheet, he tries to not think about the tiger. But of course in this game when you try not to think of a thing, then you do. For a long time, he sits staring into the demon black above his bed. But eventually, everyone must sleep.

*The tiger walks on the soft pad of paws. Deep in the jungle where the light is striped and supple and bends over broad-leaved plants, winding up lianas until it runs across the canopy.*

*The tiger bends to drink, pushing its tongue to the water and bringing it into its mouth. It hears the cry of an animal, feeling it down deep in its stomach. Ears turn, trying to locate the sound. It begins to run towards the sound. Towards the blood. And the sight – the quiver of the animal's flank, eyes widening in the blue-black shadowlight. And it is on it. A mouth clamped hard around its neck.*

The possum is on the front step when they wake. Wallace blames Tangent, who looks up at him like he is a fool.

Didima appears in the doorway, her hair tangled with sleep. She sees the corpse and wrinkles her nose. 'Can you get rid of it please, Wallace.'

'I'll get rid of it, Didima,' says Rudra and, picking it up by the tail, walks quickly up the hill behind the house. Tangent dances along behind, snicking at the possum's bloody snout.

Up above the house, the rocks form a ragged escarpment that runs back along the creek and into the hinterland. Rudra realises that wherever he leaves the possum, Tangent will just try to drag it back with him. He is small, but he's a plucky little thing.

'Go home!' Rudra shouts at him.

Tangent cocks his head in answer and turns an excited little circle.

'Go home, Tangent. I need to get rid of this possum and I don't need your help.' Why is he explaining this to the dog? The dog doesn't care. He sees meat.

'Go home!' Rudra kicks out at him, but he nimbly jumps to one side. He tries to outrun him but after a minute of exhausting scrambling up the hill, he stops to find Tangent standing there with his tongue out.

Then he strikes upon an idea. Gathering rocks from about him, he forms a rough cairn with a hollow centre. Into this he places the possum and slips a flat rock on top. Tangent sniffs round the cairn but can't get inside.

Rudra sits. From here he can see the curve of the creek into the lagoon that sits behind town. He can see his own house roof from here and *Paper Tiger* at mooring in the bay. His father has not been to sea for days. He seems to have lost hope now that someone else might soon own his boat and his house.

*What has become of this summer?* thinks Rudra. He remembers when summers were a stretch of sand and bright water. When all he needed to do was run home and fill his belly before returning to play. When his bike and his mates and coming back on dark were all that mattered. *Is this what adulthood is going to feel like?*

# 15

RUDRA FINDS HIMSELF, SURPRISINGLY, at the library in Umina. He can count on his elbows the number of times he has been here. But he needs the internet. During the school term he has access, but in the holidays he is stuck. It will come to their home *over Cord's dead body*.

From the outside, the library is a turd-brown building built in an H (...for *Humdrum*, for *Ho-hum*, for *Happenstance*) with narrow windows and an angular tiled roof. Inside, books stand to attention on the shelves, idle and ignored, their dusty breath full of half-forgotten words.

He signs into a computer and googles Baghchara. There is a flood of angry articles about the sunken island. Rising sea levels are blamed. Melting ice-caps. Deforestation. Humans are parasites. *This is what happens when you leave the lights on,* they say. *An island dies.*

How he will get there when it is time? What map he will use to find a place that exists now only below the water? He wonders how Didima must feel, belonging to a place to which she can never return – her sense of unbelonging. Is there even such a word?

Then he stumbles on a new article from *The Times of India* – 'Baghchara Island Rises'. A senior scientist from Jadavpur University tells the journalist it is *a revelation*, claiming satellite pictures show its gradual re-emergence – like a mudskipper – from the waters of the river. The journalist visits the site and there it is – only the spire of a *mandir*, a temple, probing the air above. *It will all come back*, the scientist predicts, *little by little*.

This feels like the fluttering of birds inside Rudra. He can barely contain his excitement as he pulls the article from the printer and catches the last bus back to Patonga.

There in Wallace's little room it begins to end.

'I brought you something, Didima,' Rudra says.

But now the article seems so insignificant in his hand. He knows she will carry away all her stories like bones in a blanket. It is a selfish thought and Rudra tries to push it from him, but when he bends to kiss her on the cheek, the smell of her fruity breath causes it to bubble over.

'So tired, Rudra.'

'I'll ring for a doctor, Didima.'

'No, Rudra. What is the use? I am just old, that is all.'

'I'll call Mum then.'

'Yes, call Nayna.' Didima smiles weakly. 'I would like to see my girl.'

Tangent gets up and turns three circles before settling back on the bed. Seagulls keen outside the window.

Rudra makes the call. 'Quickly,' he says, before putting down the phone and returning to Didima's bedside.

'The island,' he says. 'Baghchara. It's coming back.'

Didima blinks away the mist. 'Baghchara is coming back?'

'It's true, Didima. I'll read it to you.'

He reads the article slowly, pausing when Didima closes her eyes, when her breath stalls for a moment, or quickens to a pant. *Is this what dying looks like?* When he finishes, he folds the paper and slips it into Didima's soft hand. She looks up at him. 'Baghchara is rising,' she says. 'From sadness,' she says.

'Yes.'

She props herself on her elbows and takes a sip from the water glass beside her bed. She closes her eyes and speaks. 'Dokkhin Rai is swimming behind the boat. So silent. The men will never hear him. His whiskers are sharp and his tongue will take your skin. Be careful.' She grabs him by the hand. 'Don't go into the forest, Baba.'

'It's Rudra, Didima. Your grandson.'

She blinks her eyes. 'I can go back now.'

'Wait for Nayna. She's on her way.' Rudra feels angry with her – this betrayal of leaving.

'The forest, Baba. The full moon. Bonbibi cannot help you tonight. Dokkhin Rai is too strong.'

'Didima, you're here. You're in Australia.' But Rudra is not even sure of that anymore.

'So far,' says Didima. 'So far away.'

There is a small altar to Bonbibi on the windowsill. She is riding the tiger – Dokkhin Rai – his stripes violent black bars over his yellow flanks.

'Tell me this story. The one about this altar,' says Rudra, hoping by doing this she will wait at least until his mother arrives.

Didima inhales deeply as if coming up for air after a deep dive.

Her voice is barely a whisper. 'Listen while I tell you the story of the Lady of the Forest.' She closes her eyes as if remembering something she learnt by heart – a long time ago, when she was a little girl, sitting in a village that was soon to disappear.

'Bonbibi is important to Muslims and Hindus. In the rest of India this would not happen, but in the Sundarbans, Hindu and Muslims share this goddess.

'It is said that she was born to the second wife of a holy man from Mecca. When his first wife demanded he get rid of his children, he abandoned them both, Bonbibi and Shah Jongli, in the forest. They lived in the forest for seven long years, raised by a deer.' Her voice is cracking with the strain of the story. Rudra props her head forward and helps her sip from her water glass.

'After seven years the holy man, Berahim, rescues his children and they visit Mecca. When Bonbibi and Shah Jongli try on some magical hats, they are carried at once to the Country of the Eighteen Tides – the Sundarbans.

'They find the land under the control of an evil prince – Dokkhin Rai – who is demanding of them sacrifice. Bonbibi and Shah Jongli will not stand for this. And so begins the battle of good over evil, humans against the power of the deep forest. Eventually, Dokkhin Rai is subdued and the people of the Sundarbans no longer have to live under the yoke of the wicked prince.

'But Dokkhin Rai still lives in the jungle; even now, Rudra. He is like the danger, the dark, that lives inside us all. When he decides the time is right for sacrifice, he will take the form of a tiger. Then you had better beware.'

She points her crooked finger at the altar. 'See the small man in Bonbibi's lap. That is Dukhe, the honey collector, whose name means "sadness". He was betrayed by his greedy uncle, Dhona – whose name means "wealth". Dhona promised him up to the Tiger God for the price of a boatful of honey and wax. Dukhe, abandoned on an island as a sacrifice, heard the roar of Dokkhin Rai, eager for his blood. He prayed to Bonbibi and she heard him and sent her brother Shah Jongli. Shah Jongli fought Dokkhin Rai bravely, and the evil god, fearing for his life, escaped.

'A local holy man brokered a truce between the people and the tiger. It was agreed that only those poor and pure of heart could enter the forest and they must come with empty hand, without weapons. They must take only what they need or Dokkhin Rai will have his revenge.' She smiles at Rudra, placing her small papery hand over his. 'Light some incense for Maa Bonbibi, Rudra. She will protect us all.'

Rudra picks up some incense, lights it and waves the purifying smoke over Bonbibi and Shah Jongli, then over the small, frail form of Didima. 'Protect us,' he whispers.

When Nayna arrives she insists on calling a doctor.

'Such a woman of science,' Didima says. 'It is wasted time.' But she is happy when Nayna places coconut *ladoos* on her table. Happier still when she sits by her bed and rests her head on her lap. She strokes Nayna's hair until the sun falls behind the hill and the shadows creep from the room. Still the doctor does not arrive.

It is fully dark when Rudra hears his grandmother's last breath escape her. It is not a gasp. Didima does not seemed shocked at leaving. Nayna calls her name softly but, of course, she doesn't answer. They both sit there with her. Even when the doctor arrives in a borrowed boat, Nayna will not let go of her hand. The doctor leaves eventually and still they maintain their vigil. Wallace comes home from his evening at the pub, and presses cups of sugary tea into their hands, insisting they drink.

Rudra does not sleep. Instead he sits motionless, propped against the wall until first light, feeling his own breath come and go. Sometimes the pain catches him by surprise and a sob jags its way out, followed by the sting of tears. And when they find their way to his mouth, these tears are salty. Of course they are, because he is from the sea and has always been and will always be. It is in his blood – on two continents. And he wishes he could splice these two halves of him together. And he wishes Didima had managed one more day of stories.

Rudra opens the bag of coconut *ladoos*. He pops one in his mouth and places one before Bonbibi. *Protect us.*

On the way back from the crematorium, he carries the ashes on his knee. They are in the ute and he is wedged between his mother and father. At this moment, he feels like a child again. There is something comforting about his parents' bodies on either side, protecting him from the world. But through the windscreen the world keeps coming.

'We should have been there,' he says.

His mum sobs. His dad glares at him. 'Four grand they wanted to charge us.'

'It's Didima.'

'She doesn't care. If she did, she would have left the cash.'

'She did, Cord,' says Nayna, wiping her eyes with the back of her hand. 'The money she got from selling her house. The only money she had.'

Cord takes his eyes off the road. 'We'll need that money to keep the bank off our back.'

'No,' says Nayna. 'That is not happening. We need to take her back to the Tidelands. That is what she wanted.'

'She is dead, Nayna. She. Doesn't. Care.'

'I care,' says Rudra.

His mum takes his hand. 'I care too,' she says.

'Then both of you can walk,' Cord says and he stops the car. They are still two kilometres from home and it is getting dark.

'Cord, please.'

'Get out!'

'Dad—'

'Out, I said.'

They shuffle out of the ute and stand on the roadside.

'Walk'll do you good,' says Cord, and takes off in a spray of gravel.

They are left staring after his ute as it disappears out of sight.

This time it is Rudra who takes his mum's hand. 'We'll be okay.'

'Maybe,' she says.

It scares Rudra that even his mother is unsure. 'Let's get walking,' he says, just to stir the air with his voice.

As they crunch along the soft shoulder of the road, the sky turns to tempered steel. The air cools and Venus rises.

'The Evening Star,' says his mum. 'We call it Shukra. It's believed that he brings good fortune.'

'We could use some of that.'

'We surely could.'

They continue on in silence for a while. Didima's ashes seem to weigh nothing to Rudra. 'Mum?'

'Yes.'

'Is this all of Didima?'

She looks at the urn. 'I expect so.'

'It doesn't seem enough.'

Nayna lets out a sharp, surprising sob. 'I should have done more for her, Rudra.'

'She told me about what happened.'

'About what?'

'You running away. The dowry. Everything.'

'Such a complicated thing between mothers and daughters.'

'And fathers and sons?'

'That too.' Nayna wipes scoops a tear from the corner of her eye with her fingernail. 'It wasn't even her fault. It was Baba who came up with the crazy marriage scheme. Oh, he was the solution-*wala*, alright.' She shakes her head. 'Still, he was just doing the best he could with what he had.

'I blamed her though. She was my mother. She had climbed out of the muck of poverty and superstition and married outside her caste. She had been educated. In those days, this was something remarkable. Even now it would be considered very brave or very stupid. I hated her for her hypocrisy, Rudra. You know what that means, right?'

'Yup.'

'Of course you do. You're sixteen. You know pretty much everything.'

'True.'

'I'm glad your *didima* got to know you.'

'Me too.'

'I wish you could have met your *dadu* too. He was a good man. Even with what he did, he was a good man at heart.'

Rudra is sure he can hear the stars charging through the sky, grinding at its edges. Things had become so complicated. He had started the holidays with one clear story – it belonged to him and he understood it perfectly. Now summer's flat blanket was bristling with a hundred thorns of unclaimed narratives, some that he would surely have to make his own.

'We have to take her back,' says Rudra. 'To her island.'

'We do.'

'Dad's not going to like it.'

'He isn't.'

They keep walking until all that remains is their footsteps and Shukra, the clear, bright planet, crossing over their heads. It is very dark when they come to the hill that overlooks their little town.

'*They* look like stars,' says his mum. 'All those winking house lights. Our town is a constellation.'

'Mr DeNicola told us when you look at space, it's like time travel.' Rudra's words echo off the escarpment. 'The stars we see might already be dead. It takes so long for the light to reach us that we are looking back in time hundreds or thousands of years.'

'Maybe it will take our town that long for its death to reach the outside world.'

'What do you mean?'

'Maybe its light has already gone out. Maybe we just can't see it from up here.'

'That's a bit sad, Mum.'

'Yes.' She kisses him on the cheek. 'And we have probably had enough sadness for one day. Are there any more of those *ladoos* left at Wallace's?'

'I think I left a couple.'

'Excellent – let's celebrate your *didima*'s life.'

Wallace breaks out a bottle of old muscat he's been saving for a special occasion. They sit out the front peering into the dark.

'So when you going?' asks Wallace.

'I'll book the tickets tomorrow. We might get a flight out by next week,' says Nayna.

Rudra wonders about India, about the place Didima insisted is his home. A place he has never seen and of which he knows only what little Didima managed to leave behind.

'Mum?'

'Yes, Rudra.'

'Do you know anything about this?' He hands her the hunting photo he has removed from its frame.

'Where did you get it?'

'I took it from Dad's office.'

'You're lucky he didn't catch you.'

'Do you know who these people are?'

'The man with the beard and the turban is a Sikh. I am guessing it was taken in India. And this man...' She holds the picture to the kero lantern. 'He looks like your great-grandfather – Arch Solace. Your dad's grandfather.'

'And *that*,' says Wallace, 'is a tiger. Don't hold it too near the lamp, Nayna. That old paper will burn pretty easy. You know what this means, don't you, Rudra?'

'Not really.'

'That thing we pulled out of the bay – it's a tiger skull.'

'It is.' He knows it for sure now; deep inside him.

'And your great-grandfather killed a tiger in India.'

'Looks like it could be.'

'He brought the skull back here.'

Rudra looks at the picture again. 'How did it end up in the bay?'

'*Paper Tiger* is not the first Solace boat, Rudra,' says Wallace. 'Your family had a boat go under. I don't know exactly when, but I know where.'

'Where?'

'Flint and Steel.'

'Where we pulled up the skull.'

'Yup.'

'That's just too much coincidence,' says Nayna.

'Dokkhin Rai will have his revenge,' says Rudra, remembering his *didima*'s words.

'Rudra, what is this rubbish?' Nayna's eyes are wide with anger and surprise. 'I didn't escape the Sundarbans to have it follow me here. It's just superstition and nonsense, stories to scare little children and fool the gullible. We are educated people.'

'I'll put the billy on and make us a cup of tea,' says Wallace. 'It's been a big day. You can stay here tonight. I'm guessing Cord won't be on the road looking for you.'

He goes inside. The phone rings and he reappears, thumbing over his shoulder. 'For you, Rudra.'

Rudra leaves his mum in the guttering lamplight and picks up the heavy old receiver.

'Y'allo.'

'Ruds, it's me,' says Maggs, 'Been trying to get hold of you. No answer at your place.'

'Didima died.'

'Shit, man. I'm sorry. When's the funeral?'

'There wasn't one.'

'Is that some kind of Indian thing?'

'That's some kind of Cord thing.'

'He's a bit of a dick, your dad, isn't he?'

Rudra swallows the night air. 'I'm going to India.'

'No shit?'

'True.'

'When.'

'Soon.'

'Can you bring me back one of those pyjama suit getups?'

'Sure.'

'You scared?'

'Plenty.'

'Hey, did you ever get that thing back from your dad again?'

'It's a tiger skull.'

'A tiger skull? From in the bay off Patonga? Shut. Up.'

'It's complicated.'

'It's beyond complicated.'

'I need to take the skull back to India.'

'Why?'

'To stop the dreams. To set things right.'

'You know that you're saying this stuff out loud, right?'

'I don't know how they're linked but they are.'

'Well, mate, have fun with your craziness and all.'

'I will.'

'And call me when you get back.'

'I will.'

'And we'll have a surf or something.'

'Sure.'

'Seeya.'

'Yup.'

The line goes dead.

Rudra wakes late. His mum is still asleep and he leaves her be, sneaking out to where Wallace is squinting into the mid-morning sun. The photo of the hunting party is on his knee and there is a cold scum on top of his tea. Rudra sits down beside him.

'What's next?' Wallace asks.

'We take Didima's ashes back to India.'

'And the skull?'

'It goes back too.' He wants to tell Wallace more. How the skull belongs to a tiger god, who has been out for revenge all these years, and how returning it will stop the dreams and the killings. Instead, he says, 'It's the right thing to do.'

# 16

IN THE DARK OF A MOONLESS NIGHT, Rudra rows a dinghy out to *Paper Tiger*. Over the past two days, he has watched from Wallace's house as Cord moved his life to the boat – one tinnie-load at a time. Damp clothes hang over the gunnels and net winch. The boat sits lower in the water, sadness settling like so much ballast in its hull.

It is as if Cord's life is contracting – that he is giving up more and more each day. Soon there will only be a dark smudge where he once was, a ring on the water marking that final point where his flat stone once skipped across the surface.

Cord's ute is not in the foreshore carpark. Still, Rudra has wetted the rowlocks so the oars don't squeal. He will slip quietly on to the boat and work quickly. Get it all over and done with before his dad returns.

He reaches the boat and climbs on deck, moving towards the cabin with his torch probing the dark. There is a screech and Rudra swings the torch quick enough to catch a gull tumbling down from the cabin roof. In its confusion it almost blunders into Rudra. He can feel its wings graze his cheek and then it is off, low across the water, mewling like a saltwater ghost.

The cabin door is locked but Rudra reaches on top of the frame and his fingers find the key. He sucks up a breath and slips it into the door, hearing its serrated edge trickle through the lock barrels. He turns it and feels the latch ease out of the striker. Then he turns the handle.

He opens each of the lockers in the cabin and looks inside. Nothing. There are boxes of stuff stacked beside a mattress and he begins sifting through them. It is just old junk: his dad's football trophies; a framed photo of his grandparents – stiff and solemn; a rubber band ball; a set of chipped china cups. And then he pulls out a photo album.

His dad held on to an old-style camera long after everyone had gone digital. Rudra remembers him grumbling that it would never last. *Digital photography is junk food*, he said. *The only reason that people like it is that it's quick and cheap.*

Rudra opens the album. The plastic film has ruffled and made the photos look bleak and tacky. The first one is of him and his mum on *Paper Tiger*. He is a baby: a small pink, pinched face, eyes closed and mouth open, and a pupa body tightly swaddled in a blanket. It must have been winter because his mother is wearing a beanie. He recognises it as one of his father's and he can't believe that sometime, long ago, they would love each other enough to share clothes.

His mum looks like she is about to say something or has already said it. Something joyful because she is smiling through the words, and he knows then they must have been happy together. Once. Upon. A. Time.

Must have been happy. It feels like it was always as bad as this and that Cord Solace has never loved. It is easier for

Rudra to believe this than see the possibility of change – for good or bad. It is simple to see life as static, like a photo, but there are frames and frames stretching back and forward from this captured moment. And frames to come that Rudra cannot know.

It was once explained to him that photography is just light captured over time. If the light decreases then the time needs to increase to compensate.

Light and time. Rudra can see the picture of his mum and him was taken close to Lion Island. Above baby Rudra's round head, in the background, is the mouth of the cave – dripping with foliage. It is dark and it looks like that mouth is about to consume the child. Eat it whole.

The next photo, directly below, is the same scene, maybe with a second or so gap between. His mum's smile has dropped slightly, her words sipped away by a wind that has begun to chafe at the bay. The mouth of the cave seems to have grown but it may have been a change of angle or light.

In another, below again: Rudra is struggling and crying and his mum looks as if she is about to drop him. The cave mouth seems even bigger, the light muffled by cloud.

Rudra shudders at how quickly things can change. Why would his father want to capture such a thing and hold it forever? He can understand the initial mistake: the almost-automatic winding on of the film and clicking of the shutter. But why save the next two shots when the first was the perfect moment.

It is then he hears the moan of the outboard and knows his dad is returning. Quickly, he switches off the torch and replaces the album. He needs somewhere to hide. There is a cardboard mover's box up near the front window. Inside it – a couple of towels and not much else. He clambers in and pulls the lid over.

The outboard gets louder and soon he hears the tinnie clashing with the hull of *Paper Tiger*. Then, his dad climbing on board and pulling the tender to the mooring line. A silent moment while he ties it off. Opening the cabin door. Pausing. Knowing he had locked the cabin, that he always locks the cabin. Turning the light on.

Rudra holds his breath. Shuts his eyes on the violence that he knows will take place. Steels his body against it – making his body tight and impervious to pain. A ball of iron.

He waits. While his father moves around the cabin, picking things up. He can smell him. The odour of fish that never leaves. And something else – alcohol. A thing he rarely touches. The smell is deep – pub deep – a smell that Rudra has noticed in the men and women who make it their lives. Whose meat is marinated in beer and cask wine. It can't be his father.

But it is his father. He knows it in the way he moves about the cabin – like he owns every space, even the air; this final place. And Rudra can feel him claiming it, stealing the breath from him and calling it his own. And he shakes uncontrollably. The shaking becomes a roar and Rudra can taste acrid diesel smoke in his throat and hear *Paper Tiger's* motor tack-tacking as its pistons and valves slowly warm. His father leaves the cabin, casts-off the mooring, returns and throttles the boat round in an arc out to sea.

When the boat stops, Rudra is pretty sure he knows where they are. If he can just get out of the box maybe he will have the time to jump overboard and swim to land. It is dark and the sea is full of things he cannot see but the danger here is greater.

He lifts the flap of the box a little. His father is outside. He can hear him talking and thinks it must be on his mobile. Now is the time. Rudra tries to stand but he has been curled inside the box and his body does not want to unfold. The box tips and he lands heavily on the floor. He holds his breath and his father's voice stops.

He crawls from the box. His head is bleeding from a gash above his eyebrow. He staunches the flow with the corner of a towel and creeps to the door. Peering out, he can see the outline of Lion Island and the dark bulk of the headland leading round to Umina. Good. He can swim that far if he strips to his undies and kicks off his shoes. He just needs to reach the water.

He pulls himself upright. His dad is holding something, mumbling drunk. The sweeping light of the Barrenjoey Lighthouse combs the sea. Coming...coming. The white beards of waves like phosphorous. The light streaks from the stern of the boat to the bow, illuminating Cord Solace for a moment.

His father turns the skull on the tips of his fingers. So precarious. So precious. A thing that must go back. And, even though it knows salt water, it does not belong in the sea. Rudra runs towards him. He clocks the look on his father's face and it seems like defeat. He sees the skull tip, balance for a moment on the thick prongs of his dad's fingers, then fall over the gunnel.

Without thinking, he dives after it.

The water is a shock – thin and dark and cold. He surfaces, gulping air, sees his dad's face over the hull of the boat as the lighthouse arm swings over. Then he dives, and as he goes he kicks off his shoes and his shorts and pulls his shirt over his head. The water feels slick on his bare skin. It is deep here and he cannot possibly find the skull, but still he dives.

He dives down until the air brings fire into his lungs then he claws his way to the surface. It is a long, long way up and he can see the light from the boat dancing up there but not getting any closer. Finally, he surfaces.

'Rudra! Get in the boat!' But Cord's yelling is without menace, the fire in his voice nothing but a guttering glimpse.

Rudra gulps air and dives again, swimming down in a slow arc that he imagines the skull will have taken. And when the burning comes to his lungs again he keeps going downwards. The water gets colder. And colder. He feels the leather of kelp against his face and he holds on as a surge tries to carry him off. Then he sees a bright patch of light and he pulls himself along the weedy bottom towards it. The air is festering inside him. He wants to gulp at the water but knows that will be the end.

His fingers find the holes – the eye sockets – and he plunges them in and grabs the skull to his chest. The skull warms him. He looks above to the oval of light on the surface of the ocean that should mean home. His world. And although his lungs are screaming for fresh air, he lingers for just a moment. The sweeping arm of the lighthouse touches the surface so lightly, a caress. He would like to stay down here forever just watching it all go by above. Light and time – a perfect exposure.

But he knows he doesn't belong. His pulpy lungs are telling him to rise. And slowly he goes, gripping the skull to his chest. The water glows inside him. He is slipping upwards.

Someone told him once to never trust an animal that walks sideways. And the way it takes the landscape so seriously makes him want to scream. It fills his whole vision and wills him to rise. And when he does, the sea comes from him in a burning rush. It pours from him, stinging his throat.

The crab scuttles back to the safety of the rim of seaweed at the high tide mark. There it watches him. Him, as tall as a tree and clutching the polished white skull of the tiger to his chest. Him, brandishing a new-found bravery.

After the dark of the night before, the day seems clean and right. He feels good, even though he is only wearing his undies, and the morning is chill.

But the mainland shore is a good swim away and he knows enough about sharks to fear them. There are rules for dangerous dogs and nesting magpies involving territory and respect. Same goes for sharks. The channel is a known spot. They'll be there for sure, nipping penguins and fish from the water. Most likely they were there last night too and, if he'd thought too hard about it, he would never have jumped from the boat.

It will take him ten minutes, at a lick, to make the other shore. Holding the skull will slow him down though. Plus, swimming with one arm will make him look and feel like a wounded animal and those vibrations will excite any sharks big enough to take him.

He searches the high tide mark and finds enough nylon cord to make a strap. He passes it through the nose then down and out through the mouth. The lower jaw has been attached to the skull with old copper wire. He takes a turn round the jaw with the cord, to make sure he doesn't lose it, and slings the whole thing over his back.

The water seems benign – a scattering of baitfish easing past the rocks, a flat mirror with clots of weed breaking the surface. As he wades off the point, he shivers with the early morning chill. *Suffer in your jocks*, they would say.

When he reaches the other shore he'll need to walk round the point and through the reserve, coming out at Dark Corner and then having to cross the beach to get to Wallace's place. It'll be mid-morning by then and the tourists will be there.

*One thing at a time*, he thinks. *First the swim.* He feels the power in his body, the muscles in his arms and legs under tension; the lightness of himself skimming across the surface of the sea – sixty per cent water already, come from the sea and always returning. Him, with sea people on both sides of the family.

The strokes become automatic and the rhythm calms him. The skull, nuzzling between his shoulder blades, sets him to thinking about its owner. The tiger that killed his great-grandfather on one side and, in turn, was killed by his other great-grandfather. All this happening over sixty years ago in the jungles of the Sundarbans and bouncing down through history before coming to rest at his feet – the world's biggest coincidence. Is it possible that his family on both sides are linked by this one terrible event? Were his mother and father brought together by something far more powerful than chance? Or is all this just lies – another convenient story to trick him, the gullible kid?

He recalls his mother and a much younger him, scribbling letters on the sand for the sea goddess to take – a myth created to protect him and to dispel his fears. But more often he would listen to Nayna debunking the myths of *her* childhood – gods and goddesses crumbling before her strong, sweet voice. She would tell him to believe only in what he could see, to shrug off superstition and acts of faith. Now, one half of him wants to believe, while the other knows it to be lies.

His hands rise and fall from the water – like the blades of an oar, or the cups of a waterwheel. The strange thing about thinking, he realises, is the more you try and do it, the harder it gets. The slow rhythm of this swim is enough of a distraction that the thoughts keep coming like waves on the shore.

Can he, Rudra, take this skull back to where it came from? A place his *didima* waved goodbye to as a little girl and now can only return to as ashes?

Halfway across the channel now, with a side rip carrying him towards Pearl Beach. His hands slice the water and it comes over his head in silver strings. And with each stroke the far shore comes closer. He imagines the shallowing, the floor rising up to meet him. He sees his shadow flying over the sand. It's like a desert below. And he knows out in the kelp forests fish are hunting, and there are hills and valleys like on land. And the fish are silent as they hunt, and they cast small shadows.

# Land of eighteen tides
## *atharo bhatir desh*
### ল্যান্ড অব এইটনি টাইড্স

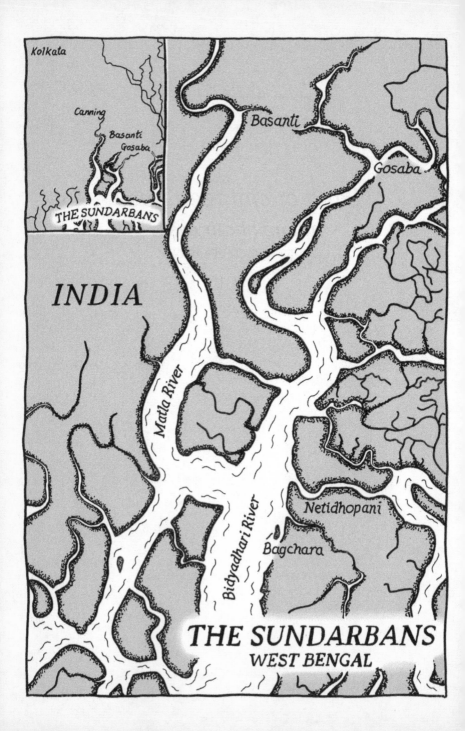

# 17

CAN YOU OPEN YOUR BAG, SIR?

Why?

Just open your bag, please, sir.

What's wrong, Rudra?

They want me to open my bag.

What do you need him to open his bag for?

I just need to check inside, madam.

What for?

Would you prefer to do this in private?

No.

I'll do it, Mum.

Good lad.

Okay.

What's this?

Ashes.

Ashes?

Ashes.

What ashes?

Not what, whose.

Whose ashes?

*My grandmother's.*

*I don't think that's allowed.*

*You don't think.*

*Mum, I can handle this.*

*I'm sure it's not allowed.*

*By who?*

*You mean by whom, madam?*

*Don't be pedantic.*

*Mum!*

*He's being pedantic, Rudra.*

*By India. They won't allow it.*

*Pretty sure they will.*

*How do you know?*

*I'm Indian.*

*By birth?*

*Yes.*

*But not a citizen?*

*No.*

*Well, I'm sure you can't just bring ashes into India.*

*You're Border Security, right?*

*Yes, madam.*

*Australian Border Security?*

*Yes.*

*Is this a risk to Australia?*

*No, madam.*

*I think we'll let India worry about this one then. Put it back in your bag, Rudra – we have a flight to catch.*

*Sorry. My mum...*

*Don't apologise for me, Rudra. Let's go or we'll miss our flight.*

*Lucky he didn't see the skull.*

*Lucky, Rudra.*

'Hollow bones,' says Nayna once they are onboard.

'What?'

'It's what makes birds light enough to fly.'

'And?'

'We don't have them.'

'True,' says Rudra. 'But we have this plane.'

'This plane is built by people, Rudra.'

'True.'

'And engineers and such – they tighten bolts and repair fuel lines and replace tyres.'

'I hope so.'

'And they are human?'

'I'm not sure where you're going with this.'

'Humans make mistakes and I can't stop thinking that the mistakes they made, maybe last night when they were tired, or this morning when they skipped a coffee break, might mean that this plane will fall out of the sky. Because,' she pauses to take a sip of water, 'we do not have hollow bones and were never meant to fly.'

'Mum.'

'Yes, Rudra.'

'You're a woman of science.'

'I am a reasonable woman, Rudra,' she snaps. 'But reason tells me this machine should not fly. I know the physics behind air travel and all – lift, thrust, drag. This I understand. But really, we are breaking the rules by doing this.'

'We'll be fine, Mum.'

'How do you know? You're only sixteen.'

Soon enough, they are taxiing to the runway. On the runway now, nose pointed at the water. Then they are thrown back in their seats and Rudra feels the growl of the beast in his belly, and the wing-shaking calamity of too much speed so soon. And a leap into the air, cursed by pockets of chaos, unseen, lurching drunk, this way and that. It makes him want to cry and laugh. He feels his teeth unscrewing and his ears lumpy with pressure, and he grins wildly at his mum but she is staring intently at the screen on her seat back, the tail camera showing way too much, and it not disappearing despite her blinking it away like a bad dream. Nayna, a woman of science, rational, knowing this bird doesn't fall as often as a car will crash, but there's still the possibility. And then they're bouncing through pavlova cloud stretched as far as forever, meringue of the gods.

When the seatbelt sign goes off, it triggers a calm in Nayna Solace. She, trusting now that the danger is over until landing, shrugs at Rudra.

'See – nothing to worry about,' she says.

When they are over the huge red heart of the country, Rudra looks down and imagines himself a tiny speck on the map below. It turns out that the Central Coast is not the whole world after all and that all-the-worries-that-ever-were are unseen from this altitude.

After hours of blood-coloured sand and mulga, they are still in Australia and Rudra begins to grasp the immensity of their country and this planet. He watches a movie, then another. He eats an impossibly small meal on a stupidly small tray, grazing elbows with Nayna. He tears open a foil-capped cup, spilling orange juice on his lap, drinks a bitter cup of tea, sits in biscuit crumbs. He starts a Bollywood movie as they set out over the ocean, volcanic cones of islands snaring cloud beneath them. The movie exhausts him with its singing and crying and gangsters and laughing and choreographed dancing piled on top of each other like layers of exotic, gaudy cake. Soon he is asleep with his mouth open, waking frequently to gasp at the dry air.

They stop for fuel in Singapore, swooping to the runway, his mum's damp hand round his wrist. They rise again in a flossy sunset, over container ships, dark blocks in the harbour, water like polished copper.

Somewhere, on nightfall, over the Andaman Sea, an island's lights wink up at Rudra and he feels a flutter of excitement rise in his belly, knowing they are drawing close to mainland India. He walks down the aisle to the toilet, past people with their heads thrown back in sleep, their kids glued to inflight games. The toilets are both occupied and Rudra waits with an old woman. She smiles sweetly at him, covering her missing teeth with the fringe of her sari.

'*Namaste*,' she says, pressing her hands together.

'*Namaste*,' replies Rudra. It is the first time he has greeted someone this way since his whispered childhood. *Namaste*, meaning *I worship the god within you*. Back before, when he was little and his mum would teach him, out of Cord's earshot. Even as the beachside hippies borrowed it to wear with their bindis and henna tattoos, he would practise this word behind closed doors.

They stand in awkward silence, before the old lady asks, 'Are you going home?'

And he looks out the porthole at an absence that he knows must be the Bay of Bengal. To him India is just a story, a phantom pain where a limb never grew. India, gone before it was there.

'No,' he answers. 'Just a holiday.'

When the woman reaches for his hand, he flinches. Then the toilet door is unlocked and a man escapes, squeezing past and lurching down the aisle like a doomed bride. When Rudra turns back, the old woman and her awkward question has gone.

When Rudra gets back from the toilet, his mum is in the window seat, conjuring land from the blackness. 'Do you want your seat?' she asks.

He shakes his head. 'You take it for a while. I'm going to read.'

He sits in the aisle seat, a gap between them, and picks up the novel they are sharing. Two bookmarks are chasing each other through the pages. His is the photo of his great-grandfather's hunting party at the temple. He has trapped it here within this book so he can recognise the point where they must drop the skull – there in the depths of the Sundarbans forest.

He turns the book over in his hands and it feels just right. When he thumbs the pages, they exhale an inky promise of things good and bad and things in between. The cover is a duotone in blues and yellows – three figures in a boat over mirror-water. One silhouetted in the bow, frozen, casting a net. Another figure at the stern – a woman maybe, a sari pulled over her head – steering. In the middle, a small child seated facing forward, wondering what his father will pull from the depths of the river.

'Good book?' The old woman he met outside the toilets is sitting across the aisle. He puts his finger at his page, shows her the cover.

'Aaah,' she breathes. 'Looks so nice.'

He smiles and opens the book again.

'Amitav Ghosh,' says the woman.

'Sorry?'

'The author of this book you are reading. It is Amitav Ghosh.'

Rudra looks at the cover. 'Yes,' he says.

'Very famous, this one. Is the book good?'

'It is.'

'What is it about?'

*The Hungry Tide* is about a woman with Indian parents going to the Sundarbans for the first time. *It's like a metaphor*, Nayna said, handing him the book on the train to Sydney. *For your journey*. Rudra looked at her. Metaphors. Why can't the thing just be the thing?

But the book ends up being alright and he is hooked a couple of pages in. Like nothing he has ever read before.

'It's about a woman…and a man…and a river.'

'So nice,' says the woman.

'Yes.'

'I have read this book once before,' says the woman.

'Why did you ask me what it was about?' says Rudra.

'I was just making chit-chat.' The woman looks wounded.

'Sorry, I didn't mean…' Rudra shuts the book and lays it on his lap. 'My family is from the Sundarbans. I'm going there for the first time.'

'Oh,' says the woman, her eyes suddenly glossy, crow's feet puckering at their edges. 'You will love it. I was there as a child. Many, many years before. There were tigers and the forest was so thick. We went on a boat and my father, well, he was a manager in a tin-plate factory, but then he became like a native. He was fishing and he was talking to the honeymen. It was truly a wondrous time. I will remember this one forever.'

'It sounds awesome.'

'It *was* awesome,' she says. 'I am from Jamshedpur, Golmuri side, originally. It is not such an *awesome* place. Mainly steel town – Tata steel plants and such. The hills nearby were wild when I was little but more and more it is being tamed. What is your name, grandson?'

'Rudra.'

'Such a strong name. Rudra, are you happy about going home?'

'India is not my home. I'm from Patonga on the Central Coast.'

'Is that not your mother?'

'My dad isn't Indian.'

'That doesn't matter.'

Rudra changes the subject. 'Why are *you* going home?'

'I am getting old. It is my time to die. I must be near the Ganga, you see, so they can burn me there and put in my ashes.'

'The Ganges?'

'Yes. My son, he does not understand, he works in IT and he has married a fully Australian girl. My grandchildren, they don't speak Bangla or Hindi. They play basketball and they eat meat pies – such disgusting food, I cannot tell you. But I beg to my son that he show them where they are from, just once, so they know it. It is important to know the little pieces that make you up. Even if they are very long ago.'

'I guess so.'

The plane sneaks up on the Indian mainland, chasing the delicate chains of light that, dazed with cloud, run haphazardly through the darkened country.

'That's the Sundarbans,' says Nayna, her finger hovering over her birthplace. Rudra stares down but can't penetrate the black forest edged with light. He has seen maps of the great delta, though, stretching from India across to Bangladesh. Wondered at its lung-like appearance, the capillaries streaming with mud, coursing their way to the Bay of Bengal.

Soon, the lights begin to thicken like clouds of bio-luminescence in a warm, dark ocean. Then they are above Kolkata.

# 18

'WELCOME TO NETAJI SUBHAS CHANDRA BOSE International Airport. The local time is ten-twenty pee-em. The temperature on the ground is sixteen degrees Celsius. If Kolkata is your home – welcome home. If you are a visitor, then *namaskar* – welcome.'

The tarry-scarred runway makes the ride to the gate a bumpy one. Then, even before the seatbelt lights go out, Indian businessmen are jumping into the aisles and wrestling their huge carry-ons from the overhead lockers. They stand between the seats, some with fresh *tilak* marks on their foreheads, snorting and shuffling plastic bags of duty-free. Still they have to wait ten minutes, then fifteen minutes, before the steps are wheeled to the doors. When the doors open, the plane inhales the subcontinent.

At the top of the steps, Rudra pauses. There is a different smell to the place – not quite smoke but not quite air. It burns as it goes down. It is a lot cooler than he would have imagined, but it is winter and the Himalayas are only five hundred kilometres to the north.

Inside, the terminal is new. Everything looks polished and empty. There are two queues for immigration – one for foreigners and another for Indian nationals.

'Which one, Mum?'

'We are foreigners, Rudra,' she says.

When they get to the desk, the immigration official studies their passports.

'What is the purpose of your visit?'

'Pleasure,' says Nayna.

'Have you been to India before?'

'I was born here.'

He looks at her and shrugs, stamps the passport. '*Namaskar*,' he says. 'Welcome home.'

They pre-book a taxi to take them to their hotel and wrestle their bags outside to the waiting cab.

The driver squashes their luggage into the boot of the cab – a strange old-fashioned affair. 'Where is your chitty?' he asks Rudra.

'Chitty?'

'Here.' Mum hands over the receipt to the driver.

He looks at it and shakes his head. 'This is not number one hotel, Madam. May I make one recommendation?'

'No.'

Rudra notices a shift in his mother's voice, a certain impatience he has never witnessed.

'Okay, Madam. As you wish.' He opens the door for Nayna, then rushes round the other side to open the door for Rudra who has, unfortunately, already let himself in. He shakes his head at this breaking of the rules, gets in himself and turns over the cab. It growls but refuses to start. The driver pounds the steering wheel and mouths some angry words. This prompts some rapid-fire Bengali from Nayna.

He rocks his head. 'Sorry, Madam. Sorry, Sir. This is very naughty taxi.' Nayna clicks her tongue disapprovingly.

'Hindustan Ambassador. This car born close-by Kolkata, driven by Madam Sonia Gandhi, also number one taxi from *Top Gear* show. You know this show?' The car's engine fires, and the driver slams it into gear and jerks it into the traffic. '*Top Gear*, *na*? Mister Jeremy Clarkson, Mister Richard Hammond, Mister James May. *Top Gear*.'

'We don't watch the show,' Mum has pulled her scarf over her face to block the fumes welling in the cab.

'In *Top Gear*, they race all taxis from around the world. Number one was Hindustan Motors Ambassador taxi.'

'They have been around forever,' says Nayna to Rudra.

'But not now,' says the driver. 'Now they shut their making place. Sadly, Madam, it is the death for the Ambassador.'

'I remember riding in an Ambassador car when I was very small,' says Nayna. 'On your *didima*'s lap with your *dadu* driving. I don't know where the car came from; maybe we borrowed it.

'It must have been my first time in a car and I remember marvelling at how my father knew how to drive – his big hand on the gearstick, his feet working the pedals, the indicators ticking, the sound of the horn. We travelled from Basanti to Kolkata during the great festival of Durga, passing decorative buildings made of cloth and paper, trucks carrying statues and people dancing to the crazy-happy music. How wonderful the seats smelled and how beautiful was the bonnet's curve above the road. The insects rushed to our headlights and smeared so thick across our windscreen that we had to stop and wash them off.' Nayna looks at Rudra. 'It's sad to think that it's all over. That India's homegrown car won't carry excited children to festivals anymore.' She laughs lightly. 'But maybe I'm just being nostalgic. I, more than most, know that everything must change.'

It is after midnight when a sign announcing *Beamish Hotel* appears in the headlights. The words are in spidery script and garlanded with a string of fairy lights. Half the bulbs are blown, which makes Rudra feel unaccountably sad.

The driver removes their bags and waits for his tip. Nayna hands over fifty rupees and he looks at it for a moment as if it could, and should, magically double in value.

A small guy in a stained but well-ironed velvet jacket takes their bags. Rudra places him in his early twenties. He has an impressive shovel-shaped goatee and a nervous manner, and his jet-black hair is greased into a glossy helmet beneath a colourful cloth cap. 'I am Raj,' he says. 'From Nepal.' He pronounces it *Nay-paul*. Then he whispers, behind his hand, like a stage villain, 'And I very much like Amitabh Bachchan.'

'Who?' asks Rudra.

'He's a Bollywood movie star,' Nayna explains with a sigh. 'He's pretty old.'

The man frowns. 'He is still number one movie star, Madam. That is why I am in India.' He pauses. 'To be.' He waggles his head. 'A Bollywood star.'

'But Mumbai is fifteen hundred kilometres away.'

'Yes.'

'And...that's where Bollywood is.'

'I know, Madam. It is okay.' Raj smiles and starts climbing the stairs. 'If you need anything, anything at all, I am your man.' He winks at Rudra. 'These bags are very heavy. Have you brought duty-free Scottish whisky? I can get you an excellent price. If you would wish to sell, you need only ask.'

'No Scotch.' Nayna looks weary and cold and tired of Raj's oversharing.

'Or maybe cigarette. Also good price.'

'We didn't buy any duty-free,' Nayna snaps.

Raj looks crestfallen. He bites his lip. 'Most sorry, Madam. It is not my place.' He heaves their heavy bags up the entrance steps to the Beamish.

From the doorway, a woman with a pile of startling orange hair glares at them. She shouts something at Raj, who mutters under his breath.

'Welcome,' she says to Rudra and his mother, extending her arms, her glare transforming to a saintly smile, 'to the Beamish Hotel. A grand experience awaits.' Behind her, a woman in a sari, bent double at the waist, slowly swishes dust bunnies across the floor with a grass broom. 'Since nineteen forty-two,' continues the woman, pausing for effect. 'And all modern convenience.' Raj drops the bags on the steps and puts a *beedi* between his lips. 'No smoking!' shouts the woman, and Raj spits the cigarette into his palm. 'We are pleased to offer you.' Another pause. 'Hot water geysers in all rooms.' She smiles. 'Full wi-fi.' Pause. 'And old-world charm.' She nods as if accepting an award. 'Do you have a reservation? Of course you do. Have you travelled far? Of course you have. Everyone has travelled far. I, myself, am from Romania. Like Mother Teresa – our own Kolkata Saint of the Gutters. God rest her soul.'

'Macedonia,' says Nayna.

'Excusez-moi?' the woman asks. This sounds more like French than Romanian to Rudra.

'Mother Teresa was from Macedonia,' replies Nayna. 'Originally.'

The woman's face darkens thunderously and Raj seems to shrink into himself. 'My name,' says the woman ponderously, 'is Ionela Ursu.' She turns full to face Nayna. '*You*.' She punctures the air with her finger. 'May call me Mrs Ursu.' Then she moves around behind the check-in desk. 'Passports, please.'

When they are signed in, Raj carries their bags up the winding staircase to their room. 'You have made an enemy of Madam Ursu.' He shakes his head. 'Mistake.' He opens their door and jerks his head for them to enter.

The room is spacious. The ceiling is high and there is a large window looking over the hotel garden to Sudder Street. The curtains are faded and dusty, but there is an air of what-once-was about the place, as if it could rise at any moment and rush back to its former glory.

Raj puts their cases on stands and opens the bathroom door. 'Hot and cold water, on tap, twenty-four-seven hours.' He opens the tap to demonstrate, and it performs to the best of its ability. 'There is one small problem with pressure often. These are very old pipes.' He backs out of the bathroom. 'Next is telephone. Direct to lobby. Here you can order food in your room if you choose. Maybe it is late and you wish some *pakora*, here you may order – but not too late, Madam would not like this.' He looks around conspiratorially. 'If you are needing *anything*, you may ask me. Even…' His eyes widen. 'A taxi or some such thing. I can give you tours booking. Or even *make* tours. Clothes washing.' He mimes pounding clothes on a rock. 'But never smashing buttons. Or movie ticket.' He holds one fist in front of his eye and turns an invisible handle with the other as if this is a game of charades. 'Train reservation – I can make myself. This will save you standing in line forever. Have you ever been to Howrah or Sealdah stations?'

At this, Nayna nods wearily.

'Then you never want to go again, *na*? I can be your man-in-waiting, in the line, buying those tickets. I can be doing all the things you hate about India. The British left behind too much red tape and no scissors. Raj will be your scissors.'

'Raj.'

'Yes, Madam?'

'You talk too much.'

'Sometimes, yes, Madam. As you wish, Madam.' Raj bows and backs out of the room.

'Raj,' Nayna calls after him.

His head pops around the doorway. 'You rang, Madam?'

'Thank you for your offer.' She pushes a hundred-rupee note into his hand. 'We'll get back to you.'

'Of course, Madam.' He looks at the note with a joyous smile. 'I shall be in-waiting.' The air in the rooms swirls as he retreats, and leaves blow through the window from the tree outside.

When they finally lie down, their backs on the thin cotton mattresses, their heads on starched, threadbare pillowslips; when they have washed the travel grime and Kolkata's soot from them; when Rudra has placed the skull and Didima's ashes beneath the bed; Rudra cannot sleep. Outside, all the dogs of Kolkata, all the dogs of the world, gather together, and they howl and howl and howl for all the crimes that have been committed against them. And as well as howling they occasionally bark, and that bark is like a beggar's cough – in it all the shit and filth and disease of the city. Autorickshaws and taxis roar down Sudder Street, and car and motorbike horns infiltrate the closed window like Morse code. They are not in Patonga anymore. Silent, calm Patonga. And the funny thing about silence, Rudra realises for the first time, is that you only notice it when it is not there.

Morning is soft and slightly cold, but it comes with car horns and the smell of burnt ghee. Rudra looks over to his mum, but her bed is empty. When he goes to the window, he notices that just outside the gates of the hotel is a makeshift stall where a man is frying something in a huge deep pan.

He brushes his teeth, rinses with bottled water, pulls on clean clothes and wanders downstairs.

'Morning, Mrs Ursu.' He nods his greeting.

'Rudra Solace,' she says. 'Such as great strong name – "the roarer", god of storms and winds.'

'I don't know about that, Mrs Ursu.'

'You can call me Ionela.' She places her hand on his arm.

'Have you seen my mother?' asks Rudra.

Her hand withdraws. 'No,' she answers. 'And that lazy good-for-nothing Raj has been gone all morning with all his chores and whatnot still to do. Does he think this hotel runs itself?'

'I wouldn't think so.'

'Well, he acts like it. I should sack him, only his father worked for me until his sad demise. God rest his soul. And he sends money to his mother in Nepal. God have mercy on her.'

'I'm going for a walk, Mrs Ursu.'

'Now, Rudra, I have asked you to call me Ionela.'

'Ionela.'

'That's better. Be careful of the beggars and the pickpockets – and don't talk to the street children, they have head lice.'

Rudra ignores the comments, leaving the hotel and walking to where the sweetmaker has set his stall near the front gate. He nods his greeting to the man, who is filling a cloth with batter from a jug. When it is full, he squeezes it over the wok of hot ghee so the dough squirts out in a squiggle. Instantly it solidifies and begins to turn golden. He continues, looping round interconnected squiggles, like a complex signature, into the smoking liquid. Finished, he prods the squiggles and pushes them around with a pair of metal tongs. Then he draws them out, one at a time, breaking them from their brothers, and placing them in a shallow bowl of syrup.

'Jilapis,' he says and offers one to Rudra.

Rudra takes a bite and the hot dough releases syrup into his mouth. It is delicious, sweeter than anything he has ever tasted. He sits beneath the shade of a tree, allowing syrup to drip down his chin.

'Good?' asks the sweetmaker.

'Delicious.'

The sweetmaker gives a satisfied waggle of his head. He takes one himself and sits beside Rudra. They sit eating side by side, looking up through the leaves to the winter sky.

'This tree is peepal tree,' says the man. 'Is possible holy Buddha meditated under this one.'

'This tree?'

'Not this tree. But also this tree. Bodhi tree they also call. Enlighten tree. Freedom from suffering tree.'

'Are you a Buddhist?'

'Hindu.' The man points to the postcard of Kali, the ferocious black goddess, on his cart. 'And you are?'

'Nothing. I don't have a religion.'

'Christian?'

'No religion.'

'Buddhist, maybe?'

'No. I don't believe in anything.'

The sweetmaker is silent, and the words hang for a while and mean more than they were ever meant to.

His mum's arrival saves him from the awkwardness of the situation. She breaks through the front gate with Raj, holding a bunch of papers in the air.

'We got it!' she yells.

'What?'

'Permission to go to the Sundarbans. Raj is a genius.'

Raj smiles broadly. 'I am,' he admits, 'a slight genius.'

'But why do you need permission to go to the Sundarbans? It's your home.'

'It's complicated, Rudra. India is complicated. Even when you are an Indian. And I gave up that when I became an Australian. When I married your dad.'

They go inside for breakfast.

'Indian or English breakfast?' asks Mrs Ursu.

'Indian,' they reply.

Mr Ursu snorts her disapproval but shouts something about *dhal* and *aloo paratha* through to the kitchen.

'When do we leave?' Rudra asks his mum.

'Raj got us tickets on the morning train to Canning. We'll catch a ferry to Gosaba and then we'll work out this complicated thing with Baghchara Island and that skull and your *didima*'s ashes.' She exhales. 'It's going to be some trip, Rudra.'

'It is.'

'You ready for this?'

'I reckon I am.'

'I reckon you are too.'

# 19

CROSSING THE CITY IN A YELLOW Hindustan cab during rush hour requires a special kind of inner calm. This driver does not have it. Instead, he has crazy eyes and a mate who rides beside him, shouting in his ear and egging him on. Like the sweetseller, the driver's deity of choice is Kali. There she is, stuck to the windscreen, with her swollen red tongue, fangs and electric blue skin, dancing on the corpse of a dwarf, a severed head in one of her four hands, a sword in another. Kolkata, *Koli-kata*, 'field of Kali' – this city is alive with her energy.

The traffic is like congealing blood – the cars, trucks, buses, trams, cycle rickshaws, autorickshaws and motorcycles are platelets in need of thinning.

'Do you know the word *cacophony*?' Nayna asks Rudra.

He shakes his head, numb with the noise. On every taxi bumper and truck tailgate, the phrase *HORN PLEASE* is painted, multicoloured, ornate, as if it is a minor law. In this, their driver is the most obedient road user of all, his hand bouncing frequently on the centre of his steering wheel, the horn incessantly sniping at every nearby vehicle or pedestrian.

They come at Sealdah Station from an angle. It is a long building, plastered with billboards and painted in the colours of the Indian flag. Nayna haggles with the driver while Rudra wrestles their bags from the taxi.

Inside, the station is chaotic. There are people sleeping on thin cotton cloths on the concrete. The grassy smell of *beedis* – cheap Indian cigarettes wrapped in *tendu* leaves – comes off the crowd like noise. Trains push into the station and swarms of passengers crowd onto them, some clambering onto their roofs, others swinging from the doorways.

Porters in bright red shirts swarm down the platforms, swooping on passengers and carrying off bags on their rag-covered heads. *Chaat* sellers, preparing their spicy snacks in paper cones, sing out for business. Their huge brass pots gleam in the murky light, towers of tomato and onions guard the borders of their carts, piles of *dhoop* weep cloying smoke to keep the insects at bay. It is barely past breakfast-time but people are already hungry, cramming food into their mouths before they catch the early train.

'Nayna! Rudra!' Raj strides across the platform, his bright cap cocked at a jaunty angle.

'What are you doing here?' asks Nayna.

Raj smiles sheepishly, moving from foot to foot. 'I…' he begins. 'Mrs Ursu…' He waggles his head and smiles.

'We can't take you with us, Raj,' says Nayna.

'But I am special guide.'

'You're from Nepal,' points out Rudra.

'But I speak Bangla.'

Nayna puts a hand on his arm. 'I speak Bangla too.'

'But I am a man.' Raj, sensing he has said the wrong thing, tries to recover. 'India is very scary place for women,' he offers. 'Sometimes too tricky. I can protect you.'

'*Protect?*' spits Nayna.

Rudra has seen a change come over his mother since she has come home. It is as if Cord's weight has been lifted from her. 'I don't think he means—'

'I think I know what he means, Rudra.' Nayna pulls her thin scarf back across her hair. 'You should go back to Mrs Ursu, Raj.'

'I cannot go back. She is not a very kind woman.'

'We have to go. Rudra get the bags.'

They force their way through the crowds on the platform, eventually squeezing onto a carriage and finding an empty seat. Nayna gestures for Rudra to sit down. She smiles apologetically. 'No seat reservations on local trains, Rudra. It's only just over an hour to Canning. You take the first shift in the seat.'

The carriage continues to fill with people. Villagers returning home with city-bought goods – plastic bags and cloth-covered bundles. Men in pressed business shirts. Babies with dark-rimmed eyes, children clutching their cones of *chaat*. Weary women in faded saris sit on the floor. Young guys crowd the doorway. Rudra looks out the window, searching for Raj, but he has disappeared.

'Do you think that was a bit harsh?' he says to his mum.

'*Protect us*, he said. From what?'

'I don't think he meant you couldn't look after us, Mum.'

'Then what did he mean, exactly?'

'I think he was just trying to be helpful.'

She hangs her head. 'You're right,' she says. 'I'm just tired and grumpy. I called him a genius this morning. I should have been kinder.'

The train groans and glumly lumbers from the station, shedding *chaat* and *cha* sellers, and peddlers of gaudy bangles and plastic guns, hair extensions and lottery tickets. The sweeper boys jump through the doors and roll laughing onto the verges, punching each other and roaring like Bollywood villains.

The train takes a while to leave Kolkata behind, and during that time Rudra is exposed to the entire rail-side population voiding their bowels onto rail ballast. The slums tuck themselves against the rail line, sometimes so close that Rudra can see beyond their plastic curtains into single rooms where oil lamps show posters of movie stars and blue-skinned gods; where sheets of plywood are tricked into thinking they can be roofs, and sad-eyed children hang limply from their mothers' arms. It scares him, how unpolished and dangerous it is.

Finally, the country opens its green quilt beneath the watery blue sky. Fields of cows, tickbirds perched on their backs, chew with loose-jawed boredom. Boys whir stones into crops, releasing clouds of finches. At small stations, *cha* sellers board with huge aluminium kettles and clusters of bisque-fired cups. Nayna orders one each and they sit sipping it, tasting the clay beneath the sweetness of the tea and milk, taking in the earth and letting it rest there. And when the last sip is gone, Rudra stares at a single cardamom pod in the bottom as if it is part of his fortune. He pulls it out and bites into it, sucking the seeds from the husk and breaking them between his teeth so they release their fragrance. And he wants to hold on to this moment forever, as if it means everything, as if this is the very taste of home. He realises now what Nayna has being doing all these years – guiding him slowly, through food and scraps of language, to know himself and where he belongs.

In Canning, they leave the station and look for a bus. But the bus has gone and the next one, a taxi driver tells them, will only leave after two hours, or maybe not at all. Nayna shakes her head and translates for Rudra.

'Do you trust him?' he asks.

'No,' says his mum. 'But he *could* be telling the truth.' They look around at Canning – a place on the way to somewhere else – the filthy *dhabas* with their displays of fetid curries, watery *dhal* and cardboard trays of eggs; a couple of sulking hotels with fat men glowering in their doorways; ring-tailed dogs that might form a pack if they had the energy; the ground rustling with foil packets that once held betel nut. And the taxi driver himself – a man with sideburns and shiny slacks and a wide-collared orange shirt – everyone's creepy uncle, leaning in with a frightening sideshow grin.

'Shall we leave this place?' says Mum.

'Sure,' says Rudra. 'How?'

'I think it has to involve this guy.' She nods at the driver, who is now keeping the other taxi and auto-rickshaw drivers at bay with sour mouthfuls of Bangla. Nayna puts her bag on the ground and smiles at him. The negotiation begins. There is a lot of pointing at the sky and a worrying moment where he walks away and confers in whispers with the gathering crowd.

'Okay,' he says finally. '*Chalo.*' And grabbing their bags, he flings them into the boot of his cab.

The taxi, it turns out, looks far more roadworthy from the outside. There are gaping rust holes in the floor and the seats appear to be made from shredded lungs. Their driver sparks up a *beedi* and exhales a choking bank of fog. Rudra goes for the window winder but finds it gone. The one on Nayna's side is missing too.

'Please,' starts Rudra. 'Can you not smoke?'

'No English,' says the driver, his voice clotty with the fumes.

Nayna repeats it in Bangla. He snarls at her and continues puffing on the *beedi*, rolling it from one side of his thick-lipped mouth to the other with his tongue.

'Can you open your window then?' asks Rudra.

Apparently his lack of English allows this one and, grudgingly, he cracks the window a little.

They cross the bridge over the Matla River and drift down the road between fields and the occasional grass-roofed shack. It seems idyllic, and Rudra allows himself to imagine a simple life in one of these roadside huts – a cow for milk, their own rice fields. And then he thinks of Patonga – of what they have, so similar. Seemingly simple until you examine it and see the cracks, the dark gaps between, which will surely draw you down.

At this stage, the taxi coughs, whines and shudders, spitting powdery black smuts onto the road. The driver rocks backwards and forwards in the seat, willing the beast on. But, finally, it dies completely; the motor ticking softly like a fingernail on a glass. The driver pounds the steering wheel and screams in Bangla, in words that Nayna will not translate. The *beedi* is spat through the window. The door is opened. The bonnet is lifted. Through the windscreen, framed by the bonnet and the dash, a hairy paunch erupts from an orange shirt. Fingers plumb the oily crevices of the engine bay.

'What now?' Rudra asks.

'I have no idea,' replies Nayna. 'We wait?'

'For what?'

She points to the goddess postcard on the Ambassador's dash. 'Divine intervention.'

A car horn ponks behind them and another taxi edges up. Nayna smirks at Rudra. 'It worked!' she says, leaping from the cab.

Rudra sneaks out and retrieves their bags from the boot. When he turns towards the other taxi, Nayna is standing with her hands on its roof. 'Rudra, you will not believe this,' she says, nodding to the passenger.

The road is potholed and fringed with cows and cyclists. They travel in silence, for there seems nothing more to say. It is plain that Nayna is embarrassed.

He travels up front and turns to smile every now and then. He pulls out a photo of Amitabh Bachchan and shows Rudra. Rudra takes it and shows Nayna, but she looks out the window, pulling at her bottom lip.

'He didn't save us, you know, Rudra,' she says.

'Of course not, Madam,' he says.

'I am entirely capable,' she says.

'You are, Mum,' says Rudra. 'But I still think you should apologise.'

'No need, Madam.'

'I'm sorry, Raj. I am. I was mean and hurtful.'

'No need, Madam.'

'But you mustn't think I need saving. *We* need saving.'

'Definitely not, Madam.'

'We'll pay you, of course, to be our guide.'

'Thank you, Madam.'

'Did you tell Mrs Ursu where you were going?'

'No, Madam.'

'Why did you leave your job, Raj? We'll be gone soon and the money we give you won't last.'

'Madam, I needed to be risky.'

'To take a risk?'

'Yes. With Madam Ursu it was not good. If I am to live my dreams then I must begin sometime.'

The countryside eases by. A slow rain is winnowed from the clouds, turning the road to butter. Villagers sit under trees, under squares of clear plastic and umbrellas and absurd yellow rain hats, waiting for buses or life.

But Rudra and his mum and their brand-new guide, Raj (who-is-not-a-guide), keep forging on – blasting through the grey mist, swerving around dilapidated trucks and whining autorickshaws. The road grows long and silence envelops them again. And all there is to do is look out of the window and wonder what comes next.

Rudra has really no idea what to expect when they get there. His only points of reference are what his grandmother told him about the Sundarbans. The legends of Bonbibi, about the honeymen and the wood collectors, and how complete the forest is. How the river swells and blots out the landscape – mills around the protective banks, the *bunds,* nibbles at them and enters the villages like a mugger, steals the walls of houses until their roofs sigh and fall. And what Didima told him about tigers and their appetite for human flesh. About Dokkhin Rai himself.

He wants to ask his mum for more, but they are so close now that it seems unnecessary. He will be seeing the place, the people, the great rivers, soon enough. *They will be there,* he thinks, and all of Didima's stories will be made real.

Their driver is silent too. So silent that if it were not for the fact of the taxi moving on without bumping into things, Rudra could believe he was not there. Perhaps that is what makes a good taxi driver – knowing when to shut up as much as knowing when to open up. Rudra is diagonally opposite him, in the back seat, and sees him only in profile: one dark eye and a bouffant of thick, oiled hair. Half a moustache cowers beneath his cheekbone. The collar of his shirt is pulled high against his neck and he is wearing a grey woollen vest. He fumbles with his top pocket, finally extracting a small green parcel, which he quickly tucks into his lower lip. He works it for a while and Rudra can hear him sucking juice from it. After a while, he winds the window down and spits a gob of red juice at the road – a fair portion of it streaks down Nayna's window. His mum clucks her tongue and shakes her head.

'What is it?' asks Rudra.

'*Paan,*' replies Nayna. 'Betel nut.'

At least it is better than *beedi* smoke. The spitting is hard to take but at least the smell doesn't claw at their throats.

They cross another bridge and travel through Basanti – a town that is more a village – tree-lined and pleasant enough, Rudra guesses. He is bored, he realises, and wonders how people travel for years on end. What do they find so fascinating about this tireless movement? Soon, though, the road expels them from Basanti and they plunge on towards Gosaba.

'What's the plan, Mum?' asks Rudra.

'We'll stay overnight in Gosaba and then hire a boat to take us to Baghchara. We can scatter Didima's ashes. You can get rid of that skull and we'll catch the boat back to Gosaba to sleep.'

'What'll we do after that?'

'We'll be normal tourists,' says Nayna. 'Take a tiger tour. Eat crab and fish. Admire the forest from a boat. Maybe read a book or two.'

'Then what?'

'Then we'll go home, Rudra.'

*Of course we will. That's exactly what we must do.*

# 20

'A *GHAT* IS STEPS THAT ARE leading down the riverbank.'
Raj sits with the mist gathering at his ankles. Over the
Bidyadhari River lies Gosaba, but it is hidden from them.
They are sitting above the *ghat*, waiting for the Gosaba ferry.

'A *ghat* can also be a holy place,' he continues. 'Like in
Varanasi – famous for the Dasaswamedh Ghat, where
Brahma made *puja* with ten horses.'

'Made *puja*?' asks Rudra.

'Killed them,' says Nayna, looking aside deliberately. 'He
killed ten horses. Isn't that so, Raj?'

Raj looks at Nayna like she is a child and then back at
Rudra. 'It is a long-ago thing, before the age of Kali Yuga.'

'What's Kali Yuga?'

'It is a story used to keep people in their place,' says
Nayna, turning away into the mist. It swallows her whole,
burping silence.

'Finish your story, Raj,' says Rudra.

Raj softens a *beedi* between his fingers, then sticks it into
his mouth and lights it with a match. 'Okay,' he says. 'But do
not tell your mother.'

He looks at the tip of the *beedi* – its little red eye sore and bitter.

'Ashvamedha is the sacrifice of a horse. Before Kali Yuga – this age of darkness – a horse would be chosen by a king. It would be allowed to roam free for one whole year, protected by a hundred young men. Other men could try to kill or catch the horse, if they wanted to be king, but if they did not then the horse would be brought home, bathed in a river, and anointed with ghee. Then it was sacrificed.'

'Why?'

'It is a powerful *puja* used by powerful men. Everything must have sacrifice, you know.'

'Do you think spilling blood can change the way things work?' asks Rudra, thinking about what his *didima* said about the tiger god demanding sacrifice for those who defiled his forest.

'That is for the gods to decide, not me. I am only a poor man.'

Nayna returns, dragging the mist behind her. 'The ferry is here,' she says, picking up her bag.

Once the mist is penetrated, the *ghat* turns out to be little more than an isthmus of concrete sitting on the mud of the riverbank.

'It's low tide,' says Nayna. 'At high tide the *ghat* would be at the water's edge.'

Tides are something Rudra understands – the link between his two worlds. Tides – the pull of the moon on the great seas. He remembers his dad showing him how it all worked, a rare moment at the breakfast table, aged eight. Taking his boiled egg and placing it on the table. *Pretend this is the whole world*. His rough fingertip rubbing the point of the egg. *This is the high tide, Rudra. See how it bulges out?*

His mum slipped a chickpea beside the egg. *And this is the moon,* she said, working the chickpea slowly round the egg. His dad kept the egg's bulging point directed at the chickpea. *See how the tide follows the moon? The moon is doing that, Rudra. It pulls the oceans towards it as it spins round the earth. On this side – low tide.* His free finger on the blunt bottom of the egg – the part that would sit in an eggcup. *And this side – high tide.* The point of the egg, still tracking that little moon – a chickpea satellite with so much power.

And here in the Sundarbans – the land of the eighteen tides, a place where the sea claims more than beaches – the moon holds sway. He remembers his *didima's* words; how she told him of the tides that suck and pull at this low-lying delta, swallowing whole towns, disgorging corpses onto river flats and forcing people into the trees.

The concrete pad that is the *ghat* reaches a plastic pontoon arm to the river. Tied at the end of the pontoon is a skiff, laden with women and men and boys and girls, chickens, a bike, towers of hessian-wrapped parcels, and plastic bags of every size and shape. The women and men are perched on the gunnels, their saris and *dhotis* fringed with mud. Some of them have black umbrellas opened against the mist.

Nayna has already taken up her position near the bow and Raj nods for Rudra to walk down. As he nears the end of the pontoon – where it floats on the turbid water – he feels it move beneath him. He has known this rhythm since childhood, the gasping sea beneath his feet. He turns to see Raj frozen at the end of the *ghat*, refusing to set foot on the pontoon.

'Come on, Raj.'

'I cannot swim.' Raj is shaking visibly.

'That's why we have a boat.'

'But if I fall—'

'I won't let you.' Rudra goes back and, taking Raj's hand, leads him to the boat.

Once Raj is seated on the gunnel of the boat he seems to calm. 'I am from Nepal.'

'I know,' says Rudra. 'You told me.'

'We have rivers. But I am from a mountain village. No river.'

The crew casts off and they enter the flow of the river. Rudra can feel its strength as it muscles below the rough planks of the boat. This river means business.

The helmsman sits high on the stern, on a wooden bench, squinting into the mist. Three of his mates sit beside him, chewing *paan* or smoking *beedis*, waving the cloying diesel smoke from their faces. The helmsman is dressed in grubby slacks and a down jacket with the words *Most Excellent Day* emblazoned on a breast pocket. His bare toes grip the deck for balance as they cross a wake. The tiller is made from bent water pipe with great knobs of rust where it joins the shaft. The muscles in the helmsman's forearm betray how hard he is holding it, willing the boat on as it swoons towards the far bank.

Rudra is seated beside a young woman dressed in a pink sari. She is hugging a small boy in her lap; Rudra guesses as much for warmth as for love. The child has the darkest eyes he has ever seen. They are glossy like pomegranate seeds and he looks like he is wearing eyeliner.

'Why is the kid wearing make-up?' he whispers to his mum.

'It's *kajal* – kohl,' she replies. 'They believe it makes the eyes strong.'

'Does it?'

Nayna gives him a sceptical look. 'They also believe it protects children from the evil eye.'

Rudra smiles at the boy with the kohl-lined eyes, and the child buries his head in the folds of his mother's sari. Rudra rummages in his bag and produces one of the tacky koalas they bought at the airport – presents to give to streetkids. The boy's mother smiles and shakes her head.

'*Thik ache*,' Raj says. 'It's okay.'

Rudra squeezes the koala's torso, making its arms open, then clips it onto the boy's jacket. He is overjoyed at the simple toy, clipping it on and off his jacket.

Rudra turns back to Nayna. 'Where are we staying in Gosaba?' he asks.

'I have one excellent recommendation,' says Raj.

'We'll stay with your aunty,' says Nayna. 'She's your *dadu's* cousin.'

'Didima told me about her – Aunty Bansari.'

'Means *flute*,' says Raj.

'Her voice is far from flute-like,' replies Nayna.

Suddenly, the boy cries out, his fingers splayed towards his koala swirling in the river. Rudra reaches for a replacement but the boy squirms from his mother's arms and silently drops like a pebble into the muddy water.

The mother screams and tries to follow but people clutch at her arms. The helmsman begins to turn the boat, but it is a long and cumbersome procedure.

'Why doesn't someone jump in?' shouts Rudra.

'They're afraid of crocodiles,' says Nayna, smoothing the frantic mother's hair.

Without thinking, Rudra rips off his shoes and socks and jumps into the water. It is colder than he imagined, and fat bubbles stream up his cheeks. Then he rises, water ringing in his ears, and Nayna shouting, 'Rudra Solace, back in the boat!' Ignoring her, he strikes out for where he last saw the child.

At water level, the river is much lumpier and it is difficult to see more than a few metres ahead. Rudra can feel that the tide has turned and is now pushing upriver. He swims against it but can't locate the boy. The boat is still turning and Rudra, following the pointing fingers of the people onboard, swims madly for a marker he cannot see. Then the boy surfaces about five metres from Rudra, clawing the water like a drowning dog. Rudra reaches him and grabs hold of his jacket. With his hand under the boy's chin, he backstrokes for the boat. It comes round in a slow arc and hands reach for them. Rudra pushes the boy up, then climbs in himself.

He is exhausted and cold. They wrap the boy in a towel and his mother grasps him tightly, whispering in his ear. And Rudra knows what she is whispering, even though it is in another language. Has had it whispered a thousand times in his own ears – that mix of love and fury.

He grabs a jumper out of his bag and pulls it on over his wet clothes. Then he hands the boy another koala.

'*Bhaluk*?' says the boy.

'Bear,' says Raj. 'He asks if it is a bear.'

Rudra turns to the boy. 'Ko-a-la,' he says, splitting the syllables into manageable chunks. 'It means *goes without water*.'

'He wants to know if it drinks salt water like a tiger,' says Nayna.

'It lives in trees,' Rudra says. 'It drinks from the leaves.'

Nayna translates this for the boy. He looks beyond them and says something very quietly.

'What did he say?' Rudra asks Nayna.

'He wishes tigers would drink from the leaves. Then they wouldn't need the sweetness of blood.'

The Gosaba ferry *ghat* climbs the slippery bank. There are two rows of stone steps separated by a narrow ramp, up which people wheel their bikes. Nayna points out the jagged sticks reaching up from the mud like fingers.

'Those are the roots of the *sundari* tree. They're called *pneumatophores*. The roots steal oxygen from the air.'

A woman calls out shrilly from the *ghat*. 'Nay-naaaaaa. My Nay-naaaaaa.'

'Speaking of oxygen thieves,' says Nayna, 'there is your Aunty Bansari.'

'She does have a voice like a flute,' Rudra says.

'You think?'

'Played a little too hard, for a little too long.'

'Shhh, Rudra, she'll hear you.'

They hire a cycle rickshaw and Bansari climbs on with the luggage. She is plump, with tiny feet and a luminous yellow sari. Her mouth, nose and eyes are crowded in the centre of a wide face as if afraid of her immense gold earrings. 'Come on, you three,' she trills.

But the rider looks unable to pull them all, even along the flat, beaten paths of Gosaba village.

'We'll walk,' says Rudra.

'Okay, the men can walk. The women shall ride,' says Bansari.

'But I—'

'Noooo aaaarguing, pleaaaase, Nay-naaa.' She draws out every word to force her point.

Nayna climbs wearily onto the rickshaw and the rider pushes his vehicle to gain momentum, before leaping on and leaning into the pedals to keep it going.

Gosaba is laid out neatly. The houses nearest the *bund* – the sea wall – seem poorer, made of rough planks and branches with grass thatch on the roofs. But as they move further into the interior, the houses are built of brick and concrete, painted Krishna-blue or turquoise, and capped with new tin. Eventually, they stop in front of a small house with a garden edged with flattened tin cans.

'Be it ever so humble,' Bansari beams, 'there is no place like the home.' She swings open the gate so they can take the ten steps to her house.

The house is dark inside, and on the walls and every flat surface are photos of a young man. 'My son,' explains Bansari. 'He is in Kolkata studying engineering, of all things.' Rudra can tell she means, *This is actually the best of things*.

'And your husband, Pisi Bansari? I am sorry, I forget his name.'

'Nayna, you forget so quickly. Is this what living in Australia means?' Bansari gives a tight smile. 'Alas, most sorrowfully, he is departed. No longer with us, as it were.'

'Dead?' asks Nayna.

'Yes, *quite* dead,' replies Bansari, as if it is the most vulgar thing she has ever heard. 'Have you eaten?' she continues. 'I have some *rosogolla* I made specially.'

'That would be nice, thank you, Bansari,' says Rudra.

'Call me aunty, or *pisi* if you must. I think that's best, don't you?' She goes to the kitchen and lights a burner on the stove. 'I will make some tea too. You will have tea.'

'*Cha*?'

'I will not make you *cha* in this house. It is for truck drivers and policemen. You will drink tea with milk separate.' She smiles again. 'Like the British.' She moves back through the open kitchen door. 'Come, I will show you your quarters. Your guide will need to stay elsewhere.'

'But—'

'It is not appropriate. What would my neighbours say? Two women in a house with a strange man.'

Raj whispers to Rudra, 'I will make my own arrangement.' And he slips out the front door like a ghost.

Nayna purses her lips and Rudra, seeing she is about to comment, asks quickly, 'Aunty, have there been many tigers this year?'

Bansari ignores the question and opens a door. 'You will stay here, Nayna. No *charpoy*, notice, this is a full inner-spring bed. Come, put your baggages down and I will show you Rudra's room.' She pushes past them and, dragging Rudra by the sleeve, enters another room. It is plainly the biggest room in the house; a large set of double doors opens onto a small rear garden.

'It's nice, Aunty. Thank you. Only...'

'Only what, Rudra? This is my son's room. He lives like a prince when he is in Gosaba. But these days he prefers Kolkata.' She shrugs. 'It is to be expected.'

'I thought I might be able to see the river.'

'The river? You don't want to see the river. Low caste people live there. Some people call them *Pods*. I do not

181

call them *Pods* because this is a rough word,' she whispers, 'meaning *arses*. They are prawn seed collectors, *meendharas*, and honeymen. If the tigers you love so much arrive by night, it is the *Pods* they will take. They are our early warning system.' She laughs, showing gums reddened by *paan*. 'Those *Pods*, some people say that they eat their food raw and this makes their meat sweet for tigers. You should stay away from the river.'

On the plane Nayna had outlined the caste system for Rudra, or tried to. How it extends to every facet of Indian life. How people are born, live and die, locked to one idea of who they are – a priest, a warrior, a merchant or a servant. The untouchables, so lowly that they are not even a part of the system, doing the jobs no one else will. Cleaning the streets of shit, carting rubbish and burning the dead. After independence from the British, who used the system to their own advantage, the Indian government tried to dismantle it. Renaming the untouchables the *Scheduled Classes* or *Scheduled Tribes*, Nayna explained, has done little to improve their cursed lives.

'Now, tea.' Bansari, bustles from the room.

Rudra flops on the bed and stares up at the ceiling – at the patches of peeling paint like clouds. One is the shape of his father's boat, tugging insolently at its anchor chain. He wonders if Cord is still sleeping on *Paper Tiger*, his world shrunken to the decks of his floating prison. Him, deep in a bottle, with a ship wrapped around the outside. And what of his anger – is it fading or growing? How will Rudra ever return to the Patonga he once knew? It seems like a place now existing only in memory, like Baghchara – his *didima*'s island.

'Tea, Rudra. And *rosogooooolaaaas*.' Bansari's voice rings through the house.

He picks himself up from the bed and goes through to the sitting room. The tea is laid on a brass table with a plate of doughy white *rosogollas* to the side.

'So, Nayna,' says Bansari, sipping her tea. 'Tell me why you are here. Details were not so clear from your message.'

'Perhaps Rudra should explain,' replies Nayna.

'Yes, Rudra, explain your aunty why you are nearly a man and you have never ever come to visit me. Explain me that.'

'I don't—'

'Just tell her why we are here, Rudra,' says his mum gently.

'My *didima*,' starts Rudra. 'She wanted to come back home. To have her ashes scattered on her island.'

'Here? Gosaba? Such a low place. She spent much time in Kolkata also, when she was a child, you know. Before she went up in the world. Maybe it is better you take her to Varanasi where you can scatter her on the Ganga and she can be assured a high rebirth.'

'She wanted to be scattered over Baghchara.'

'Baghchara? Are you joking? That island was so terribly lowly that the river ate it.'

'But that is where Didima wanted to go.'

Bansari lowers her eyes. 'It is a pity you cannot argue with the dead.'

'Keep going, Rudra,' says Nayna.

'I am all of the ears,' says Bansari.

'My Australian great-grandfather shot a tiger.'

'In Australia?' Her eyes widen. 'Oh yes!' She nods. 'I have heard of such Tasmania tigers. Is it close-by to you?'

'He shot it in India. When he was a young man.'

Bansari considers this point. 'This is incredibly bad luck, Rudra,' she says.

'I know.' He takes a sip of his tea. 'Plus, he took the skull away with him.'

Bansari looks around the room as if Dokkhin Rai himself is skulking in the shadows. Her voice lowers to a whisper. 'Where exactly did this happen?'

'It happened here. In the Sundarbans. I think he shot it near Baghchara.'

'When was this?'

'A long time ago, Aunty.'

'How long ago?'

'Nineteen fifty-something maybe.'

'Maybe it is the same story.' She hurries out of the room and comes back with a scuffed album. 'This was *my didima*'s.' She clears away the teacups and, placing the album on the table, opens it. There are faded photos of weddings and picnics, of leaning temples festooned with monkeys, of solemn-faced men with thick moustaches. She stops on a page.

There, a photo similar to the one Rudra found in his father's office, the one with Rudra's grandfather, the Sikh, and the dead tiger. Below it, *Netidhopani, 1952.*

'What's Netidhopani?'

'It is not a *what*, Rudra, it is a *where*. Netidhopani is a place. There is an ancient temple there and some many tigers.'

'And this is where my Australian great-grandfather shot the tiger?'

'Yes. And where your Indian great-grandfather was killed before that, by the very same tiger.'

Rudra looks at Nayna. 'We think that is just a little too much coincidence, Aunty.'

'Maybe yes and maybe not,' says Bansari, her eyes as round as dinner plates. 'Dokkhin Rai has many powers. And think on this, Rudra: the Lord of the South, he could flit between tigers when he pleases – taking on the skin of this one and that one. If he was still in the skin of the tiger your Australian great-grandfather shot, he would be most angry when this happened. Who knows what he would do for revenge.'

'Enough, Bansari,' growls Nayna. 'I won't have you filling my son's head with this nonsense.' She places her cup back on her saucer. 'Maybe, just maybe, Rudra's great-grandfathers were connected through a tiger. That, I will concede, is possible. But it is only coincidence. Nothing more.'

'But, Nayna—'

'Enough!' Nayna holds up her hand. 'Rudra will return this stupid skull. And then he will forget it ever happened. There is no curse. No Dokkhin Rai. Bonbibi *will not* protect him in the forest. We will throw that skull onto that god-forsaken island and we will never look back.'

# 21

IN THE MORNING THEY SET OFF on a 'tour' of Gosaba. The tour consists of visits to many neighbours' houses. At each house tea and *ladoos* are served, sometimes biscuits with fillings that leave a chemical aftertaste. At every house, Raj is made to wait outside. But he is there when they exit, hastily plugging out his *beedi* on the sole of one of his cheap shoes, smiling like he is happy. Nayna gives him fifty rupees to *go get something nice for yourself.* And they continue on the tour, keeping as far from the water as possible.

They stop for a moment in front of a small, neat bungalow.

'This is your *didima*'s house,' says Nayna.

'She sold it to a prawn seed dealer before she left for Australia,' says Bansari. 'He is a big man around town.'

Rudra can tell from the way she says 'big man' that she does not approve. 'What's a prawn seed?' he asks.

'Baby prawns. They grow them up and sell them to fancy eateries. Many are trying to get rich from this.'

Rudra thinks back to Patonga – to his father and Wallace pulling prawns from the bay. He looks at Didima's house. 'It's smaller than I thought it would be.'

Nayna nudges a tear from her eye. 'Things are always smaller than you imagine.'

'Were you happy there, Mum?'

Bansari interrupts. 'You broke their hearts, Nayna.'

'Not before they broke mine, Pisi.'

They walk to another house, another tea stop where gossip and tea is served with 'milk separate'. Rudra begins to build a map of the Sundarbans in his head. But it contains no roads, or tracks, or trees, or buildings, no rivers or ponds. It is a map of people – who is doing what to whom and why. The *Adivasis*, the indigenous people on the 'down' islands, are not to be trusted. The men from Anpur are poachers. The *Pods* are getting above their station, what with all this prawn seed business and new money. On and on it goes. All the tea and gossip leaves Rudra feeling sick.

He excuses himself for a toilet break. Free of the tangle of tongues, he walks towards the river, finally glimpsing it between the mud walls. As he climbs the *bund*, the protective wall of sticks and clay, the river flares with promise in the midday sun.

In the shallows, a girl is wading. Rudra squats down and watches her. She is dragging a frame made of four bamboo poles strapped together with wire and nylon cord. A mosquito net has been bound to it, and two ropes form a harness. She passes along the riverbank, waist-deep in the water, pulling her makeshift net against the current. Stopping about twenty metres up-stream, she trawls the net to the bank and scoops whatever she has caught (surely something small) into an aluminium pot. Then she starts again, working her way downstream.

As she passes Rudra, she flashes her bright white teeth at him. He smiles back and holds up his hand. Then, realising how stupid he must look, he sweeps the hand over his head as if smoothing his hair. The girl laughs, skipping through the water with her net skimming behind her.

Rudra thinks he might be brave enough to call after her when he hears the sour flute of Bansari's voice. 'Rudraaaaa. Rudraaaa. Rudra! What are you doing down by the river? You will catch malaria or dysentery or some such. You worry us sick when you wander off like that. Stay near. This is a dangerous place.' She prods the air with her bottom lip and scowls at the prawn seed collector. 'Come back home and I will make you a nice milk tea.'

'I think I have had enough milk tea for one day, Aunty.'

Bansari's lips tighten. 'One can never have enough milk tea, Rudra.'

Back at the house, Bansari busies herself with lunch preparation while Rudra and Raj sit outside.

Raj says, 'Do you think I could smoke?'

'You're an adult, Raj,' replies Rudra.

'Yes, but your aunty.' He waggles his head. 'She is *formidable*.'

'Your English is very good, Raj.'

'That is one tremendous benefit of working at the Beamish Hotel. Very many English customers.'

'And Mrs Ursu.'

'Not one such benefit.' Raj pulls out a bundle of *beedis*, extracts one and, popping it between his teeth, lights it with a match. He offers the pack to Rudra.

'No thanks.'

'Because Aunty?'

'Because they stink like burning cow shit.'

Raj considers this for a moment, then shrugs it off.

'Raj?'

He squints through a cloud of smoke. 'Yes?'

'What are you going to do after this?'

'I am going to go and have one drink at the English Wine and Beer Shop.'

'I mean after we leave.'

Raj pulls the *beedi* from his lip, pecks a fleck of tobacco from his tongue. 'Maybe Mumbai.'

'You wouldn't go home?'

'I cannot.'

'Why?'

'Home is not where I left it.'

'You mean your village has gone?'

'No, it is still there.'

'I'm not following you, Raj.'

'My home is very small now. Much smaller than when I lived there. When I call my village and speak to my mother, she seems – I am ashamed even to say this – she seems not so clever.'

'She's become stupid?'

Raj winces at the suggestion. 'She has not *become* that way, Rudra. She has stayed the same. It is I who have changed.' His *beedi* has gone out. He strikes another match and relights it, rolling it through the flame. 'This is why I cannot go home.' Raj's face brightens. 'But in Mumbai there is Amitabh Bachchan. There is Bollywood, and the houses of the stars. I will go there and I will become a star.

One Nepali actress has made it very big in Bollywood –
Manisha Koirala. And I will be number one Nepali actor.
Maybe we will marry. Amitabh Bachchan will come to us
for milk tea and I will cook him *biftek* and potato au gratin.
We will have an apartment in Colaba.'

This all seems extremely unlikely to Rudra, but he
doesn't have the heart to raze Raj's dreams.

'And where will *you* go after India?' asks Raj.

Rudra thinks about the skull nestled beneath the bed
in his aunty's house. Soon, he will return the skull and his
*didima*'s ashes. Then it will be done and he can go home. He
will begin year eleven. He will surf with Maggs. And in the
end he will, most likely, become a fisherman, like his father,
his grandfather and his great-grandfather – the hunter of
Dokkhin Rai. The sea is inside his blood. Cursed, or blessed,
on both sides.

This is all possible. In a most-likely world, it is prob-
able. But he feels like he is at a tipping point now, hovering
above a different path. What happens next could push him
over. And then the town he has known his whole life may
no longer exist. Not in the same solid, dependable way it
has his whole life. Then it will be gone forever, as surely as
Didima's Baghchara.

# 22

WHEN RUDRA COMES YAWNING FROM HIS ROOM in the morning, his mother's face is grey as cloud. She sits by a cold cup of tea, picking at the quicks of her nails.

'What's wrong?' he asks.

'It's your father.'

'What?' Rudra feels the panic. It's hard to love Cord Solace, but it doesn't mean he doesn't. 'What's happened?'

'There was an accident. In the water.'

The room goes cold. Rudra falls into a chair. 'Is he alive?'

'They choppered him to Sydney. He's in intensive care.' She takes his hand. 'I have to go back, Rudra.'

'We'll go together.'

'No, you have to finish this. You can do it. With Raj, and with Bansari. She means well.'

'Maybe we can do it together, quickly.'

'I have to leave today. There's a flight tonight. I can be in Sydney by tomorrow. I need to go.' She picks up her teacup. It is delicate china, so thin he can almost see her fingers through the other side. 'Your dad, he wasn't always... I don't want you to think badly of him.'

'You need to stop defending him, Mum.'

'I feel responsible.'

'That's ridiculous.'

'I know it is.'

'I'll help you pack.'

'And you'll stay? You'll finish this thing?' Her hands are fluttering near his.

'I will.'

'You'll need to hire a boat to get to Baghchara. You'll have to catch ferries and buses and trains to Kolkata. And then you'll have to fly home by yourself. It's a lot.'

'I got this, Mum.'

She grasps his hand. 'You call me, okay? Soon as it's done and you're heading back to Kolkata.'

'I will.'

'Oh God.' Nayna suddenly looks panicked.

'What?'

'Your aunty, she doesn't even have a mobile. It'll take forever to get a message to you.'

'It'll be fine, Mum.'

'Oh, Rudra. I'm sorry it turned out this way.'

'Stop apologising.'

As the ferry pulls away from the *ghat*, Rudra feels a sob warbling – a caged bird – in his chest. He wants to release it, but Bansari and Raj are here and so many strangers. He knows it would bring shame on his aunty for him to cry like a child here in public. Instead, he waves to his mother, feels the cord that has tied them together stretch and break as the boat chugs to the far bank. He thinks of things he should have said; things he needed to ask. And now it is too late.

They discuss the boat they will need to take Didima's ashes to Baghchara.

'No motor,' say Rudra.

'But motor is faster,' says Bansari. 'And less common. Fishermen are not to be trusted. Also, what if dacoits attack?'

'Dacoits?'

'Bandits,' whispers Raj. 'Pirates.'

'We'll be okay, Aunty. I don't want my *didima*'s ashes mixed with diesel fumes.'

'But—'

'Aunty, I am in charge now.'

She flinches as if he has slapped her. 'So like my son. You young folk think you know it all.'

'We will be fine, Aunty. Raj will find us a good boat.'

Raj returns before lunch with a fisherman in tow. The man is grey-haired. His arms are strong from rowing and he walks with a bow-legged strut. He is wearing a dirty *lungi* and a torn singlet.

'This man is number one boatman in Sundarbans.'

'Does he speak English?'

'I speak Bangla,' says Raj. 'And for this there is the same charge.'

'Does he know Baghchara Island?'

'He says he says he knows of this place.'

'Can he take us there today?'

Raj speaks to the man in Bangla. 'Why not,' he reports.

'We should pack some food. The boatman says we should hurry if we want to catch the outgoing tide. Otherwise we must wait until tomorrow.'

Bansari packs them lunch – boiled eggs, *roti* and a thermos of tea. She tells them to return before nightfall – the river is a dangerous place at night, *what with tigers and all, and dacoits too, poachers with no regard for human or other life, worshippers of Kali*. They set off to the river with Bansari calling after them, 'Tell your boatman to boil all the water. Ten minutes, minimum time.' And, 'Make sure he has a mosquito net. They are more deadly than tigers.' And, 'Don't trust the boatman, he is a *Pod*.' Rudra squirms at the comment, but soon she cannot shout loud enough to reach them and they continue in silence.

The boatman's name is Malo and he walks with a confident grace between the houses. In the beginning, he passes many people without speaking but as he gets closer to the water, more and more people call out to him. Some slap him on the back as if to say, *Well done, Malo, you caught yourself a rich foreigner*. Rudra wants to tell them how his family is from the Sundarbans, how his *dadu* was a solution-*wala*, but even if he had the language he doubts it would make a difference. He thinks back to when the surfer, Judge, roused on him at Box Head. How he called him a curry-muncher and told him to go home. *To here?* The tidelands are a place that is not quite sea and not quite land. He is a scrawled message in this intertidal zone, not sure to which world he belongs. He grasps his grandmother's ashes tighter.

When they reach the river, Rudra is dismayed by Malo's boat. It is shaped like a seedpod sliced in half, identically tapered at the stern and bow. No more than six metres long,

194

its worn planks are riddled with wormholes. The smooth, oiled deck has a makeshift shelter of roped branches and a mottled bedsheet. The stern and bow lift gracefully from the water, but at midships, the gunnel is within a couple of hand spans of the river. A tiger would have no trouble clambering onboard. Two boards, on edge, run down that midship section; Rudra imagines they might stop Malo toppling into the water when he sleeps.

Malo wades towards the boat, turning to beckon them. Raj looks at Rudra. 'I cannot swim,' he whimpers.

'You won't have to. It's only up to your thighs.'

'But if I fall…'

'You won't fall. The boat is very close.'

'I cannot go on this boat.'

'You have to.'

'Cannot, Rudra.' Raj folds his arms. 'Will not.'

'Then you should stay.'

'But who will help you to speak Bangla to this man?'

'I'll get by.'

'You must not go.'

'Yes, I must, Raj. I'm not turning back now.'

Rudra gives Raj some money. 'This is your pay for today – for accommodation and food and a little extra too. The next three days upfront.'

Raj looks at the money. 'It is too much,' he says, his voice thick with emotion.

'Mum insisted.'

'Oh, Mummy.' Raj wipes at his eyes with his free hand.

Rudra smiles. He takes the backpack containing the tiger skull from Raj and, slipping Didima's ashes in with it, he wades out to the boat.

'You must not drown,' calls Raj. 'Or get eaten by a tiger. Mummy, she would not forgive me.'

Rudra clambers on board and settles himself. They pull away. Slowly Raj's small figure becomes a twig in the mud – one arm raised, immobile. Then, he is obscured by a bend in the river. Rudra looks down at the skull nestled between his legs, at his grandmother's ashes in their cheap plastic container. He feels an immense sense of the purpose of this journey – to set things right, to put everything back in its place. To remove a curse.

He looks over the boat. It's not so bad. Strong enough, he reckons. And the fisherman, Malo, seems like he knows what he is doing.

A shape moves in the shade of the shelter. The shape gathers itself into the sunlight and Rudra sees that it is the girl from the river – the prawn seed collector. She is wearing lime-green *shalwar* pants, touched at the bottom by river mud, and a *kameez* shirt with cuffs of spidery silver brocade. There is a bright gold hoop in her nose. Rudra is struck dumb.

Malo speaks to the girl and she nods happily. 'I am Gitanjali,' she says to Rudra. 'You can call me Gita if it is simpler for you.'

'You speak English?'

'You're surprised that a lowly *meendhara* speaks anything but Bangla?'

'I didn't—'

'Of course not.' She smiles at him. 'I am only having some fun with you. What is your name?'

'Rudra.'

'Rudra is a good name. Have you come to see the tigers?'

Rudra takes the container with Didima's ashes from his bag. 'I'm bringing my grandmother home.' Before Gita can ask any questions about grandmother-in-a-box, he continues, 'Are you coming with us?'

'I'm here to help my father.' She nods towards Malo. 'It is just we two now since my mother died.' Her shoulders rise to a shrug. 'Would you like some *cha*?'

Malo's gaze follows them into the shelter where Gita pumps a little kerosene stove, lights it and places an aluminium pot of water on to boil.

Rudra feels an awkward need to fill the silence. 'So, you're a prawn seed collector?'

'And what of it?'

'There's nothing wrong with...Really. I didn't mean... My father is a fisherman. I am too...sort of.' The words come tumbling out, blanched of meaning.

'Catching prawn seeds is not my life job,' says Gita. 'I'm just earning enough to get to college in Kolkata. Then I'll wave this place goodbye.'

'Will you come back?'

'There is too much caste rubbish here. High caste, low caste. Marriage things. It is hard being at the bottom of the pile. Hard to be a woman or girl. All this up-and-down-island rubbish too. It will be good to leave.'

'Do you like pulling the prawn nets?'

'I do not like it and I do not hate it. It is good for money. Many, many woman do this job now. And it is making them stronger for the first time. Giving them some way with their life.' She spills loose tea into the pot, stirs in milk and a good handful of sugar. 'But I do not want to wade in the mud forever.'

'Will you show me sometime?'

'What?'

'How to pull the nets?'

'It is woman's work. The village boys will laugh.'

'That's okay.'

'Then I will show you, Rudra. You can be the first boy *meendhara*.' The *cha* comes to a rolling boil and Gita stirs it before turning the stove off. She pours it into three little clay cups and hands one to Rudra. 'My father needs *cha*; it is a strong thing wrestling the river.'

Gita leaves the shelter and hands Malo his *cha*. He nestles the oar between the crook of his arm and his shoulder, and drinks while occasionally pulling or pushing the oar to maintain his course. The ebb tide does most of the work for him, pushing them towards the sea. Soon they exit the main flow of the river and enter the channel that separates Gosaba and Bally Island.

'Can you ask your father if I can steer?' asks Rudra.

Malo reluctantly hands over the steering of his boat. Immediately, Rudra feels the power of the river in his muscles. He pumps the oar to increase their speed and bathing children sing out to him from along the shoreline. Sunlight snicks through the villages, combs the *bunds* and stands of mangroves.

When they clear the island, the river broadens and Malo takes over. There, finally, on the left bank is the wild Sundarbans he has read about – the Sajnekhali Wildlife Sanctuary – the dense forest where tigers hunt. Where honeymen and woodcutters and poachers risk their lives.

Malo points to a low branch where a shirt has been tied like a flag. '*Bagh*,' he says – tiger.

Gita says, 'The flags warn other forest workers of a tiger attack. Mostly it is these workers that get eaten. Sometimes when a tiger is most hungry, it will go to a village and steal a goat or sometimes a child. It is not often.'

Rudra scours the forest with his gaze, imagining yellow eyes with pupils black as night. Watching him. Blood curdled by salt water. Whisker twitch. Mosquito itch along the barred flanks.

The forest goes on forever. Soon it is on both sides, bending down to sip the water, roots plunged in. The tangled breadth of it makes Rudra gasp for air. An hour passes and then two – still the forest.

Then Malo calls out, 'Baghchara!' jerking the tiller and pivoting the boat into the current. Gita rushes to the bow and throws a gnarled rock tied to a jute rope into the water. The boat lurches backwards for a moment before the anchor takes. Then they are static, with the river pouring by them.

'I don't see anything,' says Rudra. 'Where is Baghchara?'

'We must wait for the tide to drop,' says Gita. 'It is below.'

She cooks a pot of *dhal*, lacing it with small green chillies. They eat it with Bansari's eggs and *roti* and wash it down with sweet *cha*. Malo rolls out a straw mat and is almost instantly asleep.

Rudra brings the skull from his bag and hands it to Gita. 'This is the tiger my great-grandfather shot,' he says.

She holds it reverentially in her hands, nose to nose with the beast. 'This is a big tiger.'

'It could be the biggest.'

'Was it a long time since?'

'A very long time ago. But I must bring it back.' He takes the skull back. 'This skull could belong to Dokkhin Rai.'

'The god?' Gita smirks.

'You don't believe me?'

'You sound like a villager. My father too believes such things. Dokkhin Rai, the tiger god, and Bonbibi the protector. But they are losing power here in the Sundarbans. Kali is the new goddess. She is giving power to the lowly people. The *meendharas* and the forest workers.'

'You believe in Kali but not in Dokkhin Rai?'

'Bonbibi and Dokkhin Rai is an old story. This is a new time for which we are needing new things. Even gods and goddesses must change.'

'Maybe,' says Rudra.

'Your great-grandfather shot this tiger?'

'Yes.'

'And he took it from its place?'

'Yes.'

'Everything wants to go back to where it belongs.'

Rudra looks out across the water. 'I have a friend back home,' he says. 'He works on my dad's fishing boat. He told me about prawns and how they long for a place they have never seen – the river where their parents lived before they spawned them out at sea. How they crawl and swim back when they are ready.'

'What is this meaning of *long*?' asks Gita. 'Doesn't this mean…' She stretches out her arms.

'Longing is wishing for something,' says Rudra. 'It's like a strong wish.'

'Desire?'

'Yes – desire. The prawns *desire* a home which they have never seen.'

'Prawns are stupid,' says Gita. 'They have no beauty. They cannot speak or sing or paint a picture. They are food.'

'Maybe,' Rudra says. He is unable to say exactly what he means, spiralling into the idea like Cord's boat tracking prawns. 'My father told me about a bird called the muttonbird—'

'This is a funny name,' says Gita. 'Mutton is goat, *na*? A bird that is also a goat.'

'—how they travel from Australia to Russia and return. Every year, many die. In spring our beaches are thick with their bodies.'

'They should just stay in Russia,' says Gita. 'Or not leave Australia. They are stupid too.'

'There is something that drives them. Something that makes them leave and something that makes them come home. Like a boomerang, Gita. Do you know this thing?'

'No.'

'It is a curved flat stick. You throw it and it comes around in a big curve and lands back at your feet.'

'That is also a stupid thing. Once a stick leaves it should stay left.'

Hours pass. The sun drops lower in the sky. Finally Malo wakes up, yawns and lights a *beedi*. He looks lazily across the river and then points to something in the middle distance. Rudra follows his finger to a spot on the water. Yes, he sees it, something black, breaking the surface.

In another fifteen minutes the tide goes slack. As if this is the signal he has been waiting for, Malo shouts to Gita to pull up the anchor. Then, taking the oar, he rows furiously for the black shape. As they approach, Rudra can see it is the top of a building.

'*Mandir*,' says Malo.

'It is one temple,' says Gita.

'Is it Baghchara?'

Malo nods as he steers towards the *mandir*'s steeple. It is made of carved stone and the water bends slowly around it. On the far side Gita throw the anchor again. It snags on something, holding the boat fast.

'There is a whole village below,' says Gita and Rudra imagines the birthplace of his grandmother slowly giving itself to the river, grain by grain, and washing to the Bay of Bengal. He imagines the walls and the paths and the wells and temples, the shrines and the *ghats* – all dissolving as if in a dream.

Pulling the plastic tub from his bag, he removes its lid and looks at his *didima*'s ashes. So grey, some lumps that could be bone or teeth. A strangled sob escapes him. Gita comes to his side, her hand light on his elbow, guiding him to the boat's gunnel.

There, facing the spire of the *mandir*, he raises the tub high. The birds on the riverbank fall silent. There is only the sound of the river straining against their hull. He tips the tub, setting the contents free.

At that moment an unfortunate breeze lifts from the riverbank and carries the ashes back across the boat. Without warning, Didima is in his eyes, in his hair, in the curved passages of his ears. She is spread over the rough deck planks.

He looks at Gita and she is fighting a smile. He knows it can't be funny, that he should never laugh at these moments. He brushes Didima from his hair. Shakes her from his clothes. It is not funny. He concentrates on the dust that is Didima. Gita fetches a broom and sweeps most of Didima into a small pile. Together they carry her to the edge and give her finally to the river – the place of her birth.

The bubbles that could be laughter subside and the grey ash floats on the water. It swirls slowly around the *mandir*'s spire, then it becomes nothing. A great emptiness opens inside Rudra. Her ash now mixed with river clay and *mandir* stone and the great waters of huge rivers bleeding from the subcontinent. His grandmother, his *didima*.

Gone.

The birds begin first, nervously chattering into the silence. A monkey shrieks. The world continues.

'I am sorry, but my father says we must turn for home on this tide,' says Gita.

Rudra removes the photo from his book. He hands it to Gita. 'The tiger skull has to go back to this place.'

She studies it. 'This place is Netidhopani?'

'It's where the tiger was killed.'

'There is no time. We left too late in the day.'

'But I have to return the skull.'

'It will be dark soon, Rudra,' says Gita. 'My father says when it's dark, the Tiger God will come. For this he has not made *puja*. We must go home.'

'What do *you* think?'

'There are tigers in that forest. We cannot see them but they can see us. If we stay here at night on this open boat we will be in very much danger.'

'We have to return the skull. I have come so far.'

'Rudra, you must listen. My father knows this forest.

This is not joking. Tomorrow we can go back here.'

'That'll be too late, Gita. Tell him we'll pay double.' Rudra pulls a pile of rupee notes from his pocket and shows it to Malo.

'It is always about the money with you *gora*.'

'I'm not a *gora*,' says Rudra. 'My mother is from here.'

'Even so, you cannot just buy everything.'

'I know that. But I have to return the skull.'

'Tomorrow is safer.'

'I need to get home, Gita. Back to Australia.'

'So soon?' asks Gita. Rudra can't be sure if it is disappointment in her voice.

'I just have to.' Rudra cannot explain about Cord. About the water in his lungs and the dying light of the Solace fishing empire.

Rudra tries to hand the money to Malo but the man shakes his head, speaking to Gita in Bangla.

'My father says it is not worth this money. That we might all die.'

Rudra knows it is wrong to put them all in danger like this, to go against Malo's advice. But he must return the skull, then return himself. He could miss his flight if he wastes another day on the river. And what if Cord dies? What then? Nayna's words echo inside Rudra: *You'll finish this thing?* She is a force of nature, like the tide – strong and determined. And half of her is him.

He pulls more money from his backpack. 'This is everything I've got on me.'

Malo takes the money from Rudra's hand, muttering something to Gita.

'He will do it,' says Gita, turning her head away in disgust. 'I hope there is the time before it goes dark.'

# 23

'THIS IS THE PLACE OF THE SNAKE GODDESS – Manasa Devi,' says Gita.

They are rounding the head of an island, slipping into a small, slow tributary of the Bidyadhari River. Malo pumps the oars and they wend their way up the narrow waterway.

Gita hugs her arms to her body. 'It is not a good place.' They break through clouds of black flies. Mangroves weep into the water. Tree roots stick up from the mud like rows of shark teeth. 'Only tourists come here looking for tiger. There are too many.'

'Tourists or tigers?' Rudra asks.

'It is not funny,' says Gita. 'Also, we cannot stop at this place – it is forbidden. My father's boat could be taken.'

Rudra stays silent. He feels like a fool. A fool with money who has bought his way here against local advice. There are so many rules that he does not know; things he doesn't understand.

*You'll finish this thing?*

Before long they pull up at the jetty at Netidhopani. There is a heavy cyclone wire fence and a gate with a lock on it. Gita ties the boat and Rudra steps off.

'This is a very bad idea.' Gita steps onto the jetty behind him. 'Stop walking away,' she calls. 'Why are you climbing? Do not climb the fence. Throw that skull from here. Inside are tigers. Tigers!'

Rudra moves down the path, past the watchtower where eager tourists search for tigers, protected by officials with guns. It is approaching evening now and he knows it is a battle with the dying sun.

'You will get us both killed.'

He turns to see Gita. She has climbed the fence and is walking the path towards him.

'You shouldn't have come,' he says.

'You are a stupid boy.' Her words are like bee stings. 'What do you know of this place? Do you think you can just walk here like you own it?'

'I—'

'Don't,' says Gita. 'Let's finish with this before the tigers wake from their afternoon sleep.' She looks at the skull in his hands. 'Where will you leave it?'

He doesn't know. The dreams that came after they dredged the skull from the bay have eased. Some of them were so terrifying he was sure they emanated from this object. *It's just a skull.* Those dreams seem eerily familiar now he is standing here, like this is the place that conjured it all. *You little weirdo.* This jungle path, the light. He knows what his mum would say. *Rudra, you heard the stories. You saw the photo. Your mind did the rest.* But those dreams were so real.

'Rudra, we need to hurry,' says Gita. 'Where will you put the skull?'

'The temple. It should go back to the temple. I saw it in a photo. Dokkhin Rai.' He shakes his head. 'The tiger.' That's better. 'It was killed there.'

'The temple is further up the path.'

'How do you know?'

'My family has lived here a long time. Before this jungle was turned back to the tigers. It's this way.'

Rudra follows Gita further up the path. They take a fork and after a short while they arrive at a clearing. There are the ruins of the Netidhopani Temple – its bricks blood orange in the fleeing sun.

'This is an old place,' says Gita. 'Four hundred years.'

Rudra approaches slowly, the skull warm in his hands. He crosses the hearth of the ancient temple, down a path worn smooth. And to the altar, nothing more than a pile of bricks made weary by the rain and wind. Onto this, Rudra lays the skull; he feels it leave his hands, his fingertips sticky. He turns and hears the day crack open. Where there were no clouds, suddenly they are crowding – pushing in from the wings of a great stage. Chunks of sky, now made furious, and rain dotting the backs of his hands, on his neck and ears.

They turn to leave.

A roar explodes from the jungle. The temple bricks chatter like teeth. The roar inside his gut is an earthquake. The crooks of his arms ache. He looks at Gita, hugging her own chest. The backs of his knees burn with fear. His breath quickens and blood drums in his ears. His heart rattles. His mouth fills with dust.

The tiger steps into the clearing. Each paw is the size of Rudra's head. As they meet the ground, huge curled claws flex out. The animal snarls, whiskers a spray of white above the shocking pink tongue, teeth yellow and curved like slivered moons.

It moves forward and, with each step, the world trembles. Rudra is frozen on the temple steps.

He feels the world slipping from him. Smells the tiger's musk, the pant of its breath. Its muzzle is pulled back and teeth exposed.

This all begun long before Rudra was born. His two great-grandfathers – one a tiger victim, the other a tiger killer.

He falls to his knees in front of the great tiger; bows his head. Flattens his body on the ground. Submits. The tiger's breath pours over him like hot sea. It roars and the world is skun of light and sound. Rudra falls into the abyss.

He feels a cool hand on the back of his neck. 'What are you doing?' It is Gita.

He is lying on the ground, his left cheek flat on the twigs and earth. 'The tiger—' Nothing further will come.

'What tiger?'

Rudra looks around him. The temple is at peace. The skull is resting on the altar, a chunk of fading light through the ruined doorway. Soft rain is falling.

'I saw it. I saw the tiger.'

'We must go or we will see many tigers.' Gita takes him by the hand and leads him from the temple grounds.

Malo is silent when they get to the boat. It is too dark to navigate the river and the tide has swung against them. They bed down for the night, the boat's deck hard beneath the thin straw mat. In the forest, tigers are hunting.

When the grey dawn arrives, Gita makes breakfast. Rudra eats slowly as if tasting everything for the first time – the charred wheat of the *roti*, each spice in the *cha* a bright pixel on his tongue.

Malo says something and Gita translates.

'He says Bonbibi kept us safe. That we are lucky she was with us because there are many tigers. He says we should get back to Gosaba before Dokkhin Rai wakes up and wants his breakfast.'

They are moored in the middle of the river, as far from the tiger forest as they can be. As if reading his thoughts, Gita says, 'Sundarbans tigers must swim for hours to cheat the tides.'

She moves to the stern and washes the cooking pot in the water, breaking the *dhal* crust from the rim with her fingernails. The flecks of food float across the river's calm surface, attracting small fish.

Malo shouts, nearly making Gita drops the pot in the water. She rattles a response, clearly angry at almost losing their cooking pot. Malo sucks his teeth and, stomping to the bow, pulls up the anchor.

'What was that about?' asks Rudra.

'Village talk.'

'What was he saying?'

'That I disrespect Dokkhin Rai by washing my pot by his forest, in his water. That he will be angry.' Gita shakes her head. 'Tigers do not care about such things.'

They enter the Bidyadhari River just as the tide begins its rush back in. Rudra can see it happen before his eyes – the mud being consumed, monkeys hunting crabs, gingerly picking their way back to the safety of the trees. This tide helps to carry the boat back to Gosaba. And again, Malo barely has to row; only correcting their course with a decisive tug or push on the oar.

Rudra cannot believe it is over. That he has laid his grandmother's ashes in her homeland. And that he has completed something that his great-grandfather set in motion over sixty years ago. The skull is finally back where it belongs. It is over. No more dreams of death. He can return to Patonga and his old life. Cord Solace is as tough as they come; he will surely recover from his near drowning. And maybe, just maybe, Rudra will go back on the boat until the end of the season. Make his dad proud, then work things out from there.

# 24

THEY ARRIVE BACK IN GOSABA IN TIME for lunch. Raj is there to greet them and sets off to let Aunty Bansari know he is safe. Rudra follows Malo and Gita to their small mud house by the river. They sit on the floor kneading balls of rice and *dhal* and popping them into their mouths. Rudra looks around the single room – two *charpoy* beds, a small dung-fired stove, in one corner a long spear with dark, polished handle.

'What's that for?' he asks Gita, nodding at the spear.

She shrugs. 'It is a long-ago thing. We do not use it anymore. Now it is just for looking.'

'Is it your father's?'

'It is his father's father's, maybe more. We call it *Tiger Killer*. But really it is only a spear.'

They go back to their food for a while, scooping food from their aluminium plates.

'When will you leave Gosaba?' Rudra asks.

'When I have the money for college I will go to Kolkata. Maybe after this prawn season.'

'Do you think you might come to Australia one day?'

She smiles. 'Australia is very far.' They continue eating for a while before she asks, 'When will you go to Australia?'

'I need to leave for Kolkata tomorrow. My flight is the next day.'

Gita seems annoyed. 'So today we could have taken the skull to Netidhopani?'

'I couldn't risk being caught on the river and missing my flight.'

'You speak of *risk*? What of our lives?'

'I'm sorry, Gita. My dad is sick and my mum – I need to get back to her.'

She gives him a head waggle that could mean she forgives him, or thinks he is an idiot, or possibly both.

'I need to call Australia now. Is there somewhere to do that?'

'The man who runs the phone place likes a very long lunch. It is better if you wait two hours minimum.'

When they finish eating Gita gathers the tin plates and the cooking pot and together they wash them, flicking water at each other with their fingers. When Malo stretches out on his *charpoy*, Rudra asks Gita, 'We have a while until I can make my call home. Are you still going to teach me how to pull the prawn nets?'

'The village boys will laugh,' she says.

'I can take it,' says Rudra.

They cross the *bund*, carrying Gita's prawn net and a plastic tub to hold the *meen*. When they are waist deep in the river, Gita shows Rudra how to hook the straps over his shoulders. The mud is slippery and Rudra has to claw his toes into it for purchase. He strains into the net and pulls it in one long pass, parallel to the riverbank.

'Again,' says Gita. A clutch of young boys have gathered to watch. He takes another long pass, closer in this time, feeling the net bump across the bottom. The boys are laughing and pointing, making comments in rapid Bangla.

'They are saying you will make a good wife,' calls Gita. 'That your husband won't have to collect honey. They ask how much will be your dowry.'

'You cannot afford me,' shouts Rudra. Putting his head down, he drags another pass of the river. When he makes it level with Gita again, he is out of breath. He unhooks his straps and, choking the net as near the frame as he can, drags it to the bank.

Gita empties the net into the tub of clear water. The prawn seeds are transparent, as thin as straws.

'It is very many,' says Gita.

'Really?'

'Not really – it is very few.' She sees his shoulders slump. 'But it is okay, they are quite big and full of health.'

'Where do you sell them?' asks Rudra.

'You will see the dealers when we walk home. They work for groups who farm the prawns and sell them when they are fat. It is dangerous business. Many have guns. There is poisoning of ponds. Everything is dangerous here.'

'Even pulling nets?'

Gita looks at him as if he is mad. 'Yes, it is dangerous. Very, very much. Some crocodile. Some shark. Some woman dies from water disease.' She washes the net back and forth in her tub to release the last of the prawn seeds. 'It is very dangerous being a *meendhara*.'

'What does Malo think about what you do?'

'Sometimes he is not happy. But when the money comes it is better.' She lowers her voice. 'You cannot eat happiness.'

'True.'

'His brothers, my uncles, they are not fishers. They are honeymen. They say we are bringing bad luck to the Sundarbans. They say prawn seed collecting is stealing and we have no respect for Bonbibi. They say that is why men get killed by tigers. Because the forest is angry.'

'And you don't believe that?'

'These men know nothing.'

They take turns pulling the net for the rest of the afternoon. It is hard work and Rudra's calves ache from walking in the mud.

They see a boat preparing to leave. Four men jump on board. They have bundles tied with string.

'Isn't that Malo?' Rudra points at one of the men on the boat.

Gita nods. 'Yes.'

'Is he going fishing?'

'No.'

'What then?'

She seems embarrassed. 'They are blackworkers. Woodcutters. They are going to the forest.'

'Isn't it a bit late in the day? You and your father told me how dangerous it is in the forest at night.'

'Yes, but the forestry department do not work at night.'

'Why is Malo going? He's a fisherman.'

'There are not so many fish these days. He needs the money.'

'Who is that guy?' Rudra nods to an old man whom the others are helping into the boat. He doesn't look able to swing an axe.

'He is a *bauliya*. I don't know the English.'

'A shaman.'

'You have *bauliya* in Australia?'

'No, but my *didima* told me about them.'

Rudra walks to the boat. 'Can I talk to the *bauliya*?' he asks Gita.

'What do you want to ask him?'

'About what he does.'

She talks to the *bauliya*, then turns to Rudra and says, 'He wants that you would pay.'

Rudra pulls out a fifty-rupee note and hands it to the man. The man speaks a few slow words. He holds Rudra's gaze as he talks, then looks to Gita to translate.

'He says he keeps the party safe.'

'How does he do it?'

'Magic.'

'Can he show me?'

'No.' Gita takes Rudra's arm. 'He cannot show you. For that you have to go to the jungle. Maybe he keeps a bit of *sundari* wood under his tongue. Or puffs his breath on the forest earth. This doesn't work. Many blackworkers worship Kali now. She is better for violent jobs like poaching and woodcutting.'

'And collecting *meen*?'

'Yes. Bonbibi is old news. I have been already telling you this.'

They turn to go but the old man calls them back. He pulls a red cord from his bag and begins to tie it round Gita's bicep. '*Na*,' she says. 'You should have this, Rudra. You need protection more than me.' She takes the thread from the *bauliya* and, looping it twice around Rudra's arm, knots it tightly.

Across the river, storm clouds gather. Tongues of lightning lick the far bank.

'The rain is coming,' says Gita and they gather the net and the tub full of *meen* and climb back over the *bund* to the village.

Immediately, they are accosted by an aggressive dealer who fires rapid Bangla at Gita and sneers at Rudra through his fake Ray-Bans. He smooths a thick, oiled moustache with his forefinger and thumb and indicates to Gita to put her tub on the ground. Rudra wonders if this is the man who bought his *didima*'s house. He immediately dislikes him.

Bending over, the dealer stirs the *meen* until they are a whirling mass. He rattles off some words, then stands up, shaking his head. Gita silently picks up her tub and begins walking away. The man is furious. He shouts at her. But Gita ignores him.

As Rudra catches up, he asks, 'What's going on?'

'He thinks because I am young, because I am a woman, he can cheat me. I can get double what he offers. The *meen* are out of season, there are big needs – Kolkata and abroad.

'Even so, the price is not like before. Now there are hatchery places in Orissa and Andhra Pradesh. The money is going and I must earn rupees so I can leave this place.'

The man catches up and grabs Gita by the elbow. She shrugs him off and lets fly with a string of Bangla. The man is clearly caught unawares. He swallows and smiles. He wrings his thick hands and talk softly to her. But Gita turns from him again. He calls after her and, this time, whatever he says makes a difference because Gita places her tub back on the ground.

The man calls over a boy with another tub of water. Gita squats on her haunches and, bringing a white cockleshell from her sari, begins scooping *meen* from one tub to the other. Rudra can see her lips mouthing silent numbers. The dealer stands over her, growling instructions. She flicks the blood-coloured, dead *meen* onto the path. It takes her half an hour to count them and by the time she is finished, rain has started to dot the dirt around them. The dealer mutters at the sky and hands over some filthy hundred-rupee notes.

Placing the tub over her head as a rain hat, Gita motions for Rudra to follow. They run down the path to her father's house as the rain turns the dust to mud. Laughing like children, they enter the house.

Raj emerges from the small mud hut in which he has been renting floor space. He smells of cow dung smoke but his hair is still immaculately combed and his shirt is well-pressed and whiter than ever. Rudra doesn't know how he manages these small everyday miracles.

It turns out he has been busy arranging ferry tickets and their connecting train. He has also called ahead to the Beamish. This last task caused him some grief. He relays the conversation to Rudra, playing both parts as they walk to the Public Call Office.

'Madam Ursu, she says: *Raj – I don't know such a person. I do remember a boy called Rudra and he is welcome at the Beamish Hotel.*

'Raj says: *We are catching the train from Canning tomorrow. Please have one room for Rudra Solace.*

'Madam Ursu says: *I do not take bookings from servants*.

'Raj says: '*I am not a servant, I am a guide. You do not know someone called Raj. This is a new person.*' Raj finishes triumphantly, 'I play her at her own game.'

The PCO is no more than a tin-roofed shack with an ancient rotary dial telephone. The owner examines the piece of paper Rudra hands him, then carefully spins the number into the machine. He passes the receiver and Rudra listens to the ringtone, imagining it echoing in the hallway of their house in Patonga.

A day has passed since Didima's ashes were scattered at Baghchara and the skull was returned to Netidhopani.

He counts forward the five-and-a-half-hour time difference. It will be night in Patonga. The fishing boats may be at sea. All but *Paper Tiger*. His father's boat will be at anchor – holding a vigil for Cord Solace in his hospital bed.

The phone rings out. He tries again. Nothing. He calls Maggs's number and after three rings, it is picked up.

'Yo.'

'Maggs.'

'Rudra?'

'It's me. I'm calling from India.'

Rudra can feel the nine thousand kilometres of copper that strings them together. The warbling seethe of the ocean, the echo and crackle of the empty desert.

'How is it?' Maggs asks. 'Did you get my pyjama suit?'

'Not yet.'

'Did you see a tiger?'

'I'm not sure ... Maybe ... Almost.'

'Cool. Did you drop the skull?'

'I did.'

'You still having them crazy dreams?'

'They're gone. I met a girl, Maggs.'

'She cute?'

'She's a prawn fisher.'

'That'll make your old man happy.'

'I doubt it.'

'So you getting married?'

'Idiot.'

'My dad had an accident.'

'I hope the stains come out.'

'Stop being a fool. He fell into the water.'

'Is he okay?'

'I don't know. My mum flew home to be with him.'

'Shit. That's pretty big.'

'There's been a whole lot of bigness about this summer.'

'It'll be one to remember, alright.' The line goes quiet and Rudra looks at the earpiece of the old phone as if it is responsible. Suddenly, Magg's voice breaks back in. 'I guess I'll see you when you get home.'

'I'll be hopping on a plane day after tomorrow.'

'Then I'll see you then.'

'I missed you, mate.'

'I don't want to marry you.'

'See you soon.'

In Bansari's house, mildew crawls from under the beds. Fat raindrops peck at the tin roof. It begins to leak and Bansari rotates her cooking pots in a complicated choreography across the floor, catching the drops. When the generator fails, there are kerosene lamps, sputtering out a yellow light that falters in the dark corners.

Rudra tries to read but the light is so poor that his eyes begin to hurt. He yawns his goodnights and goes to brush his teeth. Raj has been allowed to stay tonight. He is singing Bollywood hits quietly to himself as Rudra shuts the bedroom door.

The darkness is complete. It even swallows sound, burping back the tallow honk of frogs. The thinnest blade of light under the door allows that there is still a world. That and Raj's song and the rain. Rudra feels his thoughts circling like the *meen* in Gita's tub. Tomorrow he will be starting the journey towards home. And, as he thinks of what that means, he is suddenly immensely tired. He closes his eyes against the dark and tonight, he knows, he shall not dream of tigers.

Swimming, the tiger's wake broad across the night river. He comes unbidden. Up with the tide he swims, salt sending him furious with desire. Over the *bund* silently, swiftly, pushing forward on the pads of his feet. He insinuates himself like a sliver of *sundari* wood under the skin. Behind him, pugmarks swell in the mud. The village is dark but he can smell what he has come for. The sweet scent of blood like perfume on the light wind. The closest huts with their fat infants and grandmothers are easy pickings but he is after something sweeter still.

His feet drum the beaten ground. Rounding the corner of a mud house, he waits at a window, whiskers pulled back, twitching. Flexing out his claws, he pulls himself onto the sill, perches there for a moment, balanced. Then, lightly down inside. Gone like a puff of smoke from the outside world. As if he has never been.

But inside, his tail swishes from side to side. He pushes his nose in the air, giddy with the smell of the human. His lips pull back. Teeth angle in the dark. He sees the spear leaning against the wall and snarls at its forgotten magic.

She sleeps alone – her father gone into the forest to steal yet again. He nuzzles the flesh. Her throat is soft and bright as the moon and, as his tongue rasps across it, she wakes.

Rudra sits upright in bed. Something is wrong. He pulls on clothes and grabs the torch from his bedside table. He runs to the *bund* to where muffled shouts pepper the soft air. His torchlight breaks into the darkness on the path and soon he is near the river. There, a large group of villagers has gathered around Malo and Gita's house. They are carrying torches made from *sundari* branches and *lathis* of solid dark wood.

*What is going on?* he asks with his shoulders and puzzled eyes.

'*Bagh!*' they cry. Then, 'Tiger!' in English.

He pushes to the front of the crowd but when he tries to enter the house, hands wrap around his biceps and hold him. A low, rumbling growl comes from inside. Rudra breaks free and lunges through the door.

The room is cut by firelight and darkness. There, in the far corner, made of flame and shadow, is a tiger so huge his shoulders are halfway up the walls. He owns the air between them. Gita lies beneath him, a black stain gathering on the mud floor. Without thinking, Rudra grabs the ancient spear leaning against the wall. The tiger roars his warning. The red *bauliya*'s cord tied around Rudra's bicep bites into his skin. The tiger snarls. Rudra lunges at him with the spear. The tiger dodges and, picking up Gita's body in his massive jaws, leaps for the window. Rudra thrusts the spear again. This time it finds the flank of the tiger, slipping into flesh. He snarls in pain but will not drop his prey. Scattering the villagers, he makes for the *bund* with Gita.

Rudra runs outside. The villagers are frozen by disbelief and fear, their limbs gone heavy, torches snuffed on the ground. A trail of blood leads from the window towards the *bund*. He flicks on his torch and follows the trail, hoping against all the odds that Gita has survived. Maybe she is just unconscious and the tiger has dropped her. He crosses the *bund*, slipping on the slick mud. He gets to his feet and continues. The torchlight picks out blood, so much of it – some Gita's, some the tiger's. Down the far side of the *bund* and to the river's edge it goes, before disappearing into the water.

For a moment Rudra stands there, staring into the night. A wake laps at his toes. The tiger is gone. And with him, Gita.

# 25

'HE BELIEVES IT IS HIS FAULT,' says Raj. 'He angered Bonbibi by cutting wood, and she deserted him and his daughter.'

Rudra is mute. The words have been torn from him. He cannot believe the violence of this place. How quickly and easily things can change. How do people live here?

They mourn a bloodstain – a ragged stripe that terminates at the water's edge.

Malo runs a wet rag over his windowsill, turning the black stain to bright red, to pink and then to nothing. When he has finished, Rudra hands him the spear – its tip stained with tiger blood.

'I tried,' he says.

Malo throws the spear to the ground and mutters something in Bangla.

'What did he say?' Rudra asks Raj.

'Nothing.'

'What did he say?'

'He says that now Dokkhin Rai will come for you.'

Rudra knows what his mother would say – that Dokkhin Rai is a story told to scare village children at night. A myth pieced together to reason with this complicated and uncaring land, to order the chaos of blood and death. *Gita was going to college*, thinks Rudra. By next season, she would have escaped.

He looks down at his packed bag – lighter now without the skull and ashes. So much left behind. The ferry is leaving soon and he doesn't know what he can say to Malo. Hasn't the words, even in English, to fill the gap.

As they leave her house, Bansari smothers Rudra in a hug. There are huge glossy tears in her eyes. He realises then how complex people are – that they are not just characters in a book with cookie-cutter traits and emotions.

'I will miss you, Rudra.'

'I'll miss you too, Pisi Bansari.'

'Call me Aunty.'

'Yes – Aunty.'

'Will you return?'

'Of course,' he says, not knowing if it is true or not.

'Give my love to Nayna. And to your father. I wish him all the best.'

'Thank you. For everything.'

'Even too much milk tea? With milk separate? And old people's gossip?'

'All that.'

He picks up Raj from his hut and together they walk towards the *ghat*. As they are about to board, Malo arrives;

half the man who strode through the village on the day of their first meeting with a rich foreigner in tow and his ambitious daughter waiting on his boat.

As Malo approaches, Rudra offers his hand to shake, but instead Malo grabs him and holds him close – like a brother or a son. Rudra can feel his body shaking. Raj places a hand on his shoulder and, as Malo breaks away, he hands Rudra a book.

Rudra boards the ferry with Raj and it pulls away. Malo turns through the crowd of waving people. They are waving at the young man in a badly stitched suit, a bundle of books tied with string balanced on his knees. And they are waving at the family of six with battered cardboard cases. They are waving at three teenagers, travelling back to school, and at a farmer with a basket of solemn ducks. They keep waving until their smiles and tears vanish, until they are no more significant than mangrove roots.

Rudra focuses on Malo crossing the *bund*. His tears are not visible from this distance, but Rudra knows they are there. Just because you can't see something, it doesn't mean it does not exist. The book that Malo gave him is in his hand and Rudra flips it over to read the title – *Gitanjali* by Rabindrinath Tagore.

'*Gitanjali* means song offerings,' says Raj. 'Malo could not read. I think this was truly Gita's book.'

Rudra opens at random to a line in English.

*By what dim shore of the ink-black river, by what far edge of the frowning forest, through what mazy depth of gloom are you threading your course to come to me, my friend?*

The ferry makes mid-river and the tide sucks at it. Downstream, in the deep forest around Netidhopani, stripes of light will fall across the paths and the abandoned temple and a tiger will amble up from the water. His muzzle will be masked with blood and he will lick at the wound on his rump. Turning, he will sniff the air and catch the scent of something familiar.

They near the far *ghat* and, as the crowd pulls their bags and bundles closer, Rudra breathes deeply. He smiles wearily at Raj, white-knuckling the gunnels of the boat. Rudra is going home; repeating the whole journey in reverse. He feels the bungee cord stretched between him and Patonga – his umbilicus, which has been tugging at him since he left. All he has to do is relax and the cord will bring him home.

The taxi to the station delivers them without incident, and then there's the trip back to Kolkata. *Cha-wallahs* come and go. Men with fists of bright toys, sweet sellers, *chaat* men with paper cones of nuts and spices. Through the barred windows, stations come and go, fields and villages. Kids jump on and sweep the train, collect plastic bottles and a few coins. Musicians play, and a man with a cobra in a wicker basket pulls off the lid and lets Rudra peer inside at the wicked silver-grey coils. Despite all this, the day is drab and Rudra knows the snake charmer has pulled the cobra's teeth. The *cha* is watery and the music seems grotesque.

Rudra thinks of Gita. How can he not? He tries to see only the landscape, but that thin smear of blood across the windowsill and the drag mark across the dirt path eclipse everything. He imagines what it is like to have a tiger's jaw tighten like a vice around your neck.

Even though it is an impossible thought, he cannot help but feel she paid for something done by his great-grandfather all those years before. That this awoke a great cataclysm of events that are reverberating even now. He knows that Nayna would wave this away with her hand. Would scrawl these fears on the high tide mark and tell him that the sea goddess will remove them. That goddess of her own making for her new land. A goddess made like all, she would say, to fill a particular need.

The train pulls into the station of a small town and Raj buys them both an ice-cream through the barred window of their carriage. The day is warm and they sit licking the melting treat from their arms.

'What will you do now?' Rudra asks Raj. 'Will you go to Mumbai?'

'There is always Bollywood.'

'Yes, there is always Bollywood.'

'And when I make it famous, you must arrive to visit. I will also have a special room for you and Mummy. And maybe your daddy too will come, even.'

'Maybe,' Rudra says, unable to picture Cord Solace on a crowded Kolkata-bound train, licking ice-cream from his forearm. 'Do you think you can make it in Bollywood, Raj?'

Raj's brow furrows and Rudra is reminded of wave patterns on a sandbar. 'Yes, I will make it. It is my dream.'

'But there is already one Amitabh Bachchan.'

'But not one like me. I will be the Nepali one.'

# 26

AT THE BEAMISH HOTEL, MRS URSU is trapped, like a fly in amber, on the steps out front. Her orange hair is an inferno in the deepening night.

'Welcome,' she says, extending her arms. 'To the Beamish Hotel. A grand experience awaits.' She pauses, peering into the dark. 'Oh, it's you.'

'Hi, Mrs Ursu.'

'Hello, young man. There is a message here from your mother.' She brushes down her gown, measled with sequins. 'Raj, take his bags to two oh four.'

'But he's not a porter anymore—'

'It is okay,' says Raj picking up Rudra's bags.

They walk up the stairs and Raj swings the door open. He places Rudra's bag on the stand and opens the bathroom door. His voice sounds automated.

'Hot and cold water, on tap, twenty-four-seven hours.'

'Raj, you don't have to do this.'

Raj shrugs.

'You're the Nepali Amitabh Bachchan!'

'Am I?' Raj opens the window and breathes in the smoky

Kolkata night. 'Maybe it is too much for me to do in one life. My village is very small. My life is very small. I escaped to Kolkata. Mumbai, maybe it is too much.'

There is a morning, then an afternoon, then an evening, merging and swallowing each other until night clambers across the courtyard and through the gate to the peepal tree. Rudra is stuck on his bed – an island engulfed by dangerous seas, tricky tides, whirlpools and waterspouts. Raj brings him *dhal* and *parathas;* he brings him sugary *cha.* The plates and glasses crowd the bed like flotsam and jetsam.

Rudra reads, like it is a new thing. Not because someone has told him to, or because he has to write an essay on it, or answer comprehension questions, but because, now, right now, he is looking for answers. It is urgent. He feels it like a dart in his blood. Some words reach down inside and grab him by the gut and make him want to cry out in pain. And others, well...they make him want to strangle the English language.

The book is *Gitanjali.* The copy Malo gave to him on the *ghat.* The pages are so thin that the words on each page are ghosted with the ones preceding. The language feels old – if he had the word *archaic,* that might go halfway to describing it. He has searched this book for clues all day and into this night, hoping it will give some meaning to what has just happened. Instead, all he can remember is a tangle of blood and bone and teeth. He clings to the book as his *didima* may have wrapped her fist around a talisman – a magic trinket that may have cost her ten rupees.

*Gitanjali* was translated by Rabindranath Tagore into English and published in 1912. So many *thees* and *thous* and *dosts*. A language of poetry that died, and should stay dead, now and forever. A language that the word *flowery* was invented for.

He sees Gitanjali, the flesh-and-blood girl, walking across the *bund* with her prawn net slung over her back, never translated. And again sitting by the river, reading this very book – her finger worrying the stanzas, lips untangling the words as she might unpick a snarl of twine. On this page, Rudra notices, there is a lick of river mud. On the next, a smear of blood where a mosquito, pressed flat, has leaked across the paper. He presses his nose to the book, hopeful of something other than dust.

'What are you smelling?' It is Raj in the doorway.

'Don't you knock?'

'Sorry, sir.'

'I'm not sir, I'm Rudra. You know that.'

'Sorry.'

'It's fine. I'm reading the book Malo gave me – Tagore.'

'Do you want to see where he was burnt?'

'Who?'

Raj points at the book. 'Rabindranath Tagore. The poet.'

'Why would I want to do that?'

'You need to not be so sad.'

'By visiting a crematorium?'

'Maybe, sir.'

'Don't call me sir. It's weird.' Rudra sits upright, the world spinning after so long lying down. 'Sure, let's go to the crematorium.'

Mrs Ursu is drinking brandy and watching TV in the lobby. She doesn't see them as they sneak by and out of the Beamish. Raj hails a cab and they set off for the Nimtala burning *ghat*.

They hit the river at ninety degrees, at twenty kilometres an hour, bouncing over the railway track – a dark corridor with dangerous bundles of rags that might be human. To the left, the double drapes of the Howrah Bridge vault over the Hooghly River. Its symmetry is pinched upwards, bleeding gaudy light to the water. Even at this late hour, the bridge is infested with traffic – cars and buses, blaring trucks and plodding bullock carts, cycle rickshaws and people on foot.

They leave the taxi on Strand Bank Road, the smell of rank mud and smoke grasping at their clothes.

'This way,' says Raj, and they cross the stone hearth to the *ghat*. As they enter the courtyard, a bamboo stretcher borne by a group of sweating, chanting men pass them.

'...*Ram Nam Satya Hai, Ram Nam Satya Hai, Ram Nam Satya Hai*...' The parcel is topped with orange marigolds and tinsel. '...*Ram Nam Satya Hai, Ram Nam Satya Hai*...'

It takes Rudra a minute to realise that the white shrouded figure is a body.

'The name of the god is truth,' says Raj. '*Ram nam* – the name of *Ram* – is breath, is truth.' He indicates the shrouded figure. 'This body has breath no more.'

Rudra tries not to inhale the smoke, knowing it is full of teeth and hair and flesh. There are two pyres in the open courtyard at various stages of burning.

'There is not so much burning here now,' says Raj. 'People with much money will go to Varanasi. There they are getting a better rebirth. This Hooghly River – it has some Ganga water inside it but it is not so pure. The poorly people – they are burning in the electric *ghat*.'

'Electric *ghat*?'

'Yes. Cheaper. Not very much smoke. Good for the environment. They have timetables and screens like a railway station. They even have a mobile phones app to tell when is the right time for arriving.'

Rudra looks at the fizzing, smoking pyres nearby – at the men pushing the sandalwood logs with long poles, arranging the bodies so they burn better. If he were a poet, like Tagore, he would say *we are fuel for a greedy world, we are tiger meat, we are ashes*. But he is not Tagore. 'But this traditional way,' he says, 'it's more holy, right? Better?'

'It is slow. And these men.' Raj looks around. 'They breathe smoke, they drink too much whisky, they push the skull and the bone into the fire, and their child will do also.'

They move down to the *ghat* itself – a pockmarked series of steps, slimy with river mud. There, a woman floats a tiny lamp onto the river. Next to her, a family of tired westerners cast handfuls of ashes into the water. Rudra wonders at their shared pain, the lives they are remembering. The river will take these offerings and carry them to the Sundarbans. There, a girl whose name means *song offering* once lived. There she pulled a prawn net. Rudra closes his eyes.

'Everyone will die,' says Raj, as if he knows what Rudra is thinking. 'Everyone you see, and then their child and their child. Funeral fires in Varanasi – the fire of Shiva – are burning for three thousand years, making everything clean. They will burn forever.' He claps his hands as if finalising the thought. 'I promise to show you Tagore-ji's memorial.'

Rudra had almost forgotten why they had come. So they turn from the river, past the fires and through an archway. There, without fanfare, in front of them is the memorial for India's greatest ever writer.

'They *chose* those colours?'

'Some people, they do not like it,' replies Raj. 'Every new politician makes it new colours.'

It is dumpy, it is gaudy, it is ugly.

'Do you think he'd like it?'

'Which person?'

'Tagore.'

'He is dead.'

'But if he was alive.'

'But he is dead.'

This could go on forever but Rudra knows Raj would win – he has the patience and persistence. Instead they move back into the cremation grounds. As they pass the funeral pyres, Raj nods at a woman in white, staring directly into the flames. 'She is a widow,' he says. 'It is usual she would be only at home. But, yet, there she is.'

The woman is too close to the radiating heat. Her skin is dull and loose around her elbows. Her hair is a bunch of brittle twigs beneath her sari. She might catch fire.

'Sometimes in the olden times it was needed that the widow do *sati* – that she burn on her husband's fire. The government do not allow it now. Sometimes it still happens. Maybe over many hundred years all of our old, bad things will be taken by the government.'

'What about the other things? The good things – the ceremonies, the festivals and languages? The beautiful stories?'

'That will also go.' Raj shrugs as if this is a done deal.

Rudra feels the red cord the woodcutters' *bauliya* gave to Gita still on his arm. *You need protection more than me,* she'd said as she handed it to him on the riverbank. And that very night a tiger dragged her from her room. Slipped her silently into the river and swam away.

It is time now. With his mission done he can make a final offering. He pulls at the cord until it cuts into his bicep. When it breaks, he feels the release in his muscle and a tingling where it once was. As they walk back past the funeral pyres, he casts the cord into the fire.

He can't be sure it is anything – just a trick of the light, a flare of the fire that might make the extinguishing of a holy item more than the mere burning of a cotton thread. 'Did you see that?' he asks Raj. But Raj is intent on lighting his *beedi* – rolling it through the match-flame.

# 27

THE TIGER DRAWS HIMSELF FROM THE FOREST like a filament of night, the dark knives on his pelt exhaling shadows. He is not running and not walking. It is a pace that will allow for kilometres of village paths, of *bunds* and paddy fields and the vast gleaming snakes of train track. His hunger is tinder-dry inside him. It rattles like a bone in a cage.

He pauses only to drink and the closer he gets to the city, the more he can taste it – a film of oil and soot dribbled over puddles, and over streams that thin into veins. The city is not his place and that troubles him.

When the metal tracks shake and hum, he knows to retreat to the verges, to allow the noise and light to pass by. Mud huts pump tin music into the air, cow-shit smoke dimples the night. And still he keeps on, feeling the rhythm in his shoulders and in his rump. The soft trumpeting of his footfalls, calling, answering a mantra that checks his stride.

The spaces between grow smaller. Things start to pile on top. Wires enter and exit the wounds of houses. Mud gives way to brick then to concrete and although he does not have the words for these things, he does not fear them. He has stored the forest inside and it sustains him now.

Here everything has been scoured. Here, these people, these animals who think they are above it all, have replaced what lay beneath with everything they have made. He pities them. Because it cannot last. Because everything they throw against the world is futile. One day, when they are gone, the forest will return. This is true savagery – the art of waiting and persisting.

Soon there is too much light. It catches in his eyes and makes them flare. It burns his pelt, bleaches the fire orange to dulled rust. He trots between patches of shadow and, when the stars disappear, he begins to run.

Rudra wakes as the light in his room shudders and dies. The way to the window is paved with plates and cups. He weaves his way through and looks out on a Kolkata devoid of light. This happens, he knows, when the city flicks off the power for hours at a time. *Brownouts*, they call them, because they are not as serious as blackouts, though they can be equally dark.

Slowly, lamps are lit, bleeding pools of copper. As his eyes adjust, he sees the peepal tree and below it the hump of the sweetmaker's cart. Something is there – the slightest movement between oily shadow and night. He narrows his eyes in an attempt to drill into the dark.

He closes the door to his room and creeps down the stairway. The Beamish creaks and groans like a ship at anchor. He crosses the foyer and slips down the front steps. The sweetmaker's cart is twenty paces off.

The tiger swallows the light as if it is nothing. He sees the boy at the window and then coming down the stairs. He snarls at his arrogance.

He remembers the temple grounds, the slabs of stone cracked open with tendrils, the forest fingers pushing and finding. He still has the taste of his meal, the blood dried on his muzzle.

He recalls a man with a waxed moustache, gun glinting with starlight. Then that long-ago night slashed open with gunpowder flash; that noise, that hit – a pummel, a hoarse bark. Them dragging a broken bag of skin-and-bone, breaking shins so he fits. The stencil of a skull in his mind, carried to a far land. To a boat in the darkness, burning, set fire by madness and anger. *Flint and steel*, he cried, that madman. *Flint and steel*. And the fish singing their crazy-making song. The boat drawn down, belching clouds of air. And the skull resting, seaworms turning in eyesockets.

Rudra watches as the tiger steps from behind the sweet-maker's cart. So big that it makes him gasp. *So unfair,* he thinks. The advantage is always with the hunter. It can so rarely work out right for the prey. If only he had a gun, he could crack that skull open one more time. But he has nothing. Just bare hands. He threw the red cord into the funeral pyre. *You need protection more than me.* He curses his stupidity.

He thinks of what he has killed in his life and what he has demanded to die so he can keep on living. *We all end as food*, he thinks. He is no longer afraid and wonders if that is how Gita was in the end. Wonders if everyone surrenders at the right time.

Then he thinks about the equation that has led to this final reckoning. His mother's grandfather taken by the tiger. The tiger taken by his father's grandfather. And now him, alone on this the last night on earth in Kolkata – the city of Kali.

Kali – the black one, the destroyer. The goddess of taxi drivers and poachers. And sweetsellers. A modern goddess for modern times. The annihilator of ignorance.

The tiger looks at the boy sideways, avoiding his direct gaze. All tigers despise the look of a human face. That gloating guilt-giving stare. Something about the open ground between the features causing them to squirm.

A time past, under the sea, fish worshipped the skull, singing songs of praise that rose as bubbles in the blood. Shadows passing above and nets widening their greedy mouths to gulp and gulp and gulp. The skull beneath all that water. Not enough to keep it drowned. Uncovering itself.

Rudra doesn't speak, doesn't need to speak. He has walked the tiger paths in his dreams – from Dark Corner to Patonga Creek to Netidhophani. He understands that this tiger, that

Dokkhin Rai, is part of him, of his family. Anger and revenge have kept this going – leapfrogging their way through history. He must cut the line now and watch it tumble back into the dark. He must let go.

The tiger opens his muzzle and roars, and the leaves on the peepal tree quiver. His whiskers twitch. He takes a step back. But it is not a retreat. He turns into the shadow of the sweetseller's cart. And as he goes, he feels fingers brush his pelt, playing each one of his stripes like the string of a sitar. The wound on his flank knits, heals, scars, then disappears.

Across Kolkata lights return. TVs flicker into life. Bollywood drama flares across the suburbs from North Dumdum to Tollygunge. Cricket matches played in far-off lands erupt onscreen. The shadows that had played the parts of ghost and goddess are driven off.

Rudra feels a hand on his shoulder.

'You have been dream-walking,' says Raj. 'I was watching you from there.' He nods to the Beamish steps.

'Did you see the tiger?' asks Rudra.

'A tiger in Kolkata?' Raj smiles. 'There was no tiger.'

'I saw him.'

'Maybe so,' says Raj. 'But he was not there.'

# Central Coast return

# 28

THE PLANE COMES LOW OVER SYDNEY – the towers of
the CBD nicked with morning light. The coathanger bridge
hangs over the harbour, all dark and spidery in some steam-
punk dream. Beside it, the Opera House is a lotus grown
from the cracks in Bennelong Point.

Everyone returning is cowed by it. They sit in rows,
silently fingering beads bought on Sudder Street or flicking
through their photos of wild-eyed *sadhus* smoking *chillums*
by the Ganga at Varanasi, a camel safari (one day too long)
in the Thar Desert. Some are expat Indians, coming back
to Australia. They do not call Australia home, even though
their children were born here. Even though they have
lived here twenty years and have houses in Eastwood and
Marrickville and go to Bondi on Sunday and sink their toes
into the sand; when they spread picnic blankets, they cover
them with tiffin pots of *rogan josh, aloo gobi*, rice and *naan*.
This is not home. Will it ever be?

Outside the perspex windows, Sydney does not care for
them. And inside, their kids are on their phones, faces blue
with reflected light, sweeter than Krishna sometimes. They

took them home to meet the family – outside Chandigarh. Took them to the village where they were born. Showed them the tractor they had bought and given to their brothers. The kids were bored to tears. Hated the flat fields and the Golden Temple at Amritsar. Blushed at the ceremony and poverty. Were frightened by dogs and beggars. Were charmed by the monkeys until they bared their teeth.

And now they are all coming home. Home? The adults confused and stateless, refusing to believe the India they left behind has gone forever. The children determined to become more Australian, to never eat *puris* or *dosas*, to never visit the *gurdwara* or *mandir*, and utter those high, rattling syllables. They are practising their rising inflection even as they land, their quickfire east coast prattle that their parents can only catch half of, words that the old folk will never understand.

But there is one boy – older than the others – alone (in that, some suspicion). His hair smells of Kolkata – the charnel houses down by the river, *ghee* from a sweetmaker's pot, the bitter breath of Hindustan taxis. He is staring at the seatback and imagining a land where eighteen tides worry mud-walled houses and reclaim the *bunds*. And as they taxi to the gate, he knows it is vanishing from him, slipping back under the *cha*-coloured waters.

Cord is laid up in a four-bed ward with wires and masks and beeping machinery. Rudra recognises shame, or something very like it, as he catches his father's eye. The nurse has prepared him. Cord is paralysed down one side.

'Like a stroke,' she says. 'No air, you see. It starved that part of his brain.'

'Will he work again?' Rudra asks.

She says, 'You'll have to ask the doctor that,' and refuses to look at him, so Rudra thinks not.

He takes a chair by the bed. Damp plastic. The sweet alcohol scent of hand sanitiser. His dad rolls his head towards him, one side of his face a landslide. He doesn't speak. Not even hello. Rudra is braver now, but he can still feel the words stuck like urchin spines in his throat.

'I took it back,' he blurts.

His dad's eyes narrow.

'The skull. It's back in the Sundarbans now. Back where it belongs. The curse is done.'

*Curse.* Where did that come from? What curse? He should have said *anger* – something Cord could grip hold of.

His dad snorts, pulls the covers around him. The sheets are stained slightly around the edges, like the scum on a flood tide. He grabs a remote with his good hand and clicks on the TV. *That's all from us for today,* announces the talk show host. And Rudra, picking up his bag, exits the room.

# 29

HE MAKES THE NEWCASTLE TRAIN, RUNNING DOWN Platform Nine at Central, entering the carriage breathless and sweaty.

After the Long Island Tunnel, they cross the Hawkesbury Bridge. He remembers that night – so long ago now, it seems – when they came up under the bridge in the *Paper Tiger*. Out for prawns and mere hours away from pulling up the skull. *Dredging up the past*, Cord might call it.

Downstream, the old sandstone pylons battle the tide. Once, long ago, before the bridge existed, a paddle-steamer would cart passengers down to Broken Bay and into Brisbane Water, dumping them at Gosford – their tall hats, tweed suits and petticoats freckled with salt.

In the future, in the present, in the stinging blindness of right now, the train pierces the Cogra Point tunnel. Rudra welcomes the darkness. He has left behind the ghost island, a *bund* that does not protect, an aunt who is not an aunt, and a blessing cord from a girl he barely got to know.

They drift up beside the oyster leases at Mullet Creek, trees scudding by like ghosts, the escarpment bleeding vegetation to the water's edge. The train slows, then creaks to a stop at Wondabyne. The platform is so short passengers have to ride the last carriage to get off.

A woman and a young boy step out. A man is there, with his hands in his pockets. He is in exactly the right spot, bringing the woman's face into his hands and kissing it, tucking a loop of hair behind her ear. Rudra feels that he should look away, but he watches the man sweep the boy into his arms, throwing him into the air as if he is meant to fly. He carries him and a battered suitcase towards the crossing. Through the scratched glass of the carriage, Rudra sees their dog miming barking from a boat tied at the jetty.

They have been away, he imagines, the child and his mother. Overseas – somewhere exotic – visiting family. He, the father, has remained behind; he has to work, otherwise he would have joined them. He's an oyster farmer but he takes the time to teach his boy the things he learnt as a child – how to kill mullet and make a gumleaf whistle, the secret tracks to caves with scraped symbols and pools deep enough to lose a boy. Their house is across the river, accessible only by boat. That is their yacht tugging at the reflection of Mount Wondabyne. Everything arrives by boat. The mail is carried by the tangled-beard skipper – salt-chapped hands, trousers eyed with fish scales.

The father lowers his son into the boat. The dog licks the boy's face and they laugh. *Gerraway*, says the boy. *Make him stop*. His dad ruffles his hair. *He loves you*. He pulls the motor into life and the dinghy skips across the river. The woman sits in the bow, smells the air, lets it sit in her throat. She feels like singing. And the boy sits beside his father and is allowed to steer. The father feels like a tree beside him – solid, dependable, supple.

But Rudra is down the line as all this comes into being. Or maybe it never happens, only in his head. He wants this to be so badly. Wants a chance to have that sort of dad.

He turns on his phone and waits for the signal. Then he rings.

A woman sitting opposite him stares at him as he begins his conversation. She has a wispy beard and sallow smoker's skin.

'Hi, Mum.'

'Rudra, it's so good to hear your voice. Are you okay?'

'I'm fine.'

'How was the trip?'

'It was okay. Long.'

'And now you're almost home.'

'I have so much to tell you, Mum. Things happened.'

'What happened? Tell me.'

'When I get home. I saw Dad . . .'

'He needed to see you. How did he seem?'

'He was okay.'

'*I'm* looking forward to seeing you.'

'I'm looking forward to seeing you too. Where are you?'

'Gosford.'

'How did you know which train?'

'Us Indians, you know – fortune tellers and all.'

'You're too funny. You should have your own show.'

'You think so?'

'Not really. How's Wallace?'

'He is okay. He's working for Wink now.'

'What does Dad think about that?'

'What he doesn't know can't hurt him.'

'I guess so.'

'I'll see you soon.'

'Okay. I'll stay on until Gosford. I'll see you then. I love you, Mum.'

Rudra hangs up. The phone stays warm in his hand as if it has held some of what passed through its metal soul.

'This is a quiet carriage, you know,' says the lady opposite.

'It was my mum.'

'It's a quiet carriage.'

'I know. Sorry,' says Rudra. 'I've just been to India to scatter my grandmother's ashes. She was from there. A place called the Sundarbans actually.'

'I don't care, boy. This is a quiet carriage and you need to be silent if you're here. That's the meaning of quiet. No noise, see.'

'My friend – she was called Gita.'

*Was* called Gita. *Was* a *meendhara*. *Was* pulled from her mud hut by the river. *Was* going to college.

The woman is wary of the tears. The boy could be dangerous. 'Just keep it down, okay.'

'There's this guy too – called Raj. He's not the best guide in the world, not the best hotel doorman, smokes too much and scared as hell of the water. But he's going to be a Bollywood star.'

'I'll make a complaint, I will. This is a quiet carriage. It means, *be quiet*. No noise. People sit here 'cause they don't want to be disturbed. Then there's you harping on about nothing, taking phone calls, making a general nuisance.'

'Raj was teaching me a lesson.' The switch flicks in Rudra's mind. 'About going for what you believe no matter what people think.'

'That's it. When we get to Woy Woy, I'm telling the stationmaster. You can't just get away with it.'

'I'll finish the summer on the boat, that might make Cord happy.'

'Alright, you've had your say. Can you just be quiet now? It's not just me, you know, there's others on this carriage that deserve a bit of hush.'

Rudra smiles at the woman and she looks away.

The train pulls into Woy Woy and the woman with the wispy beard gets up, wrestling her discontent and a clutch of bloated plastic bags. The last thing he sees is her talking to the stationmaster. He gives her an ironic wave as they pull away.

They cross the spit at Pelican Island – through Koolewong and Tascott with their scattering of yachts, a Heron dinghy sailing over Brisbane Water, its sky-blue sail tightened to the breeze. *It is good to be home*, thinks Rudra.

They stop at Point Clare, pass Central Coast Stadium and into Gosford. Rudra shoulders his bag and leaves the train.

And there she is – Mum – smiling and pressing her palms together.

'*Namaste*, Rudra.'

'*Namaste*, Mum.'

They hug each other. Rudra feels her tears on his shoulder. 'It's okay,' he says.

'I know,' she answers. 'I know it is. Come on, let's go.'

They walk to where the Solace ute is parked. Mum opens the door and gets in the driver's seat.

'I've never seen you drive.'

'That doesn't mean I can't.'

'Can you?'

'Of course I can.' She lurches onto the Central Coast Highway. 'You'll need to get your learner's soon.'

'I guess so.'

'A lot of things are going to change around here, Rudra.'

'Good. They needed to.'

'Yes, they did,' said Nayna.

Instead of heading back through Woy Woy, they take the road to East Gosford.

'Mum?' says Rudra. 'Do you know where we're going?'

'I've been living here longer than you have been alive, Rudra Solace.'

'But this isn't the way home.'

'It's the long way.'

'It's a really long way.'

'There are too many left-hand turns if we go via Woy Woy.'

'What?'

'I need practise turning right.'

They motor through Green Point, Kincumber and down Empire Bay Drive.

Nayna says, 'Remember those animals that were killed?'

'Yes,' says Rudra.

'Turned out to be a wild dog in the end. Really big. Swimming back and forth over the creek and killing wallabies and possums and people's pet cats. Wallace shot it.'

Rudra doesn't know what to say. Doesn't know where that leaves his weirdo tiger dreams. Does this stone-cold fact make any of the shadowy stuff that has gone on this summer any less real? Is it the cord or the holes between that makes the net?

As they drop down the hill from Daleys Point, the *engineering marvel* of the Rip Bridge approaches. He remembers Maggs being dangled above the rip and how he fell, all brittle-boned and goose-fleshed, to the water.

'I used to hold my breath when I crossed this bridge,' he says to Nayna.

'Why is that, Rudra?'

'I never trusted those engineers even though I was always told I should.'

'And now?'

Rudra looks behind them – a trail of cars up the hill and beyond. 'You're driving a little slower than I'm used to,' he says. 'The need to breathe is greater than my fear of this bridge collapsing.'

Finally, they wind their way through Umina and up over the headland towards Patonga. A glimpse of Pearl Beach between the points, scrub blackened from recent fire, and a vapour trail scrawled across the sky.

'Mum?'

'Yes.'

'Do you think Didima is happy back in the Sundarbans?'

'Well, she *is* dead, Rudra, so I doubt there is much happening by way of happiness – or anything else for that matter. But to answer your question in another way, it's what she wanted when she was alive.'

'Yes, but so far from us.'

'She'll always be with us, Rudra.'

Rudra looks at her. 'Did you seriously just say that?'

Nayna grimaces and grips the wheel tighter. 'If I start telling you she is in the clouds and the leaves on the trees, can you please slap me?'

'I will.'

'What I mean to say is that I kept some ashes.'

'You did what?'

'I held a little back.'

'What for?'

'Your *didima* needs to be here as well. That's for us.'

# 30

THE PHONE RINGS IN THE HALLWAY. The sound breaks open the emptiness of the morning, rolls across the photos on the wall. Men long dead, a tiger. The Solace boys on the beach, the nets limp in their hands. A woman beneath a parasol stepping from a boat – caught forever between places, not of the land but not of the sea.

And others, new photos – Didima and Dadu, smooth-faced and terrified in their wedding finery. Didima with a nose-ring – a half moon; Dadu with a tightly wrapped turban, hands slim in his lap. Their hair partings drenched in vermilion that can hardly be imagined in black and white. Not daring to look at each other. And Nayna Solace in a graduation gown, flying from her parents at a speed no one could have reckoned. To a new life, a new land, a husband, a child, a renunciation. These photos showing both sides now, what with Cord Solace in hospital and all his rules broken.

Propped between the phone and a small brass elephant-headed Ganesha – the god of letters and writing – is a postcard with a triple-headed lion stamp. Slightly grubby, faded, imperfect.

*Dear Rudra and Mummy,*

*I am here – Bollywood! I have never seen Manisha Koirala still she evades me and I have not serving milktea and biftek to Amitabh Bachchan quite as yet but once I did see him in Leopold's Café in Colaba where I am having a job learning how to cook the Indian, Chinese, Continental foods and the other good things. I am having one job starting tomorrow in a film where I will be an extra character and this is one gangster film so I will be awesome. I think fame is not so very far from me now. I hope you are well. Love and namaste to your good daddy Mr Solace.*

*Your very good friend and guide,*

*Raj.*

The phone rings and Nayna in the garden, with a job application half-filled in, thinks about what she's missed and what she can go back and get. She thinks it might be Cord on the phone because he's taken to calling lately, now his speech is coming back. She ignores it this time and goes back to her application.

And the phone keeps ringing because that is what phones do when no one answers. Rudra Solace stirs. His sheet is wound into a rope that he should climb to reach his pillow. At the foot of his bed, his dreams are scattered like so much sand. If he were to drift his fingers through, he would come across pieces of the Sundarbans here and there – a *meendhara* girl, a gossipy aunt, woodcollectors and poachers, honeymen. But that tiger is nowhere to be seen or dreamt.

The phone rings and Rudra, dragging himself upright, goes to answer it.

'Hello,' he says. 'Maggs!'

The swell is massive, a glut of whitewater across the bar. The channel has lumps three foot high into which surfers are swallowed and regurgitated. The luckiest ones are getting dropped out the back in boats. Some are getting tow-ins on jet skis. It is that big.

'Maggs, I dunno, mate.'

'You'll be fine.'

'It's pretty huge.'

'It just looks big from here.'

'Reckon it'll look even bigger close up.'

'Just get your wettie on. I haven't seen a south-easterly swell like this and I'm not sitting it out.'

They push into the channel on the outgoing tide. Rudra knows immediately it is going to be hard to sit still out there with all this water churning through the exit from Brisbane Water. But he knows all he has to do is to wait it out. Maggs can snare a couple of waves and then they'll paddle in for pies and a milkshake at Ettalong. Easy done.

Of course it isn't so easy. It never is. Out there on the wild sea with men twice and three times his age – not so easy. And Maggs all over the waves; almost snaking; almost dropping in. Rudra nervous, way out on the shoulder with the kids on bodyboards, half-hearted and half-paddling. He sees Judge, avoids his gaze. Judge's dreadlocks are a salted fleece across his head. He looks smaller and a little sad; on the outer now. The older guys are deeper and the hottest surfers are deeper still, taking off with a fizzing spit, freefalling and driving hard off the bottom, freight-training down the line.

Nothing has prepared Rudra for this. He is a weekend surfer and not even that. He belongs on a boat. Here the sea is too close and too real. Here the sea can bend and break and doesn't care who you are.

He watches Maggs paddle for one. He is deep, real deep. The wave struggles and gathers behind him, reaching out its lip like a rock ledge, and Maggs drops, pushes his board beneath him, freefalls, bird-arms, hits the bowled bottom of the wave, throws a quick turn, rises to the lip, smashes it, drops mid-wave and sets a rail. The wave, angry now, vomits a tonne of water above his head and Rudra can see it fringe over Maggs – so very deep. But then Judge paddles further along the shoulder, preparing to drop in. And Maggs, now speed-crouching, racing that lip, sees him, grabs a rail. It's either hit Judge, or have the wave hit him hard, and he has to make a choice right there.

Then there is whitewater and plenty of it. And more of it. The sea is a boiling mess. The noise fills the air. And everyone abandons boards and dives for the bottom, for the sweet weed and sand.

And when Rudra rises, it is to a hissing fit of water, like someone has dumped bicarb out the back and turned the world to bubbles. And in among the white, there is red. Blood thinned by seawater.

Rudra paddles. He knows it is Maggs. Knows it. But another wave comes, bigger this time, drumming sand up inside it. It goes unridden. And he dives again, feel his board tugging at his ankle – his legrope an umbilicus.

He turns up and catches the fleeting gold of the sky before the wave burns everything.

Up again and pulling at the air. Nothing so sweet. And another wave comes, smaller this time but still deadly. Rudra waits until he can wait no more and dives again for the bottom.

Once it is past, he swims for the surface, to a world shot free of sound. Everyone around him seems stunned, pulling their boards towards them, climbing on and paddling as far free of the line-up as they can. No one wants to face another set like that.

Rudra looks around. There – in a patch of blood, floating face down. He swims towards him. Wrenches him over. Rudra can't face another death; he's had enough to last two lifetimes. A huge gash across the forehead, draining blood, lidded eyes, a flood of dreadlocks, a Southern Cross tattoo. Judge.

Maggs is paddling back out. 'I did that, didn't I?' he says, screwing his eyes against the guilt.

'We need to get him in.'

They drag Judge onto Maggs's board and together push him towards the shore, catching anything they can. Someone calls an ambulance and it arrives quickly, sirens blaring. The ambos work on him, right there on the sand. Maggs keeps people back. 'What're you gawping at, you ghouls!'

They pump Judge's chest, give him mouth to mouth. One of the ambos rushes back with a defibrillator. 'Stand back now.' They hook him up and give him a jolt. He bounces but lies still.

'Don't die. Don't die. Don't die.' Maggs is shaking though it isn't cold.

They give Judge another shock. He rises and falls; coughs a lungful of seawater onto his chest.

Rudra hears Maggs release a huge breath. 'Thank you,' he whispers to the air.

'No worries,' says one of the ambos. 'Is he your mate?'

'No,' says Maggs. 'I wouldn't call him that exactly.'

Judge blinks and looks at the circle of people. 'Where am I?'

'Ettalong,' says the ambo. 'You had an accident out in the water. These two guys pulled you out.'

Judge looks at Maggs and Rudra in turn. The gash on his head is raw. His lips move on words but they fail to exit. Rudra and Maggs turn their backs and, grabbing their boards, walk to the road. The sea continues to roar in the background. It's like they're leaving a packed stadium.

'It'll be all over *The Advocate* in big bolds,' says Maggs. 'CURRY-MUNCHER SAVES DREADLOCKED LOCAL ZERO.'

They dump their boards in the bushes on the foreshore and head to the Ettalong shops, stripping wetties to the waist. They order pies and choc milks at the bakery and sit on the bench to eat.

'So was India much chop?'

'It was sort of familiar and strange at the same time. My mum and Didima told me so much about it, and then to see it for real, I dunno, it was like something slotted into place. I felt like some part of me belonged there. And I liked it – the people, the craziness, the food and colour. I liked it a lot. I don't know why but I didn't expect to. People are always on about how dirty and poor India is, but that's just a smoke-screen for its awesomeness.'

'What about this girl you met?'

Rudra takes a sip of his milk. 'Can we not talk about that? Not just yet.'

'Tell me something else then.'

'I guess I found out that I really am half Indian. And that's something to be proud of.'

'You're half Indian?' says Maggs, mock shock all over his stupid face. 'Like Tonto?'

'Piss off, Maggs.'

They eat their pies in silence for a moment. The hot sauce drips across their fingers, and they splay their legs so the overrun hits the pavement.

'Your dad's a racist, isn't he, Rudra?'

'He can't be.'

'He hates you.'

'He does not.'

'The half of you that's Indian, he does.'

'How can you hate half a person?' he asks.

'If anyone can, it'd be your old man.'

'You're an idiot, Maggs.'

'I am,' Maggs agrees. 'But your old man, he's not Robinson Crusoe in hating on his own folk, is he?'

'What do you mean?'

'Australians hate people who come here from somewhere else – even though most do. Even though the "them" are really "us". We're just one big mongrel mob.'

'Maggs, this is hurting my head.'

'Don't think that's going to stop me,' says Maggs, but he does pause for a moment. Just to catch his breath. 'Why'd Cord even marry your mum?'

'Can we just drop it?'

'He pretends she's not even Indian. Why would he bother to marry her?'

'I guess he was different back then.'

'You think so?'

'I don't know.'

'And why (and I really mean *why* this time) did your mum marry *him*? She could have married anyone.' He knots his brow at Rudra. '*I'd* marry her if I wasn't your mate.'

'Maggs, this isn't something I want to talk about.'

'Fair enough.' Maggs balls his pie bag and tosses it at the bin. 'Two points, right there.' The ambulance rolls past. Maggs nods at it. 'Reckon old mate Judge is braver than your dad.'

'What has Judge got to do with any of this?'

'He's a racist, but at least he has the courage to come right out and say what he thinks.'

'Reckon that's bravery?'

Maggs thinks for a moment. 'Could just be stupidity.'

Rudra walks the length of the beach from Ettalong Point to Kiddie's Corner. Out on Umina Point he stops, laying his board carefully on the rocks. There is another storm coming, or the same one looping back for another shot. The swellmaker prods the horizon, sky almost black with a slice of bright light along the seam where it meets the sea. The seabirds are drawing themselves to the cliffs. The waters around Lion Island are swollen with fish. Off the southern point the water is boiling with them. The penguins are out hunting, and so too, the sharks.

Maggs was right: Cord Solace is a racist, and a coward of sorts. He is scared of the world moving on without him. The place he has known is one he can never return to. One morning he put to sea and when he returned all he had known had been swallowed. The *bund* he built against the world had been breached by tigers and tides beyond his imaginings.

'Just let go,' Rudra whispers. 'Even though it feels like giving up. Let go.' And he imagines the words drifting past the island, past the gaping maw of the Hawkesbury, down the coast, along the spindrift beaches – Palm, Newport, Narrabeen, Curl Curl. Past Freshwater where the Hawaiian, Duke Kahanamoku, introduced surfing to Australia. Past Manly – named for the whale-eating Guringai men who speared Captain Arthur Phillip. A sharp right round North Head, past Chowder Bay and Shark Island. Into the harbour, by the Opera House, once a lotus, now baring its sharpened teeth at the sky. Beneath the Harbour Bridge, walkers easing across its spine – the carcass of a slaughtered Minmi, a dinosaur a hundred and thirteen million years dead. Up through the Rocks, where the first white men and women pitched their ragged tents; along the clotted, winding streets of the city. To the hospital.

And Rudra sees Cord Solace lying in a four-bed ward with the screens pulled round. One half of his face slapped flat, watching *Judge Judy* and running the sheet hem through his hands as if it is a net. Cord shuffles off his bedclothes and limps to the window. Great boiling clouds are rolling over the suburbs. He looks through Naremburn, Northbridge and Willoughby into the guttering grey beyond. There, the outline of the pines as clear as if they are stapled to the window. The kite, uttering her keening cry and swooping across the bay. Look, the cutlass blade of the beach where he played pirates with his brother and built weed humpies through the winter, tithed to the swells and garrulous winds. He is ten years old, a muttonbird smuggled inside his gut-flecked jacket; its beak pressed into his flesh, the mechanical knock of its heart. He is ten and his father is a lump of fear in his marrow – a cancer of which he will never be rid. They walk on eggshells each night, when he's back from the sea, smelling of it, anger flaring off him like spindrift. When even the scrape of a knife on a plate could earn a 'clip'. That's what he called it, but it could cause blood. *You had the chance to be different*, Cord thinks, and a sob escapes him.

# 31

CORD SOLACE COMES DOWN THE HILL on the final day
of the school holidays. The taxi he is riding in passes Volvos
stacked with tents and toys and kids and blow-up boats;
roof-racks with boards; trailers with bikes and rods. Faces
at the window, peeled red noses, appealing to the Summer
God – the Lord of Zinc and Singlets – to grant them just one
more day before they return to the outer west of Sydney.
Three cheers for brick veneer, for morning commutes and
pale, peeling paling fences.

Cord Solace looks away in shame and disgust because
he has never known these people, though they have been
coming to his town since he was born and long before. He
has never got to know them because they don't matter and
if he ignores them they will soon be gone. He learnt this
from his father, who learnt it from his. *Don't get attached*,
they said. *They're a temporary annoyance.*

He passes the pub and sees the fish-and-chip shop is for
sale. Now some Indians will take over, and what do they
know about batter or fish? He blinks at the thought that his
wife is Indian. How did that happen? He remembers a fish

and a note and a feeling that swam up inside. Could it have once been love? And for the second time in his adult life he is moved almost to tears.

Almost – because ultimately he holds them back, as he knows he must. He's seen this taxi driver play a set at the pub every now and then, and he's known around the traps for his ship-sinking lips. And though Cord is sitting in the back seat, he knows the driver has spotted him in the mirror and it will be all around town quicker than a flash. Then it'll be over. Once they sense his weakness, they'll move in for the kill, like bloody sharks, and share the spoils between them. He is alone and has always been alone and will always be alone. Forever and ever. Ah-bloody-men.

The jacarandas are ringed with mauve carpets. *Let go. Surrender.* He doesn't understand where that voice is from. Has to ignore it, because the mullet season is still to come and there's fish to be had. How will he do it with this body slack and useless? He recalls how it used to feel – so powerful, solid, like a broadaxe. Some days he used to think he could bring the nets up without the winch, hand-over-hand – that powerful, he'd want to sing for it. It is good he has a son, no matter how useless. He'll take over now; he has the sea in him on both sides. *Maybe*, Cord thinks, *I married well in that regard.*

*Dad, I'm not going out on the boat. Not this autumn. Not ever again. It stops with me. I know our family have been fishing here since they boated over the Hawkesbury. I don't know*

*what I am going to do but I know it isn't fishing. I'm going back to school and you'll find someone else. It doesn't have to be a family member. I am still your son. I don't feel for fishing, not the way you do. It's not Mum's fault. You can't blame her. Or Didima. Things change, Dad. Everything changes. Tradition isn't a reason by itself.*

Rudra looks at the mirror as he speaks. Not out loud. Is that still counted as speaking? It's more like rehearsing, he concedes. Lip-syncing without a backing track. The mirror is speckled with toothpaste, and inky shadows where the silver backing has dissolved. He looks carefully at his face. His skin that browns too easily in the summer. His mother's nose but his father's ears and mouth. He is the product of both of them – a confusing cloud of features and blended cultures.

When two currents collide, a whirlpool begins. A whole separate thing created from the mixing of waters. Rudra is the whirlpool. He is spinning, and it is hard to know what to grasp hold of. The tides that pull and push his parents feed this whirlpool. He is at the centre of this maelstrom.

His mum knocks on the bathroom door. 'You okay?'

'Yup.' Still spinning.

'Your dad will be here soon.'

'I know.' Spinning, slower now.

There is a pause. Rudra holds his breath and the spinning stops.

'It's going to be okay,' says Nayna.

Rudra can hear her forehead lightly touch the door. He releases his breath. 'Is it?'

'Sure.'

'Mum?'

'Yes.'

'Everything is changing.'

'Yes.'

'It scares Dad, doesn't it?'

'It terrifies him.'

'Why?'

Nayna sighs. Rudra can feel her shoulders slumping. 'Change is hard, Rudra. But it's as certain as the tide. Whether you like it or not, it comes, sweeping clean what's been left. Your dad's not alone in trying to ignore change, you know. But the tide is persistent. The tide is inevitable.'

There is a knock at the door. Rudra turns down his music and goes to answer. There is Cord, leaning on an aluminium crutch, a plastic bag in his other hand.

'Why did you knock?'

'I'm not sure,' Cord answers.

It is the first time Rudra has ever heard his father use those words. 'Come in,' he says, as if his old man is a stranger. 'Let me take your bag,' he says, like Raj at the Beamish Hotel.

'I can manage,' his father says, slightly slurry, clambering down the hallway, the pictures rattling on the walls. He pauses halfway down to look at one of the new additions – Nayna, Rudra and Raj on the banks of the river at Gosaba. Rudra holds his breath, watches his father's hand tighten on the crutch.

Cord purses his lips and nods his head – *this is how it is now.*

'Cord.' Nayna comes out of the kitchen, the light behind her – a goddess, crackling with energy, the awesome Kali with blood and fire at her command.

'Nayna.' Cord – a dried sea dragon carcass collected from the beach, shrivelled, small, a husk that once filled a room.

'Let me take the bag,' says Nayna, and this time he releases it, watching it go as if it was the last thing he owned, his pride parcelled in grey plastic, bound for recycling. 'Would you like tea?'

'Yes,' Cord says. 'Please.'

They go into the kitchen and Nayna puts the *cha* pot on the stove, throws in a handful of black tea, pours in the milk, adds sugar, a stick of cinnamon, some cardamom pods. She pours three glasses. Hands him one. He accepts and holds it longer than he should, blowing across the surface. Rudra sees the tiny waves lapping at the far shore. Cord sips the *cha*, winces, puts it on the table in front of him. '*Cha*,' he says, pinching the bridge of his nose.

They sit in silence for a moment, the old house creaking around them. Rudra can hear his music still blaring in his bedroom. A thing never allowed under the old regime.

'It's like this,' Cord blurts, shifting anxiously in his seat. 'We gotta keep fishing. Can't let it go.' His voice has that tinge of slur as if the sea has not quite drained from him yet. He looks at Rudra with such fear in his eyes.

Rudra wants to cry, wants to shrink away, wants to leap into his father's lap and bury his face. 'Dad, I'm—'

Nayna interrupts. 'Rudra's not going on the boat. Not permanently. He's got other things he wants to do.'

'Like what?'

'I don't know yet, Dad.' He wrote this script, wrote it in his head and practised.

'Until you do...'

'I'm not going to fish *Paper Tiger*. I can't be you, or Grandad.'

'I want to tell you something, Rudra.'

'Stop it, Dad. You're not listening. You never listen.'

Cord's eyes darken. Clouds roll in and slashes of lightning appear in his corneas. 'I was under for a long time,' he starts, gripping the chair as if steadying himself. 'When I got caught in the nets. It was like a relief. I felt as if I deserved it or something. I spent every day of my life on top of the ocean, dragging stuff out. But I never looked under before. Wasn't even curious. I don't even go swimming – not for pleasure, anyhow. That day, the sea rushed into me, like I was a bay or something and the waves were coming inside and...' He puts his hand over his mouth. He never wanted it to come out. Why now? These secrets used to be so easy to keep. He doesn't understand what is going wrong, why everything is crumbling.

'What?' asks Rudra.

Cord shakes his head slowly. 'I heard it. Music, like a finger on a glass rim.'

Rudra remembers Didima's story. About her mother's cousin, the truck driver, hearing a song through a fisherman's oar in a Ceylonese lagoon. *Singing fish?* This is not his father. They did something to him in hospital, replaced something. A transfusion maybe? 'You were drowning,' says Rudra. 'It was probably your brain shutting down.'

'No,' says Cord. 'It was different. I'm, I dunno... different.'

Rudra feels something that could certainly be panic if he let it. 'You're not giving up fishing, are you?'

Cord looks at his hands. The glassy scars across the knuckles, the calluses like chitons on a rock. 'Not that. No.' He cups his hands to his ears as if blocking out the world. 'I don't know,' he whispers.

This uncertainty in his father scares Rudra more than his anger ever did. Cord always knows what to do. No matter what.

Nayna gathers the empty glasses. She puts her hand on the top of her husband's and speaks softly. 'Cord, maybe you need to consider getting someone else for the boat.'

Cord looks wild, frightened. 'Who?'

'We'll leave that up to you.'

Rudra wakes from a dreamless sleep. He breathes the dark for a while, lying there and letting his chest rise and fall. It gives him peace, this old house, a place he has always known – his constant. He thinks of the Sundarbans, the *bunds* keeping the sea at bay, and the tigers with their soft footfalls in the forest.

He hears the sound of men's voices, low, like thunder from across the bay – his father's and another. Getting up, he creeps to the kitchen door, looks through the hinge gap to their kitchen table. Cord's hands are splayed out like otterboards; he's trying to funnel his words into a net. Rudra shifts to see who the other person is and catches Wallace's profile between the jamb and the inside edge.

'I gotta go where the money is, Cord, and with you out of action I had to go fish with Wink. It's not like I had a choice or anything.'

Wallace has been on the receiving end of too much grief to use words carelessly.

'Understood, Wallace.'

'So, what's this about? Are you asking me back? Because I'm onto a pretty good thing with Wink. He's got the two boats now and he's paying me more than you ever did. I get a percentage too. It's a sweet deal.'

'I am going to ask you back, Wallace, and I'm going to ask you as a friend.'

'Is that what we are?'

'I thought so.'

'Well, maybe.'

'And I want to take this to another level.'

'Are you proposing to me, Cord?'

'Don't be a smart-arse, Wallace. I can still flatten you. I'm talking partners. You work the boat and get fifty per cent.'

'And long term?'

'I'm talking about long term.'

'What happens to *Paper Tiger*?'

'*Paper Tiger* stays with me. In the family. If Rudra...' His sentence drifts to nothing.

'Rudra's not interested, Cord.'

Rudra turns his ear to the door to catch what his father will say.

'Then we'll see.'

# 32

'IT'S BAD LUCK AND YOU KNOW IT, Nayna.'

'Just pass me the brush, Wallace.'

'And there's Cord to think about.'

'And the paint,' says Nayna.

'It's not right.'

'It is completely right. Isn't it, Rudra?'

'I guess.' Rudra holds the tender steady against the hull of *Paper Tiger*.

Nayna begins by sweeping a broad brush along the hull. She works quickly, once on each side of the bow and then on the stern. By the time she is back at the bow, the afternoon sun has skinned the paint enough.

Nayna smiles at him. 'Remember the sea goddess?' she asks. 'Remember leaving your trouble-words on the beach for her?'

'I was such a sucker. No way that was ever going to work.'

'You were a child. And it did work. When the tide came in and took the words, your pains were gone.'

'That was just time. You can't just erase history as easily as that.'

'True. But when the time is right, you need to have the courage and belief to let it go.'

She goes to work with the fine brush and a pot of black enamel. She works painstakingly, one hand resting on the bow, her brush-hand on top, slightly quivering. First, a straight vertical line – the air roots of the *sundari* tree probing up from jungle mud. Then a bold curve like the god-archer Arjuna's bow. And another directly below – the belly of a cow down by the river. Then a circle – a mouth opened by pain or wonder. A straight, then a curve – a *meendhara* bent to water, picking prawn seeds from her net. An upturned nine – a lucky number of sorts. A hook bothered by a dot – a mosquito? Then the last two characters repeated as if they have been stuttered in black paint.

Nayna stands back, the boat rocking slightly. She tucks a stray hair in with the handle of her brush. 'What do you think?' she asks Rudra.

'I think Didima would have liked it.'

'And you?'

'It's good...'

'But?'

'Dad's going to freak.'

'You need to stop worrying about what your dad thinks.' She leans forward to the boat again. 'I need to finish.'

Below the word she has just written, she draws a series of characters beneath a bold, straight line. To Rudra, they are a group of stray birds huddled under a roof.

বনবিবি

'I know it's Bangla, but what does it say?'

'It says exactly the same thing – *Bonbibi*.'

'Now Dad is really going to freak. Once in English was bad enough.'

Nayna shakes her head. 'Row me to the stern so I can finish that one.'

She repeats the words on the stern and on the other side of the bow. Then they row in and sit on the beach. Clouds begin to roll over Barrenjoey Headland and soon the bay is obscured by rain.

'Reckon we should have some sort of ceremony?' asks Wallace.

'No,' replies Nayna.

'Pretty sure there has to be a ceremony.'

'I changed the name with Maritime – that's all we need to do.'

'Will the rain take the paint off?' asks Rudra.

'It's oil-based,' replies Nayna. 'Permanent.'

# 33

THE TINNIE CHAMFERS A SOFT ARC across the bay, peeling the water back like a shaving of wood. The water is so pale, like the air itself. A shoal of fish careens from deep, cold water, passing underneath as if it is a cloud and they are a flock of birds.

Wallace is in the bow with Maggs, and Rudra is steering. Nayna sits in the middle, her hands flat against the seat, arms splayed like wings, hair ruffled like feathers. The fishing boats are set at chaotic angles on their moorings. The wind usually gives them a common direction; without it, they are bereft.

Rudra thinks how this town has been forever in his memory – the tall pines, the pub, the flame trees and the pier. People come and go. They thin in winter to a weeping spring. In summer they become a flood. But the things – the pines, the pub, the pier – they are constant, like beacons to steer by. The smell of two-stroke gusting from the old outboard fills him with joy. It is so familiar that he wants to talk about it in the way people speak of their grandmother's baking or the smell of mown grass.

In autumn, the mullet run from the cold river, their steely heads buzzing with new direction – swooning and fading to a song they hear so keenly. The men, sitting high on the hill, call down to the boats. And in they go with their nets, working together, running them around in an arc. The water boils white with fear and fish tails. The mullet are dragged onto the beach in a fearsome gnarl of dying. The men box and ice the fish and the birds come in: the pelicans with gullets like skin bags, the gulls setting on each other, arguing over disgorged sprats. Even the cormorants get their fill; preening their oily wings out on the pier rails when they're done. And finally, the kite spirals down from the pines and over the bay. For her, there is a single fish left on the sand. If she could read music this would be a clef – indicating the pitch and roll of death across the beach.

Rudra climbs onto *Bonbibi* – their newly named boat – followed by Maggs in his new *kurta*. Nayna and Wallace are in the cabin. It feels strange to be back here, remembering the last time – when Rudra swam from Lion Island to the shore, the skull strapped to his back.

His dad was living on the boat before he got dragged under, and it is a mess. Rudra rights a drum of oil and pushes a damp wad of blanket against the wall. He expects to find some sign of his father's repentance – a photo of Rudra as a kid, a letter apologising for being such an arse. But there's nothing.

His mum pops her head into the cabin, haloed by cerulean sky, a patch so small it would be hard-pressed to make a sailor a pair of trousers. 'You okay?'

'I'm fine,' he says.

'Come on,' says Wallace. 'Let's get this done before the whole of Patonga wakes up and sees us.'

'You're not still frightened of Dad, are you?'

'Me? I'm frightened of everyone.' Wallace pushes past him. 'I just don't let it get me down.' He fires up the old diesel. 'Make yourself useful and cast off, will you.'

Rudra goes on deck, walks to the bow and unhooks from the mooring. Wallace backs away, then slips into forward and cuts out in the direction of Barrenjoey. When they clear the headland at Dark Corner, they hang a left, as snug to the coast as their draft will allow. Maggs clambers up on the cabin roof and sits there, smug as ever. *That is something Cord would forbid*, thinks Rudra as he crosses his legs in the bow. His mum walks across the deck and crouches behind him, not saying a word.

In the silence between them, Didima arrives, smelling of *ladoos* and *dhoop* – the small cones of incense she would burn at her altar to Bonbibi. Rudra feels her there, as real as the ocean, sighing and plucking at their hull. A little girl who fled a drowning island. An old woman with skin like brittle paper. He never saw death up-close before this summer and now he has seen so much.

When the rump of Lion Island appears, Wallace slows. 'Tell me where,' he yells.

'Where do you think?' Rudra asks Nayna.

'Is there any place better than another?'

'Let's go to the seaward side.'

They motor around to the head of the great lion. Rudra tries to find the cave where he spent that crazy night with the tiger skull, but it has disappeared. Trees fall over, rocks shift and fall, things are obscured and exposed. Everything changes.

The water is a simmering blue, warm as it will ever be at the end of summer. There is something about these flooded valleys, the underwater creek lines and hillocks that makes him feel as if he is flying. *What we think we know of the world is just the tip of it*, thinks Rudra. You think an island is everything until you swim away from it. Then you see it as a mountain with its tip pushed into an unbreathable atmosphere – part of something far bigger and more connected. Like a temple spire with a whole village below.

It used to scare him to think of the size of the ocean. How it left his shore and bled out across the world, smashing every coast from the Sundarbans to the beaches of Normandy, from Tierra del Fuego to the Cape of Good Hope. You can call it by different names, but really it is one huge continuous mass of water. So big it can swallow islands, or give them back, as it sees fit.

His mum produces a yoghurt tub from her cloth bag.

'Tell me that's not Didima.'

'It is.'

Rudra shakes his head.

'Your *didima* loved curd. Every morning for breakfast. And *lassi* too.'

'How do you want to do this?' asks Rudra.

'We just shake her into the sea.'

'Without any words?'

'Do you have any?'

'No.'

'Then without any words.'

'Wait,' says Wallace, coming out of the wheelhouse. 'I got a poem right here that'll suit nice.'

'This'll be good,' says Maggs.

'You think I don't know poetry,' says Wallace. 'I know it, alright. I got more things going on than just fish.'

'Let's hear it then.'

Wallace pulls out a scrap of paper from his pocket. He flattens it against his thigh and gets the measure of the words. He rubs the stubble on his neck, then begins.

*'The fish in the water is silent, the animal on the earth is noisy, the bird in the air is singing.'*

He pauses, looks at them. Maggs is about to speak when Wallace holds up a hand.

*'But man has in him the silence of the sea, the noise of the earth and the music of the air.'*

They stand for a while in the bow of the boat with the water tocking on the hull and the waves shushing on Lion Island.

'What does it mean?' asks Maggs.

'Hell if I know,' says Wallace. 'But it sounds pretty.'

'It's Tagore,' says Rudra, remembering the lines from the book he read a thousand years ago in a room at the Beamish Hotel.

'It's a what?' asks Wallace.

'Rabindranath Tagore. The Bengali poet.' Rudra feels blood drumming in his ears. 'It's from a book of his poems – *Gitanjali*. Song offerings.' He remembers Gita's nets, the way they fought the water. Her smile. Blood mingled with dirt. Pawprints.

Wallace looks at the paper. 'Didima wrote it in the sand down by my pier.'

'I think I know what she meant,' says Rudra. 'She told me once that we should treat everything like it has the potential to sing – even a fish – as stupid as that sounds. That sometimes a song is so quiet we can't hear it.' Rudra looks at the yoghurt tub containing what is left of his grandmother. 'I think Didima was also saying that sometimes if we don't make ourselves heard then it can seem as if we are agreeing.'

They stand in silence for a moment, the only sound waves on the hull and the wind through the low scrub on Lion Island.

'Shall we scatter these ashes then?' says Nayna finally.

'I'm ready.'

Together they hold the plastic tub over the water and shake the ashes to the sea. This time, unlike the last, they do not blow back towards them. They float for a while and then grow heavy and sink. Tiny translucent fish rise and suck them into their mouths.

Wallace points his poem at the water. 'See that little fish. He just swallowed a bit of Didima.'

'That is just a little gross and freaky,' says Maggs.

'Nah,' says Wallace. 'A little bit of India is in that fish now. Reckon it may strengthen the little bugger.'

'It's ash,' says Nayna. 'I very much doubt it has any nutritional value.'

'Will you let go for a minute.' Wallace folds the Tagore poem in half and slips it back into his pocket. 'Didima talked to me about what you folk believe.'

'*Us* folk?' says Nanya disdainfully.

'When something dies it gets another life and turns into something else,' says Wallace.

'Are you becoming a hippie, Wallace?' asks Maggs.

Wallace ignores him. 'I take it to mean we're all related in some way. Everything's got a little bit of something else in it.'

Rudra sips a little of the clear Central Coast air. 'Listen,' he says, 'while I tell you the story of the honeyman and the hunter.'

# Author's note

I am not from India but my story is deeply entwined with that beautiful place. *The Honeyman and the Hunter* is about an Australian-born boy connecting with a country he has never known, and it is written with a sense of wonder rather than familiarity. The Indian content has been checked with readers familiar with that culture but some things will slip through. Such is the nature of nets.

Check out more fact and fiction on this and my other works at www.neilgrant.com.au.

# Acknowledgements

A big thank you to Carl Blacklidge – fisherman, writer and filmmaker – who speaks the language of the sea and steered me from dangerous rocks.

To Jodie Webster, who somehow finds the time and the right words. And Hilary Reynolds for her patience and care in making this novel the best it could be.

To Aritra Paul – of Stree-Samya Publication House – for her cultural reading of the manuscript to discover what was lost in my translation.

To Janine Ravenwood and Richard Tudor for the creative space.

To the Barefoot Café at Macmasters Beach Surf Club for a table overlooking the ocean.